BEV HAS BROKEN

Bev reaches toward me, touches m[...] she disappears into the van. I can't move. I have no idea what to do. I watch as the waiting driver passes us and stops at an empty pump. As he fills his tank and washes his windshield and gets back into his car and drives away. He does all of this so casually, as if everything certain about the future hasn't just been crushed and swept away.

And then I feel myself grab the gas nozzle and yank it out of the bus, slam it back onto the pump, and hit the No button with my fist when the screen asks me if I want a receipt. Then my hands are in my hair and my voice is choking out a long string of obscenities like I'm one of the crazy men waiting in shelter lines South of Market. And then I'm leaving, walking across and behind the station and out of sight from everyone and my sneaker kicks the curb over and over until my foot feels numb and swollen, and then I crumple into this pathetic heap on a nasty patch of weeds that smells like piss and garbage and yell the loudest yell of my life— louder than I yelled when Bev flew off her bike and landed hard on Nineteenth Avenue; louder than I yelled when I was six and got locked in a closet during a hide-and-seek game gone wrong; louder than I yelled when a group of us found ourselves up on Twin Peaks at 1:00 A.M. on a Saturday, drunk and exhausted but refusing to call it a night, and we felt so small with the city lights stretching forever below us, and we yelled at the top of our lungs because we were just these small humans but we felt more longing than could ever fit inside us.

Then I pick myself up and go back to the van.

OTHER BOOKS YOU MAY ENJOY

THE DISENCHANTMENTS

speak

An Imprint of Penguin Group (USA)

SPEAK
Published by the Penguin Group
Penguin Group (USA) LLC
375 Hudson Street
New York, New York 10014

USA * Canada * UK * Ireland * Australia
New Zealand * India * South Africa * China

penguin.com
A Penguin Random House Company

First published in the United States of America by Dutton Books,
a member of Penguin Group (USA) Inc., 2012
Published by Speak, an imprint of Penguin Group (USA) Inc., 2013

THE LIBRARY OF CONGRESS HAS CATALOGED THE DUTTON EDITION AS FOLLOWS:
LaCour, Nina.
The disenchantments / by Nina Lacour.
p. cm.
Summary: Colby's post-high school plans have long been that he and his best friend Bev would tour with
her band, then spend a year in Europe, but when she announces that she will start college just after the
tour, Colby struggles to understand why she changed her mind and what losing her means for his future.
ISBN 978-0-525-42219-8 (hardcover)
[1. Best friends—Fiction. 2. Friendship—Fiction. 3. Bands (Music)—Fiction.
4. Automobile travel—Fiction. 5. Secrets—Fiction. 6. Artists—Fiction. 7. Northwest, Pacific—Fiction.]
I. Title. PZ7.L13577 Dis 2012
[Fic]—dc23 2011021953

Speak ISBN 978-0-14-242391-2

"School Days" by Kim Fowley and Joan Jett copyright 1977 by Peermusic Ltd.
Copyright renewed. Used by Permission. All rights reserved.

Portions of *Melancholy Play* by Sarah Ruhl used by permission of the author.

Designed by Irene Vandervoort

Printed in the United States of America

3 5 7 9 10 8 6 4

To Kristyn,
for our first road trip, and
everything after

Used to be a trouble maker
Hated homework, was a sweet heartbreaker
But now I have my dream
I'm so rowdy for eighteen

— "School Days," THE RUNAWAYS

THE DISENCHANTMENTS

Bev says when she's onstage she feels the world holding its breath for her. She feels electric, louder than a thousand wailing sirens, more powerful than God.

"I thought you didn't believe in God," I say.

She says, "Okay. More powerful than the universe, then."

Bev is the lead singer of a band called The Disenchantments. They aren't very good, but they play so loud the speakers crackle and the bass makes your bones tremble. And they look amazing.

It's almost 3:00 A.M. I am so tired I can barely stand, but I have to stand anyway and go out onto the living room couch so Bev can fall asleep. Even though we've been best friends since we were nine, she's a girl and I'm a guy, and there are certain rules neither of us is powerful enough to challenge.

"We need to pay for those tickets," I say.

Bev nods.

"I mean, really soon, you know?"

"Yeah."

"Like, tomorrow."

"Okay," she says. "Good night."

She's getting the way she gets sometimes, all faraway and quiet, so I say, "You're tired; okay, I'm going."

I head to the door, but then I remember something and can't help myself: "I read today that the Stockholm Archipelago has more than twenty-four thousand islands. Isn't that rad? I can't wait."

She kicks the comforter to the foot of my bed, pulls the sheet over her shoulder.

"There's also this amusement park that's right in the middle of the city. An old cool one," I add, "with one of those swing rides that lift over the water."

I turn off the light and step into the doorway. I can almost picture Bev and me, circling through the sky with islands all around us. Suddenly the room I've lived in all my life with its wood floors and high ceiling and single, skinny window feels smaller than it ever has before.

Then, Bev's voice through the dark: "Don't forget about the tour. That comes first."

"I know," I say. And then, "We're almost free."

"Yeah," Bev says. "Almost."

In the morning, Bev walks out of the bathroom in her cutoff shorts and the Smokey the Bear T-shirt we got in seventh-grade summer camp, to the kitchen, where my dad and I are eating cereal and reading the *Chronicle*. She rumples my dad's hair and says, "Morning, Tom," then opens the junk drawer and takes out a pair of scissors. She shuffles back to the bathroom.

Dad looks at me from over the Bay Area section.

"My son, going on tour." He gets a little misty-eyed.

I say, "What about, 'My son, graduating high school.' Probably a little more important."

"That, too," he says, nodding. "This is a big day. A very big day. Your mother called when you were in the shower. She'll call again a little later."

I check my watch. It's 7:15 here, nine hours later in Paris.

"Bev, we have to go soon," I call into the bathroom.

"Yeah, I'm just finishing something," she calls back. "You can come in if you want."

I push open the door to find Bev with scissors raised and waves of blond hair drifting to the floor. I grab my toothbrush.

"What is this?" I ask. "A symbolic gesture?"

She chops off a long piece by her ear.

"I don't know," she says. "It's just something I felt like doing."

Sitting on the edge of the bathtub, I brush my teeth and watch her cut until her hair is as short as a guy's and the tile floor is covered. I go to the sink to spit and she puts the scissors down, steps back, and studies herself. She kind of looks like a movie star and she kind of looks like one of those punk-rock homeless kids who panhandle on Haight Street. In any case, she looks incredible.

"Rad," I say.

She cocks her head. "You think?"

"Um, yeah."

I lean over the sink to rinse my mouth, and when I stand up again, there we are, standing side by side. Bev's hair is barely a shade lighter than mine, and now almost the same length. Matching blue eyes, a similar darkness under them.

"We didn't get much sleep," I say to her reflection.

"We rarely do," she says to mine.

The phone rings in the other room.

"I'll sweep up," she says, "and then we can go."

Dad comes into the bathroom with the phone, so now the three of us are crammed into the smallest room in the house.

"Whoa, check you out," he says to Bev, and Bev laughs, and Dad nods his approval and hands me the phone.

"Bonjour, mon chéri," Mom says to me from 5,567 miles away. The distance between San Francisco and Paris is one of the many facts I've picked up from Bev's and my nights up late researching Europe. Like the number of islands in the Stockholm Archipelago. Like the fact that in Amsterdam, there are more bicycles than there are people, and Holland supplies seventy percent of the world's bacon, which is not really something I need to know considering that I'm a vegetarian.

"Comment vas-tu?"

"I'm good," I say, propping the phone on my shoulder and taking my place at my dad's desk. "I'm just about to pay for our tickets."

"C'est fantastique! I can't wait to see you." When she switches to English, she sounds more like herself. "I wish I could be there to see you off on your last day."

"I know," I say. "It's okay."

"We'll celebrate for days when you and Bev get here."

"Sounds good."

"Ready?" Bev calls.

"I've gotta go," I tell Mom.

"Good luck," she says. *"Je t'adore.* Call from the road if you can."

Dad hands me my sketchbook as I'm hanging up, and I stick it in my backpack and say, "It's almost like she's forgetting how to speak English."

He laughs, runs a hand through his gray-brown hair, and says, "Guess her language classes are working."

And then Bev and I are out the door into the San Francisco morning, rushing past the produce markets and well-dressed strangers, catching the F train up Market Street just before it glides away.

The school day is a collection of moments—five good-byes from teachers; a free period spent retrieving my drawings from the airy studio; lunch from the taco stand, our mouths full, asking, *Can you believe this is the last time we'll all eat tacos on this street corner together?* All of us answering, *No, no.*

After school I lean against the building and look at the sea of rainbow-haired teenagers. Everyone is out on the lawn with portfolios and instruments and sculptures, signing yearbooks and playing music, setting down backpacks and kicking off shoes as though now that we're free we've decided to stay here forever.

I'm sketching Bev, who sits a few feet away from me practicing the verse of a new song while Meg plucks the strings of her bass guitar. Nearby, a group of ninth-grade girls watches them rehearse. One of the girls wears a Disenchantments shirt that we made for their first show. Bev and Meg came up with the concept—a close-up of a girl's eyes with dark makeup and a tear starting to fall—and they had me draw it for them. I used Bev as a model and the first sketch turned out perfectly, and they had it printed in silver on these fitted black T-shirts that sold out the first night.

It's rare to hear Bev without a microphone, so I listen hard. She's working out the vocal melody. One second she's low and throaty, and the next she's doing this badass breathy thing. Her head is turned away from me, and I'm sketching her neck, realizing that I've never seen it this exposed. Her hair has never been so short.

"Hey," someone says, and then this guy Craig sits down next to me. "So first the tour, and then Europe?"

I nod. "We'll be around here for a few days in between, though."

"That's so cool," he says. "I respect that. You're doing something different, you know? You're getting out there."

Even though this is San Francisco's arts high school and people probably expect us all to go off and do unexpected and interesting things, everyone except Bev and me is going to college. When I told the college counselor our plan, she looked pained and asked me if I was sure, but I told her that, yeah, I was completely sure, had been completely sure since the summer after eighth grade when Bev and I found *Bande à part* in my parents' DVD collection and watched it three times in a row. The counselor was worried but I didn't let her get to me. Instead I told her about some Dutch guy who spent a fortune on a single tulip bulb, and how now there are tulip *fields* just thirty miles outside Amsterdam.

"Picture it," I told her, "fields of tulips."

She softened a little, took off her glasses.

"I've seen them," she said.

"You have? Were they great?"

She nodded, and I swear she got a little emotional.

"See?" I said. "This is what I'm talking about. If I had asked about, like, Biology 101 you probably wouldn't even remember it."

"I'm not crying about tulips."

"Yeah, but you're crying about the experience, right? Maybe not the tulips themselves, but whatever was happening when you saw the tulips, or the person who saw them with you. And the tulips were probably part of it."

"Yes," she said. "They were part of it," and then she cleared her throat and put her glasses back on and said, "Colby, going to college is incredibly important."

Eventually she gave up, and word quickly spread around campus that Bev and I were actually doing it. Leaving together after graduation. Going to Europe. And everyone wanted to talk about it, about where we were going to go and where we were going to stay, and how amazing it sounded and how they wished that they were going, too.

Now, just a couple weeks before we leave, I glance up from my drawing toward Craig and say, "Remind me what school you chose?"

Craig was in my art history class last semester. We didn't talk that often, but he's pretty cool.

"Stanford," he says.

"Wow," I say.

"Yeah, well. We're all off to college like a flock of fucking sheep, man, but not you."

Most people who hear about the plan think that Bev and I aren't ever going to go to college, that we're just going to bum around Europe forever. That isn't really what we have in mind, though. We want to spend a year there, getting to know Paris, traveling to Amsterdam and Stockholm and maybe even Oslo or Helsinki. Lately I've been dreaming about bodies of water: the Seine, the canals in Amsterdam, the Archipelago. Bev and me on trains, moving from one new place to the next.

And then whenever we're done, whenever we're ready, we're going to come home and go to college. I explained this to the college counselor and I explained it to my parents, but I don't explain it all to Craig. I just nod and say, "To each his own," and draw the curve of Bev's neck where it meets her shoulders.

Sunday

The turquoise VW bus arrives in front of my house at 7:00 A.M. The rumble of its engine dies down, the front door slams shut, and my mom's brother shuffles into the kitchen. He's smiling but bleary-eyed, wearing his usual worn Rolling Stones T-shirt and a bandanna tied around his messy hair.

"Look," he says, "I dressed for the occasion."

"Uncle Pete," I say, "you dress like this every day."

"True." He nods solemnly. Then he takes the coffee mug from my hand, sips, places it back in my grasp.

"Any more where that came from?"

I get up and pour coffee into our biggest mug. My uncle sleeps less than anyone I've ever met. Whenever someone asks him what keeps him up at night, he leans in close, looks the person in the eye, and says, *Just can't get the music out of my mind.*

When I asked Pete if I could take the bus on a road trip, I had no idea what he would say. It's hard for strangers to fully grasp the connection he has with this vehicle. Pete doesn't have a wife, but if you knew him only casually, you would assume he did. When someone asks him, *Hey, Pete, what did you do this weekend?* He'll say, *Melinda and I went to the ocean.* Or, *Melinda felt like traveling, so I just let her take me wherever she wanted to go.* By the time he says something like, *Melinda wasn't feeling so hot, so we laid low and took her for a tune-up,* it dawns on most people that Melinda is the bus, and that my uncle Pete is the kind of person who spends a lot of time alone.

I think if I had asked to borrow Melinda to move a piece of furniture, or to go to the grocery store, or for any other brief and practical reason, Pete would have turned me down. But this was about music, and as soon as I used the word *tour,* Pete's glassy eyes opened wider and he smiled a nostalgic, faraway smile. I knew then that he would say yes, and for the rest of the night, he and Dad listened to records and talked about the years they spent traveling around the country, living out of the bus, and playing small town shows. This was before Ma showed up at a South of Market bar for a surprise visit to her brother and fell in love with his bandmate who she'd heard about for years but never before met. The story is that Pete was so moved by the love between his sister and his best friend that when my dad told him they were going to buy a house and have a kid, Pete never said another word about the open life they were supposed to have, nothing about the music or the adventure. Instead, he wrote a song for my parents' wedding that became a hit on many college radio stations and made him briefly famous among a small circle of tenderhearted young fans.

Flash forward twenty years and Dad and Pete are walking me out to Melinda. I throw my duffel bag into the back and take my seat behind the wheel. Pete reminds me of how everything works—unnecessary, considering that he's been giving me weekly VW driving lessons for the past couple months—and then closes me in. Through the open window, Dad slips me a wad of cash even though I've been saving up for this, and then, ceremoniously, he hands me a credit card.

"Are you kidding?" I ask.

Dad and Pete insisted on living like hippies all through the eighties. Even now, Dad hates to charge anything.

"Your mom wants you to have it," he explains.

This makes more sense. Ma's the worrier in the family. Of course she would take a break from studying the subjunctive to make sure I was ready for unplanned expenses.

I look out the window at Dad and Pete, standing happily side by side, and I turn the ignition. Dad whoops. Pete flashes a peace sign.

"See you in a week," I say, and I pull away from the curb.

My first stop is the Sunset. I turn onto Irving Street and see Bev leaning out of her upstairs window.

"Hold on," she says when I slip out of the driver's seat.

She leaves the window. I take a couple steps back and lean against the bus to wait for her, and soon she reappears with a blue pinhole camera. A group of hipsters in skinny jeans and sunglasses makes its way toward me. Their dog strains against its leash, starts sniffing at my Nikes.

A guy with a scruffy beard glances at Bev in the window. "Uh-oh," he says to the dog. "You're messing with the photo shoot."

I pat the dog's wide, white head and tell him it's cool.

"This is perfect," Bev shouts down. "Colby, can you hold the dog's leash? Like, as if it's ours?"

The girl holding the leash laughs. I can't see her eyes from behind the lenses of her sunglasses. She hands me the loop to grab onto.

"Her name's Daisy," she says, and the group moves a few steps down, out of the frame of the photograph.

"I thought you were capturing the moment," I shout up to Bev. "Like, the moment as it really is."

Daisy gazes at me with mournful eyes, then turns to her owners and whines.

Bev calls down to me to move a little to the left, to walk a few steps, to pet the dog, to lean against the bus. When she tells me to open to the passenger-side door and get in again,

I lock the door instead and return Daisy to her group. They rub her back and scratch behind her ears and tell her how proud they are of her, and then they continue walking up the street.

The downstairs door swings open and Bev's mom steps out with her bags.

"Hey, Mary," I say.

"Hi, Colby," she says. "Hello, Melinda."

I laugh. "I'll tell Uncle Pete you said that. He'll love it."

She puts Bev's bags on the floor of the backseat and returns inside for the guitar, but Bev's walking down the stairs, saying, "Mom, just don't worry about it, I got it," in this tense, annoyed way.

Mary looks at me and shrugs. She tries to act light about it, but I can see that she's hurt, and to be honest I don't know what Bev's problem is. Mary's trying to help. But that's how Bev always is with her, and I've stopped trying to figure out why. I shrug back and give Mary a hug while Bev rearranges the bags that Mary loaded for her, and then they hug, brief and tense, and Mary tells me to drive safe and I tell her that I will.

The front door shuts, and now that it's just us on the sidewalk, Bev's whole body relaxes. She smiles.

"Hey, don't move," she says.

She reaches toward me, touches my cheekbone.

"Got it," she says. "Make a wish."

"Hmm," I say. "I wish—"

"Shh. Don't *tell* me."

She waits, guitar case in one hand, rows of pastel houses behind her, holding my eyelash between her thumb and her forefinger. So much swarms through my head that it's hard to settle on anything. How can I wish for one thing when everything is beginning? So I just wish for this feeling to last.

I nod at her: finished. She separates her fingers. My eyelash is on her thumb.

"Wish granted," she says, and blows it away.

Bev's a sculptor; she's always touching things. As I steer us across Market Street and onto Valencia, she runs her hands across the dashboard, the vents, the edges of the windows, the cloth-covered ceiling.

"Feel anything good?"

"Oh, yeah," she says. "Texture city," and we laugh and make our way through the Mission.

I turn onto 24th Street and pull over in front of the Benson-Flores household. Meg and Alexa sit outside the yellow Victorian with their two dads, Jeffrey and Kevin, boxes stacked all around them. Alexa has a notebook open and her phone to her ear. Meg's talking to Kevin while Jeffrey tapes up a box.

Bev and I slide out of the bus and greet them. Then we stand, staring at the boxes, the bags, Meg's bass, and Alexa's drum kit. The bus has a lot of space, but by the time we're done, it will also have four passengers.

"Oh, man," Meg says. She's leaning against Kevin's shoulder, twisting a strand of her pink, wavy hair around her finger. "This is going to be a challenge."

Jeffrey, stonier-faced and quieter than usual, surveys the back.

"Don't worry," Kevin says. "If you forget anything we'll bring it with us when we visit next month. Or we can mail it if you need it sooner."

The rest of us will be coming back to the city after the tour, but we're dropping Meg off in Portland. She's going to Lewis and Clark, and before the fall semester, attending a summer program for theater majors.

"You're the one who's worried," Meg says, and in response, Kevin playfully pushes her away.

"Go help Jeffrey," he says.

Alexa snaps her phone shut. "Just got us a gig at a piano bar in Arcata," she says.

"Where's Arcata?" Bev asks.

"Ten miles from Eureka."

Meg sticks her head out of the van, grabs a box from Jeffrey, and says, "Where's Eureka?"

"On the coast. A little under three hours from Redding."

"So is it tomorrow?" I ask.

She looks up at me, shields her eyes from the sun. Blue marks are on her hands—her signature peace signs. She nods, yes. Some kind of headband thing is tied around her forehead.

"Melinda is beautiful," Alexa says. "I just have to sit here and look at all of you for a second."

After she's taken us all in, she stands up and joins us. I can see the headband better now—it's really just a thin strip of blue fabric tied around her long black hair, with little bells on it that chime when she moves.

Meg and Alexa peer into the bus together like dream girls from different decades: Meg in one of her many kitschy, short vintage dresses, this one brown with a stampede of white horses galloping across it, and Alexa in her flowy, white hippie shirt and tight blue corduroys. It wasn't hard for Bev and me to figure out who should be in the band. These girls dress every day like they're going to be onstage.

Jeffrey and Kevin are trying to fit Meg's stuff onto the floor of the backseat, placing the boxes and bags at different angles with none of the laid-back excitement of Dad and Uncle Pete. When they are finished, Kevin rushes toward Meg and wails, "My little girl is leaving home!"

"I know, Dad," she says, and for a moment she looks so sad that I have to look away as they hug again and Jeffrey joins them.

Bev and I climb back into the front, followed soon by Alexa. When Meg finally takes her place next to her sister, Jeffrey appears in my window.

"You, young man, had better drive safely."

"Of course," I say.

"I want you to drive like a grandpa. Slowly. In the right lane the whole way there and back."

I laugh. "I don't think Melinda could go fast even if I wanted her to."

He nods his approval and steps back, and we all wave good-bye as I pull away.

"This is so pretty," Alexa says, looking at the diamond pattern on the seat covers as I turn left onto Dolores Street. She pulls out a notebook in which she keeps a running list of jobs she might want to have someday. "I never thought of doing upholstery before, but this is gorgeous. The energy in here is amazing. What was your dad's band called again?"

"The Rainclouds," I say.

"The Rainclouds," she repeats. "I think I'll write my play about them."

Each year, our school produces an original play. The kids who want to write it have to apply in their Junior year with a writing sample. Alexa was this year's winner.

"And they toured all over the country in this?" she asks.

"Yeah, but mostly the West Coast."

"And they had a lot of fans, right?"

"Not really," I say. "They never got that big."

"Okay, so not tons of fans, but the fans they did have really loved them."

I just shrug, don't really respond, because she states this as though it's a fact that doesn't need confirmation.

"I can feel the love in here." She nods to herself. "I can feel it in the glass and the stitches. Two best friends, playing music, searching for love."

"*Okay*, Alexa."

"What? You can laugh if you want to, but it's true. Now, you're going to want to get on Van Ness and take it all the way to Lombard."

"Oh my God, Lex," Meg says. "He *knows* how to get to the bridge."

We go through what we've brought for the ride. Meg has devoted hours to making playlists to suit any mood. She plugs her iPod into Uncle Pete's recently installed, prized stereo system, and soon we're greeted with the upbeat, flirty sound of The Supremes.

Alexa has a folder containing maps, contacts, and phone numbers. Packed in a small case are an emergency radio, a universal cell-phone charger, and a first-aid kit.

"I also brought a Magic Eight Ball," she says. "I'm trying to put a little more trust in fate."

Bev has an ancient, clunky Walkman and her camera.

"That's the cutest camera I've ever seen," Meg says.

"I've been thinking about a project," Bev says. "We should take a photograph of everyone we meet on the trip so that we remember them. Like, people we meet at gas stations and working at the motels and venues."

"I love this idea," I say. "This is so great. It'll force us to talk to people. Plus it's so documentary. It's like Leon Levin-stein."

"Who?" Meg asks.

"That photographer we studied in class, remember? He photographed almost everyone he passed on the street."

"Oh, yeah, that guy."

Alexa says, "We could keep a tour journal and leave spaces for the photos to go."

"Maybe we should alternate days that we write in it," I say.

"Who wants today?" Meg asks.

Bev says, "We need a journal first."

There's the sound of Meg rifling through her giant bag and then the sound of her saying, "A journal like *this?*" and I glance in the rearview and there's Meg, waving a large black book to the rhythm of The Supremes fading out.

"I'm a good person to travel with, yo," she says. "You need something, you come to me."

It's still morning but it's warm already. All of Melinda's windows are down but the bus still fills with us laughing, and even though I've crossed this bridge a thousand times, something feels different. The sky, the water, the people walking along the footpaths, and all the cars ahead of us and behind us—everything is larger and more possible.

"Hey," I say to Bev, "we should do this photo thing in Europe, too."

"Yeah?"

"Yeah. We're going to meet so many people. We can keep a log: where we were, who the person was, what we were talking about."

"That sounds really good," she says, but there's something about the way she says it—like she's doing her drifting away thing.

"Okay, let's think about it more. We can *refine* it," I say, using the phrase Bev's favorite teacher uses instead of saying that something's a bad idea. Bev smiles her amazing smile—that dimple in her left cheek, her one crooked tooth, from the time we crashed bikes and she went flying—and turns up the volume.

We're exiting the bridge, and "Turn It On" by Sleater-Kinney has begun.

"Nice choice," Bev tells Meg.

"I thought I'd give a nod to our origins," Meg says. "Show the Riot Grrrls a little love."

The summer after ninth grade, Bev showed me this book on the Riot Grrrl movement she found at Green Apple and told me, "I'm going for this." And I think I said something like, "Why go for something that reached its peak the year you were born?" But she rolled her eyes and I ended up admitting that, yes: Bikini Kill and Sleater-Kinney were so much better than any girl bands around now, and after a laptop screen marathon of mid-nineties concert footage with terrible sound quality but dozens of badass girls jumping around in miniskirts or pounding on drum sets or strumming bass guitars (braless, in thin white shirts), I succumbed.

Yes, it was time for a resurrection. Yes, even though she had never played music before in her life, Bev could be the one to do it. Because even though some of the Riot Grrrls were awesome musicians, the real criteria were to care about injustice, to be antiestablishment, and to be hot in a way that was raw and authentic.

A few months later Bev and I saw Sleater-Kinney play at Great American Music Hall. We stood in the crowd, older people all around us, under the ornate ceiling and red balcony. I kept looking over at Bev, who was cocking her head, letting her blond wavy hair fall into her eyes, trying to look like this was nothing new when really all of it was new: standing in this dark room so close to strangers that we seemed to breathe in unison, all waiting for the same moment.

And then the lights went out and the applause began, and Bev was trying not to smile but I didn't care about seeming cool. Instead I grabbed her hand and we wove our way through the crowd, getting as close as we could to the stage. Usually I think that's a jackass move, which is why I always get to shows early and sit down on the floor for an hour before the opening act goes on. I like to be in the front but I don't believe in cutting. There are a couple loopholes to this etiquette, though. One is if the band you are seeing is your favorite band and you arrive late because you have to finish cleaning your room before you leave the house, and another is if rumors of the band retiring are swarming across music magazines and blogs everywhere and this might be your first and only chance to see them up close and possibly be graced with a drop of hot girl sweat by one of the two singer/guitarists. Both of these were true for Bev that night, so I took her by the hand and said "excuse me" about forty times.

We ended up right next to a giant speaker, and my ears would be ringing for days but I didn't know that yet. All I knew was that Bev was also grinning by now, and Corin strummed her pretty gray-and-white guitar and sang these elastic, ecstatic notes, and Janet's drums sounded like a cross between kids clapping in unison and the best punk drummer there ever was, and right above us, so close that we could have hopped the barrier and touched her, Carrie played her guitar and sang responses to Corin's phrases, and every now and then she would squint into the lights and do these lazy hops and kicks like she was feeling mellow and dancing in her living room.

"I have such a crush on her," Bev said, staring as Carrie stood above us, her hand strumming fiercely, gazing out into nothingness.

I said, "You're gonna have to fight me for her," and we both laughed and looked back to the stage where Carrie was now moving her ankles around in some weird part-march, part-moonwalk way.

For the rest of the night, Bev hardly looked at the other two, even during Janet's drum solos, even though Corin had the cutest porcelain doll face and did things with her voice I didn't know were possible. I watched Carrie sing "Modern Girl," which was slower and had lyrics I knew by heart because Bev had been listening to it on repeat for months. When "Modern Girl" ended and the raucous, catchy songs resumed, I pulled out the sketchbook I carried and started a list of things we'd need to have so that Bev could start her band. *Guitar. Amp. Drum kit. Bass and/or second guitar. Another amp. Songs (four to start). At least two more girls.*

Thirty miles out of San Francisco, I am hit with a realization: "Our tickets!" I say to Bev.

I started looking at prices and flights a year ago but Bev didn't want to get them too far in advance. Prices were high and Bev kept talking about her cousin who always gets last-minute flights for cheap, especially when the tickets are only one way, like ours are. We know that we want to leave right after tour, but we don't know when we'll want to come home, or even where we'll be by then. We'll be gone for at least a year, so maybe we'll be living somewhere unexpected, like Norway, or, I don't know, Cyprus or somewhere.

"I should call my dad right now and have him pay for

them," I say, and I get this rush when I think about him pressing "purchase" on the website for these tickets with Bev's name and my name on them, tickets that will take us to Paris and leave us to wander Europe by ourselves.

"Grab my phone?" I say to Bev, and she opens the glove compartment where we had tossed our phones earlier so they could sit with Uncle Pete's random objects: a pocketknife and several cassette tapes, a blue feather and a gray stone carved with the Chinese character for Patience, his membership cards to the Vintage Volkswagen Club of America and the Sunset Table Tennis Club—an affiliation I'm going to have to ask him about at some point. I've never even heard him mention table tennis.

"No service," Bev says.

"Really?"

She nods and after a minute she says, "I have to pee."

I exit the freeway and pull into a McDonald's lot, and I'm about to check for a signal on my phone when Bev asks me to come inside with her and buy her a shake while she uses the bathroom.

So I stand in line for a vanilla shake, Bev's dessert of choice since forever, and she emerges just as I'm collecting the change. I hand her the shake.

"Thanks," she says.

I take a few steps toward the door and turn around. She's still standing at the counter, watching me.

"Did you want fries, too?"

"No," she says.

"You did want vanilla, right?"

She nods.

"Ready, then?" I ask, and she finally steps forward and follows me out.

Bev tells me that she's feeling tired; she needs to sleep before tonight's show, so she opens the passenger door and takes out her stuff, and then moves to the backseat. Which means that now I'm alone in the front. Alexa offers to come up to copilot, but I tell her that as long as she can keep track of where we are from the middle row she can stay where she is. I'm an only child; I'm used to spending time by myself. And really, pretty much all I want to do is think about Bev and me in Europe right now, so I pull back onto the road and as soon as I have Melinda up to an acceptable speed— something that does not happen quickly—I can relax and space out for a while. We have fifty more miles on 101 before we need to start looking for the next road.

I drive past telephone wires and Adopt-a-Highway signs and miles and miles of golden hills, and I think about Bev, lying in the back row, and I wonder if she's sleeping. I imagine her back there, staring at the diamond-patterned fabric of the bus ceiling, not seeing the billboards or the hills or any of what I'm watching out the window.

I imagine that she's thinking about me.

I picture her finding the hoodie I left on the seat, bunching it up and using it as a pillow. The hoodie just came out of the laundry last night, so she's smelling the detergent that fills our kitchen on laundry days, and the clean deodorant smell, and the aftershave I put on this morning. She's breathing it in and thinking it smells amazing, thinking that it smells like me. And just like me, she can't wait either. To spend every moment of every day together, traveling from ancient cities to tiny islands. To wake up with me in hostel rooms in unfamiliar countries. She's imagining waking up and looking at me, still sleeping in the bed next to hers.

She's realizing that she doesn't want to be in a bed without me, so she pushes aside her covers and climbs under mine. The bed is so narrow that she has to press against me in order to fit, and I can feel her breasts against my chest, her leg across my legs, and in my sleep, I reach out to hold her closer. She kisses me below the ear, and then farther down my neck, and her hand travels from my chest to my stomach, and I wake up just in time to feel—

"Colby," she calls to me from the back row.

I slam on the brakes and I hear Meg yelp and I glance back to see that Bev is not lying down but sitting up, holding her milk shake and leaning over the seat. Our eyes meet for a second. My face gets hot.

"Yeah?" I say, speeding up again.

"I need you to pull off at the next exit."

"Why?"

"We should stop for gas," Bev says.

"The tank's three quarters full."

"Still."

"But we could go hundreds of miles on this."

"Colby," she says. "I need you to take the next exit."

"All right," I say. "Whatever you want. Can someone reach my hoodie? I left it in the back."

Meg's hand appears next to me, clutching the gray fabric.

"What do you need that for?" Meg asks. "It's, like, three hundred degrees out."

"I just don't want to lose it," I say, and I drape it across my lap in a way I hope looks casual, and a few miles later I steer the van off the freeway and pull into a gas station.

I get out and Bev gets out with me. I swipe the credit card, wait for the prompt, and start filling up my already-full tank.

"Are you gonna be like this the whole way?" I ask her. "We're not going to get very far if you make us pull over every five miles."

"I can't go," she says.

"Where?"

"I can't go to Europe."

A car next to us blasts hip-hop, the bass like thunder. I swear I didn't hear her right.

"I got into RISD," she says.

Her words don't register. I don't know what she means.

"RISD?"

"I'm going to college."

Neither of us says anything. I turn toward the street, but I know her face by heart, and I can still feel her blue eyes watching me.

"Oh my God."

"I didn't think I'd get in."

"I can't believe this is happening."

"You really didn't apply anywhere?" she asks.

It's hard to breathe. There's the smell of gasoline and now Bev is taking out a cigarette. She promised me she quit smoking, but here she is with a cigarette and shaking hands, lighting it.

"Don't do that," I say. "Do you want to blow us all up? And no, I didn't."

"Nowhere?" she asks.

"No," I say. And everything seems unreal: this unfamiliar gas station, the hot air, her questions. "Of course I didn't apply anywhere. I thought that if we both said, 'Fuck college, let's go traveling,' we both meant we weren't applying to college and were going traveling."

"It wasn't something I was planning," she says.

"You don't apply to school by accident."

"I was writing that paper on Kara and one night I just looked it up and it was so easy. It only took twenty minutes."

"Kara?"

"Kara Walker. She does those silhouettes?"

She stares at the cigarette, unlit between her fingers.

"Why?" I ask.

She shakes her head. Won't answer me.

On the gas pump screen, numbers are frozen in time. A car waits behind us. And through the glass of the bus windows, two girls' curious, concerned faces stare at Bev and me, waiting to know what has gone wrong.

"Do they know?"

"No. No one does. Except my parents."

"You should tell them now," I say. "Tell them before I get back in."

Bev reaches toward me, touches my arm, but I jerk away and she disappears into the van. I can't move. I have no idea what to do. I watch as the waiting driver passes us and stops at an empty pump. As he fills his tank and washes his windshield and gets back into his car and drives away. He does all of this so casually, as if everything certain about the future hasn't just been crushed and swept away.

And then I feel myself grab the gas nozzle and yank it out of the bus, slam it back onto the pump, and hit the No button with my fist when the screen asks me if I want a receipt. Then my hands are in my hair and my voice is choking out a long string of obscenities like I'm one of the crazy men waiting in shelter lines South of Market. And then I'm leaving, walking across and behind the station and out of sight from everyone and my sneaker kicks the curb over and over until my foot feels numb and swollen, and then I crumple into this pathetic heap on a nasty patch of weeds that smells like piss and garbage and yell the loudest yell of my life—louder than I yelled when Bev flew off her bike and landed hard on Nineteenth Avenue; louder than I yelled when I was six and got locked in a closet during a hide-and-seek game gone wrong; louder than I yelled when a group of us found ourselves up on Twin Peaks at 1:00 A.M. on a Saturday, drunk and exhausted but refusing to call it a night, and we felt so small with the city lights stretching forever below us, and we yelled at the top of our lungs because we were just these small humans but we felt more longing than could ever fit inside us.

Then I pick myself up and go back to the van.

"I can drive if you want me to," Meg says when I open the driver's door. I've never heard her voice so careful.

"Nah, I'll do it," I say. I turn the ignition and Melinda's engine starts to hum, and when I get to the intersection I idle for a moment, because to turn right would put us back on the path to Fort Bragg, which is the plan, which is what they all expect, but to turn left would get me back home and out of this bus with Bev.

Probably thinking that I'm just disoriented, Alexa leans forward from her seat in the middle row and says, "Do you want me to sit with you now? Copilot?"

But I just shake my head and turn right. Like I'm supposed to.

I drive.

Soon Alexa directs me onto 128. The road narrows, the car is silent.

Out the window, delicate trees with leaves so purple they are almost black line the road. I know that we're passing everything but it feels like everything is passing me.

Rows of mailboxes for out-of-sight houses.

A barn with a sunken roof.

A hitchhiker.

Thousands of yellow wildflowers.

All of this is my kind of thing, and under any other circumstances I'd be pulling over and getting out and sketching, but I can't enjoy any of it. Instead I'm reliving the last four years of my life.

This morning, which feels like forever ago, when I said we should do the photo thing in Europe, and I imagined all of these people who exist somewhere in the world meeting us, hanging with us, smiling for our camera. Last April and May, when our friends all found out what schools they got into and decided where they would go, and started talking about Boston and Ohio, and dorms and majors and roommates, and Bev and I talked instead about plane tickets and the Eurorail, the Louvre and the eighteen-year-old drinking age. The beginning of the year, when I was writing a research paper on graffiti artists, spending hours looking at

Banksy images on London streets, and added England to our list of destinations. The end of eighth grade, when Bev and I raided my parents' old movies and watched *Bande à part* one night, and then watched all the rest of Godard's films over the next two days. And Bev said, "Let's go to France as soon as we can. Let's go the second that we're free. We'll stay the whole summer." Sophomore year, when I saw a documentary on tulips, and started dreaming about the Netherlands, and said to Bev, "We should go there, too." Junior year, when Bev said, "And Stockholm, and Berlin." I said, "This will take more than the summer." And she said, "I want to go everywhere. I want to see everything," so neither of us asked our teachers for recommendation letters, and instead we pored over maps.

So when was it that she changed her mind? It couldn't have been after December. Which means that all of the planning we did after that, everything we talked about and decided on, every time I said, *Won't it be great when . . .* and she said, *Yes*—all of that was a lie.

Up ahead to the left sunlight glints over a hand-painted sign for a farm and a street I can turn onto to get off the highway. I turn without notice and drive down the narrow driveway lined with white wildflowers and a wooden fence, and park in front of a barn. No one says anything. No one moves. I unbuckle my seat belt and turn to them. Meg is curious, Alexa concerned, their faces so easy to read. But Bev? She just waits. I don't trust myself to guess what she's thinking.

"I don't think I can do this," I say.

Alexa widens her eyes and shakes her head in denial, and Bev looks down at her hands, and Meg says, "Let's talk through this."

But at this moment I don't feel capable of talking through anything. All I know is that going on a road trip while my life is falling apart feels crazy. Driving from small town to small town, setting up equipment and tearing it down, making small talk with strangers I'll never see again—all the while searching for what I'm going to do now and seeing Bev everywhere I look.

"I don't need to talk it through."

Alexa checks her watch. She says, "All right. How about this. We'll stop here for a little bit. This place looks nice. We'll give you some time to think and then, when you're ready, we can decide what to do next."

She waits for an answer, hope flashing across her face, so I say okay, yeah, we can stop here for a while. She nods her thanks and opens the car door. Meg and Bev file out after her. I wait until they are out of sight before leaving the bus.

The air is dusty and warm, not at all like San Francisco. I lean on the bus and look at the scattered rows of apple trees that fade into the distance.

I've been waiting for this for so long—something new, life after high school. I head to the orchard, walk between the rows of trees, over and down small slopes, around the occasional empty ladder stretching up to higher branches. I want an apple, but I don't think I should pick one, so I search the ground and find one, at a spot that overlooks a river, unbruised and ripe. The river makes me think of the canals in Amsterdam that I now will not boat down, will not sit and overlook with Bev, a pair of beers in our hands. Of all of the islands in the Stockholm Archipelago that I will not discover.

I slump onto the grass and pull my sketchbook and pencil out of my backpack because drawing is the only way I'll survive this detour before going back home to start my life over, or at least try to figure out a next step. I rough out the landscape, but I don't get far before Meg and Alexa are here, hovering above me.

"Time to talk," Meg says. She plops next to me, and Alexa sits gracefully, tucking her legs beneath her.

Meg takes a giant breath. "Colby, the thing is, you have to come on the trip." Alexa nods and the bells on her headband chime, and she keeps chiming and nodding all through Meg's speech. "I know you're going to say we can just cancel the first show and, like, rent a van or something, and make up the time tomorrow. But we can't rent a van."

"Why not?"

"Because you have to be twenty-five to rent a car. Or else it costs a million dollars."

"So you want me to stay with you because you need the bus."

"Yes," she says. "True. But that's only part of it."

"What's the rest?"

"Because we need you," Meg says. "Because there wouldn't be a band without you. And it's good to have a boy with us. And because . . ."

Alexa stops nodding and fixes her dark eyes on me. "Because you're Colby," she says. "You've been with us since the beginning. You know how much this trip means to Meg and Bev and me, and I think it means the same thing to you. It's the last time we'll all be together. Also," she says, choking up a little, "these are probably the last nights I'll spend with my sister."

"Well, there's always summer vacations," Meg says.

"But by then we'll be different. We will have lived apart. It will be good, but it won't be the same."

"You guys," I say. But I don't know what to say next. They're sitting here next to me in this beautiful place, two sisters, my friends, who look nothing alike because they aren't related by blood, and they're telling me that they need me and I know that they do.

"I just don't know," I say. And I feel actually, physically injured when I tell them, "I don't know if I can."

Meg leans closer to me and says, "Just so you know, we're in shock. We can't believe this either. She never said *anything* to us."

Alexa says, "Things happen for a reason. It doesn't make sense now, but eventually it will."

I don't mean to be an asshole, but I can't help laughing. "I'm screwed," I tell her. "If things happen for a reason, I was meant to get fucked over."

She looks hurt but she nods and says, "I would probably feel that way, too."

"So will you come?" Meg asks. "You're screwed either way. At least this way you'll have fun instead of moping around your house."

"I don't plan to mope," I say. "I plan to figure something out."

"But we can help you," Alexa says. "We can brainstorm when you're ready. There are so many things you could do. I'll help you plan it."

I pull a fistful of grass from the earth.

"Without you there would only be us," Alexa says.

Just then, Bev appears in the distance, walking toward us, and I stand up and say, "There's a river over there. I'm going to check it out."

I leave them before Bev gets too close to us, and walk past the parked bus and over a short bridge. I hike down to the water, apple in one pocket, music in the other. A few people are down here—two women in bathing suits and wide-brimmed hats, a man with a dog. I put in my head-phones, pull up the bottoms of my jeans, and kick off my shoes, wade out over smooth stones into the cold water.

Soon I feel a tap on my shoulder. It's a little kid, gesturing for me to take out my headphones.

"Can you step a little that way?" he asks.

I step to the right. He bends down and picks up a stone from where I had been standing.

"I'm collecting the red ones," he says, and reaches into his pocket for a fistful to show me.

Then his dad is here, telling me as they pass, "It takes a lot of years for these stones to get this smooth, friend. A lot of years and a lot of water."

They speak with an accent, Scottish or Irish, maybe. They walk a few steps downriver, and then the dad turns around.

"Hey," he calls across the water. "I noticed you up in the orchard. You and those girls." He squints into the sun, lifts a tan, rough hand to shield his eyes. "I have to ask. Is it just you and them? Traveling together?"

"Yeah," I shout back.

He laughs and shakes his head as if this is something terrifically funny and hard to believe. Maybe it is.

"Good luck." He chuckles again, turns around. His son has become a small figure in the distance, still searching.

I put my earbuds back in and bite into my apple. It's probably the best apple of my life, and I try to enjoy it. I watch for a long time as the man gets farther and farther away and catches up to his son. Eventually, they move out of sight.

A few minutes later, in the quiet space between songs, I hear footsteps in water and smell cigarette smoke. Bev stands next to me but doesn't say anything. The next song starts and I act for as long as I can like her proximity is nothing significant.

After a while I take out one earbud and say, "I can't believe you started smoking again."

Bev runs her free hand over her hair.

"I'll quit after the tour," she says, and takes a drag.

She exhales and I step away from her and wave the smoke out of my face.

"What?" I say. "Why are you standing here?"

But I feel like I'm playing the part of an angry person, because here she is: Bev. My best friend. And even though I'm almost trembling with anger all I want is for her to change her mind.

So I just say it: "Just because you got in doesn't mean you have to go right now. You could defer for a year."

She doesn't say anything.

"Just think about it," I say.

"Believe me," she says, her voice sad, "I've already thought about it."

"Why did you wait so long to tell me?"

"I needed to be sure. I didn't mean for it to take so long."

"Was it because of the tour?"

"You would have come anyway."

"Why would you think that? There are better things I could do than be a roadie for the worst band in history."

I want to hurt her, but she doesn't flinch.

She just says, "You should come on with us tonight. Play tambourine or something. You don't need to be a roadie."

"I don't think so."

"Anyone can play tambourine. You just hit it on your hand."

"Yeah, well. I don't want to be anyone."

She shakes her head. "That isn't what I meant."

We're quiet for so long. I can hear a song playing in my headphones, distorted and far away. It feels forever ago, that Dad and Pete were standing there waving, and I was pulling onto the road, confident in what was happening next. And now this trip is the beginning of nothing. We're not going to the Archipelago or the Hilton in Amsterdam where John Lennon and Yoko Ono stayed in bed for a week to promote peace. We aren't going to spend days in Paris, drinking coffee with my mom, or see the actual paintings that we've spent years studying in books.

"Why?" I ask her. "Why did you pretend that we were going to do this?"

She stays quiet, just like she did at the gas station.

"Are you fucking kidding me?" I say. "Bev. You really aren't going to answer me?"

She looks down into the water. *"I'm sorry,"* she whispers.

"Well, thanks," I say.

"Please come with us," she says. "I need you to come."

She reaches for my hand. I don't jerk away like last time, but I don't hold hers back, either.

"I'll only come if you explain it to me."

"Okay," she says. "I will."

I wait.

"I can't do it now," she says. "But I'll do it."

"Before we get back home," I say.

"All right."

"It's the only way," I say.

"Okay," she says.

We stand in the water for a few minutes longer, not saying anything, not looking at each another.

"Colby," she finally says, "you have to find something to love."

I don't know how she can say that. I shake my head. Look away.

"Something else," she says, quietly.

I turn to her but she's looking at something far away.

So she knows.

Our school didn't want us to get too comfortable in the areas of art we chose, so we had to take at least one class outside of our focus every semester. Our junior year, Bev and I took theater. All the drama kids wanted to act, so Bev got to be the director. I stood on the stage with the others, and Bev stood in front of us, her clipboard under her arm, looking at us as if we were her tiny sculptures, perfect objects she could pick up and place wherever she wanted.

Bev got to select the play she was going to direct. With the help of the drama teacher, this guy named Drew who was so busy being a rising star of the San Francisco theater community that he got all his sleeping done during rehearsals, she chose a contemporary farce called *Melancholy Play*. I played a therapist named Lorenzo who is in love with his patient, Tilly, who was played by Meg. Lorenzo is supposed to have an Italian accent and feel nothing but happiness until he falls in love with Tilly, which happens very suddenly and for no reason except for the fact that Tilly is sad and does strange things, like open his office window during their therapy session and put her hand out to feel the rain. Like I said, the play's a farce, so when Lorenzo falls in love and makes these grand statements, I was really going for it, gesturing wildly and accentuating the accent, and grabbing for Meg, who was dodging from chair to chair, trying hard not to laugh so she wouldn't break character.

When we finished our second run-through of the scene, Bev stood up from her seat in the middle of the theater and leaned back on the armrest. She consulted her clipboard and scribbled a note.

"Okay, Colby," she said. "You need to channel something."

She left her perch on the edge of a chair and walked up onto the stage where I was standing. It was a journey: past the chairs to the aisle, from the aisle to the steps, up the steps to the stage, across the stage to me. She looked at my face and then up to the ceiling, searching for the cure to my bad acting.

"You shouldn't be that funny," she said. "The play should be funny, but Lorenzo doesn't know that. Lorenzo's serious. Lorenzo is in love. So imagine being in love and confessing it."

She stepped to the edge of the stage.

I started: *"Tilly—my mother abandoned me at a sweet-shop."*

That part was easy to say convincingly; the rest would be harder. The problem was that while I knew how it felt to be in love, I knew even better how it felt to hide it. Because Bev and I were best friends and that's the way it had always been. Because every day at our school people broke up and cheated on each other and hooked up at parties and pretended not to remember anything about it the next day. Because I feared the unraveling of everything that we had become to one another from the time we were nine years old.

"Why are you telling me this?" It was Tilly's line, but as Meg spoke I found myself looking at Bev. Her blond hair falling over her left shoulder, stopping at the curve of one of her perfect small breasts. She waited for me to continue.

I said, *"Because—the heavens have cracked open—I suddenly want to tell you everything."*

The next line caught in my throat, but I turned to Meg, who was feigning Tilly's alarm but rooting for me with her focused brown eyes, and forced it out, quieter this time, without the armor of overacting.

"I think I'm in love with you, Tilly. They say that's what happens when you fall in love. You want to tell people things. You especially want to tell them sad things. Hidden sad things from the past. Something like: I was abandoned at a sweetshop in an unspecified European country. Tilly."

I had always found that last part strange. Her name: not a question but a statement. A one-word sentence. But when I said it right then, it made sense. Not, *Tilly?* As in, *Do you love me, too?* But, *Tilly.* As in, *Your name is all I that can manage to say.*

Meg pranced across the stage to hug me, and I tried to recover from the feeling that I had just confessed my love for my best friend on the stage of our school theater with the drama teacher napping in the front row and the entire cast and crew watching from the seats.

There was a moment of silence when I thought for sure the world was ending.

Then Bev said, "That's great. That was so much better."

And we ran the scene again, from the beginning until the end.

Meg drives.

I sit by myself in the back bench seat and stare out the window. A piece of tape unsticks from the side of one of

Meg's boxes. I push it back down, use her bass case as a pillow, and try to fall asleep. When I close my eyes I picture Bev's small blue-walled room emptied of all of her stuff. Then I see mine, full of everything but her.

The bus is quiet for a long time, and then Meg's playlist resumes, and after a while, they start to talk. I hear pages turning and Bev reading, "Voice and movement. Playwriting. Method acting."

Meg says, "How will I choose!"

"Take playwriting," Bev says. "I'm taking it first semester. Let's write plays and produce them over the summer. We can cast each other."

"Only if you direct me again," Meg says. "You're the best director I've ever worked with."

I don't want to hear Bev talking about this, getting so excited over the things that I thought neither of us were that into. So I sit up, assuming that they'll move on to other topics of conversation if they don't think that I'm sleeping.

I see Bev catch my reflection in the rearview mirror and she slips the catalog off her lap. For a while they talk about nothing, and then Meg stops talking altogether and focuses on the road.

Which is a good thing, because the drive gets a little perilous. The Northern California coast has to be the most amazing place I've ever seen but it's also terrifying. One moment, I'm thinking *Oh my god: the cliffs, the ocean, the wildflowers, the hills—nothing could be better than this.* And then the next, I'm wondering why there isn't a rail on the side of the road, realizing that if Meg steered us a little too zealously around a curve, we would be plunging over the cliff, into the ocean, and that would be the end of all of us. I close my eyes and almost feel it: the denial and then the dread, falling away from the future I had every intention of reaching.

Eventually, the earth evens out, the road widens. We drive past Mendocino, a perfect postcard town overlooking the ocean, everything neat and colorful. And then, all of a sudden, the trees disappear, everything turns gray, and a sign welcomes us to Fort Bragg.

"Whoa," Meg says. "What happened?"

Alexa says, "Maybe we're just in the outskirts or something. I'm sure it will get better."

Bev's staring out the window, but in that spaced-out way that means she isn't really looking at anything.

Maybe she's changing her mind.

Alexa directs Meg off the main road, past a tattoo parlor and a few bars and an unfortunate number of boarded-up buildings. At the end of a block, we spot the red Bianchi Motel sign rising over the roofs of the surrounding stores and houses.

"This is kind of weird," she says, "but we don't actually check in at the motel. We check in at the store across the street."

We get out of the bus. Across the street is another red

sign: Bianchi Market. Next to the motel is the Bianchi Laundromat. All three of the Bianchi's businesses look a little rough. Bars on windows, peeling paint. Instead of flashing on and off, the neon vacancy sign above the motel winces and sparks.

Alexa frowns. "It looked okay on the website."

"We didn't expect luxury," I say. "This'll be fine."

"Yeah," Bev says. "It's just a place to crash, right?"

Alexa nods, like she's trying to convince herself. "And it's close to the venue, The Basement. It's just a few blocks away."

We walk single-file into the market. An R & B song from before we were born crackles through boom-box speakers. Everything is coated in dust. An older woman with faded tattoos laughs loudly with a customer. Her name tag says Peggy, and I wonder if she's a Bianchi.

Alexa strolls past Peggy, over to a girl at the far end of the counter.

"You checking in?" the girl asks, and Alexa says yes.

We crowd around the counter as the girl goes over the rules. She's probably our age, maybe a year or two older, but it's hard to tell because she looks nothing like us. She's wearing baggy jeans and thick black eyeliner and her hair is pulled back into a ponytail so tight it must be painful.

She sets a laminated paper on the counter for us to read.

NO SMOKING (THIS INCLUDES MARIJUANA!)

NO GUESTS

No loud music after 10 p.m.

No shouting or yelling

This is a family place. If you disobey the rules we will call the police!!!

"Okay," Meg says, clearly offended. "Got it." She turns to the rest of us. "We should unpack our stuff and then go somewhere."

Alexa checks her watch. "We only have until eight before we have to check in for the show."

"That leaves some time, though," I say. "We should do something."

Even though Fort Bragg doesn't seem to be the most vibrant town, I don't want to go sit around the motel room, trying to avoid eye contact with Bev. And this is our trip, the first trip any of us have ever taken on our own, with our own money and our own schedule to follow and our own decisions to make.

"So what is there to do around here?" Bev asks.

The girl shrugs. "J.T.'s doesn't card. Or there's Glass Beach."

She looks around, sees the older woman still engrossed in her conversation, and says, "I probably shouldn't tell you this, but I wouldn't unpack if I were you. Your stuff's definitely safer in the car."

Meg raises her eyebrows.

"Okay," she says. "Well, thanks for letting us know."

We turn to leave and then I remember the photo plan

from this morning, when we were crossing the bridge and my future was still something recognizable. I stop halfway down an aisle—in front of a few dusty flashlights and a camouflage-print umbrella—and say, "Hey, we're supposed to get a picture of her."

Alexa looks back at the girl, then shakes her head. The bells on her headband chime and she smiles a tight, nervous smile that means she wants to leave.

"I don't know if she likes us," she whispers.

Meg adds, "That list was kind of rude."

"It wasn't *her* list," I say. "And sure she liked us. She warned us about the room."

Bev has the camera around her arm, so Meg and Alexa look at her for the final decision.

"We're taking photos of everyone, right?" I say.

She's studying the girl, the surroundings, as if she's imagining the way the photograph might turn out.

"Let's go," she finally says, and with this decision, abandons another good plan.

We drive by J.T.'s first. It's on a side road and so shabby I would assume it was condemned if we hadn't just been told to go there.

"That man has bad vibes," Alexa says about a guy leaning up against the door. He sees us checking out the bar and sneers.

"Glass Beach, then," I say, and everyone nods their assent.

So we drive a few blocks down the main road and turn where a small sign tells us to turn, and park the car and walk toward the water, Bev's camera over her shoulder. Tall grasses and flowers grow through a barbed-wire fence on one side of the trail, and when the fence ends, the path opens to a rocky area above the water. We look over the edge. Not far below us, groups of people are spread out by the water, but instead of lying on towels and sitting in beach chairs, everyone is digging in the sand.

"What's going on?" Meg asks. "This is weird."

We hike down to find out. Once we're with the rest of the people, we discover that the sand isn't only sand. Instead, we stand on millions of smooth, small pieces of beach glass.

Alexa scoops a handful and holds the glass in her palm for us to see — brown, green, blue, and white.

"This is amazing. The pieces are everywhere."

"Yeah," Meg says. "But that's not what everyone's looking for."

All around us, people are pushing the beach glass aside, searching for something buried deeper.

"I'll find out," Meg says, and takes a few steps over to where a little boy is hunched beside a rock with a red shovel.

"What is everyone digging for?" she asks him.

"Junk," the kid says without looking up.

"Junk," Meg tells us, as if this illuminates something.

Meanwhile, a short distance away, Alexa has started digging. Meg asks Bev to use the camera, and Bev takes it off of her shoulder, hands it over, and leaves to walk along the edge of the water, picking up pieces of driftwood. Soon she comes back toward me with her arms full.

"Can I have the keys?" she asks.

I hand them to her, and when she grabs them some wood falls out of her arms. I ignore her for a little while, but it takes too much effort to stare out at the water as if I don't notice her picking up and dropping the wood, so I stop faking aloofness and take some wood out of her arms. We start up the path to the van together.

"This is perfect for carving," she says.

Bev takes things from real life and makes them small. Three-inch-tall people, centimeter-long books, every detail precise and perfect. Her senior project was the whole school: every student, every teacher, every classroom. People were touched. For weeks they crowded around the display in the library, because there they were. Even if they had never even spoken to Bev, never even had a class with her, they were there somewhere, standing or sitting in their usual spots, looking like themselves in their signature glasses or boots, some small detail that made them recognizable. Our high school was different than other schools—no football team, no cheerleaders—but like any place there were kids who were noticed and kids who weren't. Bev was definitely noticed. And then, there was her project, sitting in the library, saying, Yes, I notice *you*, too.

As we walk up to the car Bev tries to talk to me as if everything's fine. She tells me that driftwood is great for the bigger pieces because it's so soft and because it's gray, a color that works well for walls and floors.

"If I'd had this to make the theater out of, it would have been so much better," she says. "I wouldn't have made that gash in the side from digging too hard."

In Bev's version of the school's theater, Alexa and Meg and a few other people were onstage, holding scripts. I was across campus in the drawing studio, standing at an easel. Bev was two classrooms away, working on a miniature version of her miniature campus.

I unlock the passenger door and we let the wood tumble out of our arms and onto the seat. Bev picks up a piece I was carrying.

"I'm gonna use this one to carve the bus," she says.

She looks at me.

She waits. Probably to see if I'm going to talk about this with her. If I'm going to pretend that things are okay. But I don't know how I can have a conversation with her about anything until I know why she lied to me for so many months.

"Do you want to tell me now?" I ask.

She shakes her head. No. We turn back to the water.

Meg runs up to greet us when we get back to the beach.

"We're finding it!" she tells us.

"Finding what?" I ask.

"The junk," she says. "It's everywhere. Come look at my stash. Here's your camera back. I got some good shots."

She leads us down the beach and shows us what she's dug up: a plastic green army man, a doorknob, a rubber boot.

"Alexa's thing is the best," Meg says. "Show them."

Alexa beams, holds up a harmonica.

"Isn't this amazing?" she says. "Someone used to make music with this. How did it get here?"

I take the harmonica from Alexa's hand. All of the little openings for air are filled with mud and sand.

"Do you think it'll work?" I ask.

Alexa nods. "I'll clean it out," she says.

When I hand it back to her, she cups it in her hands like it's something precious.

Meg dances around us. "Let's find more junk!"

But Alexa stops gazing at her harmonica and tells us we have to go. On our way back to the car we gather more driftwood for Bev. She walks ahead, pointing out the pieces we should take, filling her pockets with pieces of glass.

The address Alexa has written in her tour planner belongs to a boarded-up house nestled in a block of several abandoned houses. We stand outside its front door as she flips through her notes, searching for a mistake or an explanation.

"Everything will be fine," she assures us. "We are here for a reason." Then, more to herself, she says, "But it just doesn't make sense. It says it right here. I have it written down in two places."

We've just been standing on the sidewalk in front of the house, so I walk up to the door. The sky is darkening, the window next to the door reflects a streetlamp. I cup my hands over the glass and look inside. An old, ripped chair. A coffee table. Nothing else. I take a step back, ready to tell Alexa that if there is a reason for our presence here, it isn't clear to me.

But then I see a piece of paper on the ground below the window. I pick it up. It has a piece of tape on the top and typed words that read: SHOW TONIGHT. USE BACK DOOR with a hand-drawn arrow pointing to the left.

Alexa appears stunned but Bev nods decisively and starts unloading the equipment from the back of the bus: the drum kit, the guitar, the bass, the microphone stand, the amps. We carry everything around the overgrown side yard, step over a fallen fence, and stop in front of a screen door.

I can make out movement from the darkness inside.

"I think someone's in there," I tell Alexa. She consults her notes, walks in front of me, and opens the door.

"Walt?" she asks.

An incredibly tall man in a ratty T-shirt and sweatpants appears in the doorway.

"Alexa," he says, smiling down at her. Then, he surveys the rest of us and adds, "The band."

He steps back, extends his arm toward the inside of the house. "Welcome to my basement."

So I'm pretty sure that this is the kind of situation parents have nightmares about: towering slobby guy in his thirties smiling down at a group of teenagers, gesturing to welcome them into the dark basement of an abandoned house. But maybe because of the instruments, or the fact that at one point he and Alexa spoke on the phone, or the semiprofessionalism of the typed-up sign that was supposed to hang out front—or maybe because of all of these things combined with the fact that only one of us is not officially an adult yet, we say "What's up, Walt," and walk in.

Walt pulls a cord and a combination light/ceiling fan switches on.

"Okay, so uh . . . here's the stage." Walt walks over to a line of duct tape that runs the expanse of one side of the concrete floor. "Everything from here to that wall is yours. Everything on the other side is for the rest of us. The tape is largely symbolic but I've found that it works."

I nod as if this is perfectly normal. Meg's nails are digging into her hand, something she does when she needs to suppress inconvenient laughter, which is often. Alexa has already moved past shock to practicality: her eyes scan the stage section of the basement for electrical outlets. Leaning against the wall, Bev appraises Walt with tremendous enjoyment.

Walt leads us on a tour around the rest of the basement. It is not a generous space, but he has it broken up into sections. In one corner is The Bedroom (unmade bed and chest of drawers) and in another is The Living Room (a sagging, floral-print couch). Next to The Living Room is The Kitchen (a mini-fridge, a cooler full of beer, a hot plate, and an overflowing trash can). And then we are back to The Stage.

"Oh," he says. "I almost forgot." He takes a couple steps backward until he is in the middle of the room, extending his arms to either side.

"The Dance Floor."

Meg can no longer contain her laughter and, thankfully, Walt joins in.

He points a smudged finger at her.

"I like a lady who knows how to have a good time," he says.

The completion of the tour seems like a good opportunity for me to show Walt the sign.

"Should we get more tape?" I ask.

"Meh," Walt says, giving an exaggerated shrug. "Everyone knows where to come. That was basically just for you guys."

Soon the girls are unfastening cases, untangling cords, plugging things in, testing sound. As they move across the basement floor, Walt gives the impression of tidying up. He circles the room slowly, ignoring the piles of dirty clothes and pizza boxes, fluffing a pillow on the couch instead, walking past a table strewn with crusty dishes to straighten a framed Heart poster. When the first person arrives, he gives up the act and grabs a beer.

Soon people are streaming in, heading straight for the cooler. A guy with a Pabst Blue Ribbon shirt and a Pabst Blue Ribbon in his hand asks me if I'm with the band.

"Yeah," I say.

"Cool," he says.

We stand next to each other for a minute.

"I already knew that," he says.

"Knew what?"

"That you were with the band. We all know each other. We all went to high school together or some shit like that. But you, A) are younger than my youngest brother, and B) have a mug I've never seen before."

"Oh," I say.

"What kind of beer you want?"

I shrug. "Any kind."

He narrows his eyes at me. Apparently, this was not a good answer.

"I'll take a beer," I say. "I just don't really know what kind I like."

When he continues to look at me like I'm crazy, I add, "I'm eighteen. I'm used to taking whatever I can get."

"Walt," PBR guy barks, and Walt appears beside him, slinging his arm around PBR's shoulder.

"It's gonna be a good show tonight," Walt says. "Did you see those girls? Those girls are smokin'."

Walt turns to me.

"I mean that with the greatest respect," he says. "Your friends are ridiculously talented and special."

"Walt," PBR guy says, ignoring everything Walt has just told him, "we need to determine what kind of beer is this young man's kind of beer."

"I need a particular kind?" I ask.

"Everyone needs a kind," Walt says.

PBR points to his own shirt. "You see that I take this seriously. You need to know what kind of beer you drink to know what kind of man you are. I, for example, am a cheap bastard."

They lean back a little to get a good look at me.

"He wears old-ass Nikes," PBR says. "Now those are some vintage sneakers. I think I had a pair like that in junior high. Where'd you find shoes like that?"

"Thrift store in the Mission," I say.

PBR nods knowingly. "Lift up that shirt a little, kid, let me check out that belt," he says.

My belt is lime-green canvas with a silver pull-through buckle.

"A little ostentatious," Walt says.

"Yeah," I say. "But it's always covered."

PBR nods. "Covered by a somewhat formfitting gray T-shirt."

"And unafraid to wear a stranger's old shoes. What do you put on to keep warm, kid?"

I pull a flannel out of my backpack.

"Yes, yes," PBR says. "I could've called that."

"Young man," Walt says. "Let us now lead you to The Library."

We push through the crowd to get to a shelf of books above the bed.

"Peruse these titles if you will," Walt says, "and tell us which, if any, you've read."

I scan Walt's collection of books: some thrillers, some Hemingway, three dated issues of *Hustler*, a few contemporary novels.

"*The Sun Also Rises*," I say. "And *For Whom the Bells Tolls*. Oh, and some of that Raymond Chandler collection, too. 'Red Wind,' right? That story's rad."

"I don't want to appear obsequious, but you're a smart kid."

"Put together, but not fussy," PBR says.

"Good-looking guy for sure. But not pretty. Strong jawline. And masculine taste in books."

"Yeah, well I don't think you had any books by women," I say.

Walt hesitates, surveys his shelf.

"Observant," he says to PBR.

"Calls it like it is."

"Mellow," Walt adds.

"So we good?" PBR asks.

"Yeah," Walt says. "I think we've found a beer for our young friend."

Walt returns with a Guinness for himself and a Guinness for me.

"Welcome to the club," he says, and moves on to a group of arriving people.

PBR and I lean against the wall of The Bedroom and drink our beers.

"So what's up with this place?" I ask.

"It's a long story but I'll tell you," PBR says. "Story is that Walt never left his parents' house. It's fucking pathetic. And then his mom got sick and died, and his dad never really had a job, at least not that I can remember. You like your beer?"

"Yeah."

"Good. Walt had a job at the hardware store once, but he got fired for stealing a tool kit and no one really wanted to hire him after that."

"Why'd he steal a tool kit?"

PBR guy takes another swig of his beer.

"Why the fuck not steal a tool kit? That shit is useful. Anyway, no one was paying the mortgage so eventually the bank kicked them out. Walt's dad moved in with some family in Redding and Walt couch surfed, mostly on my couch.

Unfortunately. That was maybe seven months ago. But the bank never did anything with the place. It was just sitting here unoccupied, so eventually Walt was like 'Screw it,' and moved back into the basement. And then—as an extra little fuck you to the man—he started hosting shows here."

As if on cue, Walt's voice comes thundering out of the speakers.

"What's up party people? We have a special band to-night. All the way from Frisco. They call themselves . . . *The Disenchantments!*"

Meg and Alexa are in position behind Walt. Bev isn't there. I scan the room for her and find her off to one side, talking to some guy who must be at least Walt's age. The guy is leaning into her, talking all close with his mouth by her ear. Bev pulls away from him and gives him this look, all aloof and mysterious but also inviting, and even though I've seen her give that look a million times before, it makes me feel sick. For the first time it strikes me, how it's so calcu-lated. She knows exactly how pretty she is and exactly how to play it. It's one thing to do that to some sleazy stranger who's at least ten years older than you are, and another thing to do it to your best friend. And now that I know that she knows how I feel about her, that she's probably known for years, it's even worse that she's doing this in front of me. Yeah, we've both made out with a lot of other people, but if I ever thought she might want something more with me, I swear, I would have forgotten about every other girl.

Alexa gives a weak hit of a drum to kick off the first song. Bev picks up her guitar and strums a chord that has no place in any tuning, standard or otherwise. The amps thunder static, unable to endure Meg's low notes. For a minute, before Bev starts to sing, they sound so terrible that anyone with a sense of humor would assume they were joking.

But as soon as Bev starts singing, two things register: first, that Bev is the most beautiful being on Earth, and second, that they are playing in earnest. That they aren't going to stop and laugh and say, *No, really? You guys thought this was real?*

As usually happens when The Disenchantments start a show for strangers instead of just kids at our school, the crowd stares at them in a stunned silence. Soon, I know, the audience members will regain their composure and start to talk loudly enough that the music is irrelevant. Once in a while they'll glance away from whomever they're talking to and remember that there's a band up there. They will admire the guitar player's gorgeous face, regardless of the fact that she can't tune her own instrument. They'll move on to the drummer and think, Who cares if she's too blissed-out to pound a beat—that concentration! Those blue-inked hands! They'll look at the bassist, too distracted by her great legs and pink hair to be bothered by the terrible static that thunders with every low note. And when Bev is singing, devastating and breathy, above the sound of everything else, they'll either want to be her or to be the person she loves, and they'll know that in spite of the cacophony of everything else, she is worth staying for.

Eventually they will remember where they are and to whom they are talking, and they'll sip their drink and say, *So anyway.* . . . I know this will happen, but I don't wait around to see it, because I keep looking at that guy looking at Bev like he's expecting her to take her clothes off for him later. And even though I know Bev wouldn't do that, just the thought of it is too much for me to take.

So I take my Guinness and walk outside to find that night has fallen and fallen hard. I can't see more than a few feet in front of me but I head away from the house anyway. The flimsy back door slams and swings open and shuts again. As soon as I get to the front they sound distant, like people I don't even know. *"You look so pretty, you look so pretty, like I cut you from a magazine,"* Bev shouts.

I cross the street and listen: nothing.

When Bev and I were kids we would sing my dad's old songs together. We listened to his cassettes until the tape thinned and broke and we had to pull the unraveled, tangled mess out of the tape deck and ask for another copy. He had an endless supply in a box in his closet. He pretended to be upset about the broken tapes, but it was no secret he was flattered. The band was long forgotten by then, but we memorized all the lyrics and learned the harmonies that he and Uncle Pete had arranged. We were a two-person cover band devoted to music that only my dad and my mom and her brother remembered.

I've walked several blocks now, away from Walt's house, toward the water. Soon I'm on the path we walked earlier, heading back to Glass Beach. A car idles where I parked the bus this afternoon and a bunch of vagrant kids gather around it, their huge, worn packs cast aside on the street.

"Hey, man," one of them says.

I tip my beer can at them. They raise brown bags in return. I keep walking, wondering what it would be like to be one of them, traveling around with no specific destination, just moving for the sake of it.

The moon is out over the rocks, bright enough that I can climb down to the water. In the darkness, the beach glass is colorless, unremarkable. Waves crash against the land and drown out the sound of my footsteps. I keep thinking about those recordings Bev and I used to make. There was one song we sang more often than all the others.

I hum the melody; the words come back to me.

Soon you'll be leaving, I sing.

I sound good. I sound older. More like my dad in the original than the kid-me in the recordings.

I sing the whole verse louder. I really belt it out.

Soon you'll be leaving
And I don't know what I'll do
You pull on my heartstrings

Till I'm tied up in you

Dad and Uncle Pete must have spent days on these songs, getting the words just right, all sweet and simple like they wanted them. They didn't even have girlfriends. All the heartbreak was hypothetical. For some reason I start thinking about Walt living in that house with his dad all his life. PBR was right—it *is* pathetic. Which makes the thought of going home after this trip terrible. I can see it: me, Dad, and Uncle Pete. Drinking coffee together every morning. Taking day trips in Melinda. Listening to records and getting high on special occasions. Once in a while my mother will call from Paris and we'll huddle around the phone to listen to the news of this one woman, the most important woman in all of our lives.

As I turn back I decide, *No*. I don't know what I'm going to do now, but I promise myself that it won't be that.

The post-show scene at Walt's house is less than beautiful. Bev and the guy from earlier huddle outside, smoking cigarettes. I pretend not to notice them as I walk past, and Bev doesn't say anything to me, either. Empty cans and bottles cover the basement floor, rendering the room demarcations irrelevant. Most of the people have already left, and those still here look drunk and tired and a little bit sad. PBR rests on the bed, a passed-out girl slumped against his shoulder. Across the room, Walt is stationed at a flimsy table, playing cards with Meg and two other guys.

I take a seat next to Alexa on the sofa, next to the card table. I'm feeling better after having had some time away. A little more like myself. She has the insert from a cassette tape unfolded, spread across her lap.

"What are you doing?"

"Reading along with the lyrics."

Classic rock crackles from a corner of the basement where Walt has set a boom box on top of a pile of laundry. It looks like it could tumble over at any moment. Women with strong voices sing over a muted electric guitar and synthesized keyboard.

"It's so eighties," I say. "Who is this?"

"Heart," Alexa says. She extends her hand, painted with the blue peace sign, and points to Walt's poster that I noticed earlier. I take a longer look at it now as a song fades out, and Walt crosses the room to turn the volume up. Two girls with heavy eyeliner and blue eye shadow stare at the camera. They're wearing black lace around their necks. One brunette, one blond; one expectant, one wistful. Skinny, some cleavage.

"Listen," Walt tells Alexa. "This one's very special."

He returns to his seat at the card table but keeps an eye on Alexa to watch her reaction. A keyboard or piano starts—I can't tell which—and soon one of the women starts singing about lying awake at night, wondering about the guy she loves. Then the drums and harmonies kick in, and she sings with this powerful classic rock voice about how she used to be independent and carefree, and now she's consumed by desire. Apparently this was the night she was going to confess her love, but he hasn't answered the phone or shown up to see her, so she lets out this kind of screaming wail and belts out the chorus again. I glance at Alexa, ready to say something smartass, but she blinks back a tear. Crying over these pathetic lyrics and synths? It knocks me speechless. I can't even tease her.

The song fades out and she whispers, "That time it was Anne singing, right?"

Walt points at her. "You got it. They're speaking to you, aren't they?"

"I love it. I completely understand what she's feeling."

I laugh and scoot closer to her so I can read the lyrics.

"You're listening to the tick of the clock?" I ask. "You're waiting to touch some guy's lips?"

She laughs and yanks the tape insert from me, wipes away a tear with the back of her hand. Blue smears on her cheek. She looks at her hand, sees what she's done. Shakes her head and laughs harder. The bells on her headband chime.

"No," she says. "But that emotion? I'm going to feel that for someone, someday."

"Add it to the list?"

"Oh, no," she says. "Matters of the heart don't go on the list. Strictly professions."

She stands up.

"I love Heart," she says to everyone in the basement. "Heart is my new favorite girl band. Meg, we should go soon."

Meg nods without looking up, and Alexa walks outside to tell Bev we're leaving. Through the screen door, I can see them. The guy stands and grabs Bev's arm, pulls her up. She stands fine, but he puts his hands on her hips as if to steady her anyway. I cough away the knot in my throat.

"Pair of aces!" Meg says, slamming her cards down on the table. The other players sigh, and she hums a victory song as she finds her bag and clicks her bass guitar case shut.

Alexa's back now and we start saying our good-byes, Heart, epic in the background, like a sound track to our leaving.

I grab a stray extension cord, help Alexa with the last parts of her drum kit. We head to the door.

"Go conquer the world, kid," Walt says.

I turn to face him and laugh.

"Okay," I say, but Walt doesn't smile.

"I'm not joking," he says.

The tape ends with a click, leaving the room suddenly quiet. Walt keeps looking at me, tired but insistent, and it feels like everyone here is waiting for us to resolve something.

I nod, and say, "Okay" again. I look straight at him

when I say it, and for a moment I try to believe that the world is something conquerable. Like I could wake up tomorrow morning, and know what I want to do, and do it. Like the anger and defeat could just lift away. Like Bev could change her mind.

The two guys at the card table with Walt start gathering the cards and shuffling, ready to start a new game. I scan the basement for the last time: tape peels off the floor, the stage area is empty again. Is this what our trip will be like? A long series of endings? Walt nods at me and then turns to his new hand. PBR brushes a strand of hair off the forehead of the passed-out girl. There's so much tenderness in the gesture that I have to look away. When I look again, PBR lifts his hand to wave good-bye. I lift mine back.

We walk into the hot room at the Bianchi Motel and Bev heads straight for the windows. She unlocks and pushes them open, one after the next, with breathtaking efficiency. Even though I am wrecked and exhausted and angry, I could still watch her open windows all night. But there are only four, and then she is finished.

A breeze comes and we all exhale, drop our bags on the worn magenta carpet, survey our options: two twin beds with brown comforters, a mustard yellow couch, the floor. Off to one side, a narrow doorway leads to a small, white kitchen. I'm probably supposed to be chivalrous and take the carpet, but I don't want to be chivalrous. So I don't say anything. If they want to claim the beds and the couch, I'll go sleep outside.

Bev lets her bag slide off her shoulder onto the couch.

"I'll take this," she says.

"Meg kicks in her sleep," Alexa says. "And those beds are really small."

She looks at me, concerned.

"I'll just sleep in the bus," I say, a brief fantasy flashing across my mind of waking up at 2:00 A.M. and driving home by myself.

But then Alexa discovers a sliding door on one side of the room with a tiny balcony.

"Perfect," she says, and lays down her sleeping bag. "I can't sleep when it's too hot. And listen. It's so quiet."

She smiles at me. It's supposed to be a casual smile, but I can tell it's a pity smile, so I look away.

"Okay, good, but there is no way we're going to sleep yet," Meg says. "The night is young, and we are free forever. Not you, Lex. You're just free for a couple months."

Alexa shrugs. "I like high school."

"I have plans for us," Meg says, which is not entirely surprising. Meg is always coming up with plans. She's the one who, in the middle of a party when everyone is content with their mild boredom, will stand up and declare it time for a game of competitive improv, or pass out copies of song lyrics so we can have a spontaneous sing-along.

She crosses the room, pulls the knit hat she wore all winter out of her duffel. Next comes a stack of paper, cut into thin strips. After that, perfectly sharpened pencils. We sit on the floor—Bev, leaning against the couch; Alexa, cross-legged, under the open windows. I lean against what has become my bed while Meg distributes the paper and pencils and explains the rules.

"So this is how it works. Everyone writes down three questions, one for every person here not counting yourself. Write the person's name and a question that you really want to ask them. It's kind of like Truth or Dare, but without the daring, and better, because the questions are anonymous."

Meg seems really excited about this, so I try not to reveal how terrible an idea I think it is. But really. I would rather drive another hundred miles down cliffs in the dark.

"Maybe we should just watch TV," I say.

But they are already writing questions, covering their slips of paper with cupped hands like fifth-graders taking a test. So I pick up my pencil and write,

Meg: Is your hair naturally pink?

Alexa: If you could describe your mood in a color, what color would you choose?

Bev: I can't believe you didn't tell me.

Once the folded strips are in the hat, Meg feels around for the first strip of paper, and pulls it out with flourish.

She clears her throat. "Alexa, the first question is for you. Are you ready?"

Alexa nods. Her expression turns serious and she brushes her long black hair away from her face and looks at Meg.

Meg reads, "'If you could go back in time and change your mind about a decision you made in high school, what would you do?'"

Meg looks like the host from a reality show, head tilted toward Alexa with an expression of mild concern and expectation. Bev absentmindedly runs her hand through her newly short hair. Her gaze is fixed above Alexa, through the open window. I wonder which of them asked the question.

"I regret not going to prom," Alexa says. "Which sounds really stupid, because I know that we all decided that we were over high school and over dances, but I regretted it right away."

"Oh no, really?" Meg says. The TV host look is gone now, replaced by real concern.

Alexa shrugs. "It's not a tragedy or anything. I can go to mine next year. But, yeah. I kind of wanted to get dressed up with you guys and wear a flower on my wrist. I bet the energy would have been great. All these people, together for one of the last times ever."

Bev says, "Everyone said the after-party was the best part, and we made it to that."

"True." Alexa nods. "But it would have been nice to see everyone when they still looked all dressed up and pretty. Before all the puking. Don't you think? Next year I'm going to go. Even if I think I'm over it. Because all there is, is prom and finals and graduation, and then it's really over."

"I don't know, Lex," Meg says. "This may be sentimentality talking. We'll check back in with you a few months from now."

She reaches into the hat.

"Question two is for Bev. 'Bev, what was the saddest moment of your life?'"

Bev's position stays the same—her legs extended across the carpet, one arm propped casually on the couch, fingers through hair—but her face darkens. I wonder about these questions, who wrote each and why all of them are so into this game, why they think it's better than just asking about the things they want to know.

But okay, yeah: I still want to know what Bev will say.

She isn't answering yet. Instead she's silent, picking at the worn pink carpet, silent for so long I wonder if it's possible she didn't hear the question, or heard it but thought it was for someone else.

"Bev?" Alexa finally says.

Bev looks up.

"Pass," she says.

"No passing," Meg says. "Against the rules."

"What rules? You made this up."

"Wait a second," I say. "'Pass' because you can't think of anything or 'pass' because you don't want to tell us?"

"I can think of something," Bev says.

"Do *I* know?" I ask. I can think of a couple moments that would make it onto Bev's sad list, mostly involving death, but for some reason none of them feel like they would be her single saddest thing.

Bev turns back to the rug. She shakes her head, no. And I can't even contain how much this pisses me off. Bev knows everything about me. Everything.

Meg says, "It's my game. There's no passing."

Alexa turns to Meg and mouths, *Stop it*. She scoots over to Bev and puts an arm around her.

I watch Bev act as though she doesn't notice Alexa's gesture, and think, *Who is this girl?* And at the same time, under that, is the beginning of a memory. I feel like there was something, once, that happened. Something that she tried to tell me, or almost told me, but never did.

"It's okay," Alexa says. "You can pass."

Meg stops pushing but cuts the consoling short.

"Question three is for Colby. 'Colby, if you could make out with any of us, who would you choose?'"

She smiles brightly at me. I lock eyes with her and force myself to smile back.

"You, of course," I say. "I'm going to go outside now and imagine it."

I grab my music and my headphones and go out onto the balcony. I lie down on top of Alexa's sleeping bag and look at the stars. Even through the closed glass door I can hear them giggling, reading my question, saying, "Bev, it's pretty clear that one's from Colby." I listen for Bev's voice but I don't hear it.

I call Uncle Pete.

"Hey-it's-me-everything's-fine," I say, which is what I've said since I was a kid and my mom's voice was panicked when I would call her from a friend's house. I'd be calling to know what time she was getting me or if I should wait to eat dinner, and she'd respond by saying something like, *Thank God, I thought you might have been hurt.*

"How's Melinda?" Pete asks.

"She's running great," I say. "No problems yet."

"Don't say 'yet.' Why would you say 'yet'?"

"Did I say that? What I meant was she's running so smoothly that I have no worries at all."

"Better," he says. "Have you been checking her oil?"

"No, should I be?"

"Do it in the morning. Just to be safe. There's extra oil under the driver's seat if you need it. Fill her up with that, not any other kind."

"Okay."

He goes on for a while, asking me more questions about the bus and how it's running, and even though he's worried over nothing it's sort of calming to answer his questions and to say yes to all of his requests.

"What are you doing?" I ask him once he seems less worried.

"I was looking through some things from the old days. Tour stuff. You've got me feeling nostalgic."

"What kind of tour stuff?"

"Some snapshots. Jesus, I was a good-looking kid. I had almost forgotten. Also, business cards from every place we played a show. Sometimes we played at people's houses. They didn't have business cards so we'd have them write their names and addresses on scratch paper to go in the tour journal."

"I want to see the pictures."

"Yeah, there are some great ones. I found one of the night your mom and dad met."

He says this and, for a moment, I feel like I'm sinking. There is a question I need to ask, but I don't know how to ask it. An uneasy feeling that's been getting stronger the longer Ma has stayed away.

"Have you heard from her?" I say.

"We talked a few nights ago. I had to keep reminding her that I don't know French."

"What did you talk about?"

"Oh, I don't know. Paris, her classes, your trip."

The sinking gives way to nausea.

"How she's so proud of you for making your own decisions," Pete continues. "Living your own life. You know, she was worried at first about you not going straight to college, but we talked about it together. I told her she raised the best kind of person: an independent thinker."

Pete, I want to say. *Something happened.*

"Because, like me, you're a traveler. But unlike me, you have a plan. And unlike your mother, you know what it is you really want. You aren't going to squander your opportunities."

"Uh-huh," I mutter.

"It's inspiring, you know that? Knowing you're out there now and soon you'll be country-hopping with Bev, spending time on those islands you're crazy about. Your dad and I were talking last night about hitting the road in Melinda for a couple weeks after you go. Visiting the old haunts, seeing how they've changed. You make me want to stir up my life a little."

I want to tell Pete everything, but how can I—especially after this? He never had his own kids, so somehow I've become the only child to all three of them, and no matter how great they are, even if they hold secret conferences to discuss my choices and praise me, it's a lot of pressure to carry their hope and admiration and worry all on my own.

I want to ask Pete to tell me what's next after all of this. But it's a question that feels too huge, too impossible. So I let the conversation end, promise a million things about Melinda, and tell Uncle Pete good night.

It's still warm outside but a breeze has picked up. I browse through song choices and settle on "Modern Girl," the track Bev listened to on repeat for the entire summer before ninth grade. I choose this song because it's connected to what I was trying to remember earlier, after Bev didn't answer the question, and even though I would rather be thinking about anything else, I can't stop thinking about what else she's keeping from me.

I close my eyes as the guitar starts.

"Listen to the lyrics," I remember Bev saying.

"They're cool. I like the donut part."

"They're perfect."

"Yeah, they're good," I said. "They're simple."

Bev started the song over again.

"Listen," she said.

"I know," I said. "I've memorized it."

She looked discouraged, and then I got the feeling that this was about more than how good the lyrics were. We were quiet. Carrie was singing, *Hunger makes me a modern girl.*

"Are you trying to tell me something?"

She turned up the volume. *My whole life was like a picture of a sunny day.*

In the other room, her mom and dad were watching TV. I could hear them laughing. There was a line between her eyebrows, her mouth curved down. The lines came again.

I tried to figure out what she meant.

"Has something changed?" I asked.

She didn't answer me.

I spent the rest of the night trying to get her to tell me what it was, but she didn't. She just played the song over and over as we talked about other things. I thought about what my mom told me in one of our many awkward conversations about Bev and me now that we were older, about how teenage girls can be complicated and mysterious creatures. My mother had never been so right about anything. Because here was Bev, sitting in the bedroom that was as familiar as my own, looking at me with the same eyes I'd been looking into since we were nine, trying to get me to understand something by just listening to a song. Maybe there was something important that she wanted me to know. But probably Ma was right. Probably all Bev was trying to tell me was that she was now older and therefore complicated and mysterious and so fucking attractive and troubled in the way that all teenagers are troubled.

So I just listened to the song and watched every gesture she made, and searched for the clues to figure her out, and then the night got later and her dad appeared in the doorway to move me out to the couch, and I said good night and thought so much about what it would feel like to touch her that I forgot about everything else.

———

Later, Alexa wakes me with a squeeze of my shoulder. She takes an earbud out of one ear. "Hey," she says, "we're going to bed now, okay?"

It must be at least 3:00 A.M. The air has gotten cooler.

"Were you talking to your dad earlier? When you first came out here?"

I shake my head. "Uncle Pete."

"I have some questions for them. Research, for the play. Next time you're going to call them will you let me know?"

"Sure," I say. "How was the game?"

"It was good," she says. "We left something for you on your pillow."

I brush my teeth with Meg. We try not to crowd each other, take turns spitting into the gray, cracked sink. Bev isn't here, but I don't ask where she's gone. She's probably outside, leaning against a wall and smoking cigarettes like someone in a movie.

I slip off my jeans by the side of my bed, and see what they've left for me. On the other side of the slips of paper, Meg and Alexa have answered my questions. Meg's says, *No, but that's sweet of you to ask*; Alexa has written, *the color of melinda*.

Bev didn't leave an answer. Of course.

I pull the comforter off the bed and settle under the sheets. Soon after, I hear the door opening and shutting, half a dozen locks being turned or slid into place. I close my eyes and imagine that an hour has passed. Everyone has fallen asleep. I feel a weight on the mattress. Bev's lips graze my ear. She says, *I need to be with you.* I turn, and kiss her, and her tongue is soft and cool.

I knew you'd change your mind, I say. And everything we do we need to do so quietly, careful not to wake the others. She gasps every time I touch her, and she digs her fingers into my back because she's never felt as good as I'm making her feel.

Suddenly, there is a clicking sound. Brightness behind my eyelids. I open my eyes to Bev digging through her purse in a white tank top and tiny yellow shorts. She's moved a lamp from Meg's bedside table to the floor next to her. I watch her open a little white tube and put stuff on her lips, and even though she's across the room I know that the stuff is clear and smells like mint and makes her lips shiny. She screws the cap back on and drops it back into her purse. She finds a pen next, rips a strip of paper from one of Meg's trashy magazines, and writes something down. Then she folds the scrap of paper in half and drops it into her bag. This is what Bev does instead of making to-do lists or writing words on her hand. I wonder what she's hoping to remember.

She sets down the bag and walks silently to the foot of my bed. I close my eyes again, and hope. There is the noise of the blanket rustling, but no weight on the mattress, nothing whispered. I look for her again. She's moved my comforter to the couch, and now she's draping it over her lap. She moves the lamp closer, takes a piece of driftwood in one hand and a carving knife in the other, and works all night long.

I know this, because I don't sleep either.

Monday

Sunlight in an unfamiliar room.

A scratchy pillowcase.

The smell of coffee and eggs and burned toast.

I open my eyes and sit up, and Meg, pink haired in a red dress, hands me a mug. Steam rises.

"You're amazing," I say.

"I know," she says.

When I carry my coffee into the kitchen, Bev is already seated with her toast half finished, reading Meg's gossip magazine. Her hair is messy, sticking up on one side. Normally I'd make some joke and smooth it down for her, but I keep my hands by my sides. I don't know what it would feel like to touch her anymore. I sit in a green vinyl chair, and Meg sets a plate in front of me.

"*Alex-a,*" she calls. "*Your eggs are getting cold.*"

There are only two chairs, so Alexa hops onto the windowsill.

She stares in wonder at the eggs and toast, and I know how she feels, how everyday things are rare and exciting when they turn up in unfamiliar places.

"How did you do this?" Alexa asks.

"Breakfast is only a part of it," Meg says. "Today is going to be fantastic. What happened is this: I woke up really early and came in here because I was thirsty. So I opened the cupboard and saw that there were plates and a pan and some mugs, and then I looked up and I saw . . ." Meg pauses for effect. I take another bite of eggs.

"This!" She points to a woodcarving on the wall. Like the well-trained art students we are, we stand and gather around it.

"It looks pretty old," Alexa says.

"Yeah," I say, "but the colors are still so saturated."

The colors are the arches of a rainbow, and a sun rising over the dips in two green hills. In black italics, under the hills, is written: *Good morning, sunshine.* Despite our cocked heads and intent gazes, this is not something that would ever hang in a museum. It's more like something a kid would make in a wood-shop class, or something left over from the seventies, hanging on a motel wall because there is no better place for it.

But, still. I like it.

"So I thought, *This is perfect!* Obviously. And then I knew right away that I needed to get it tattooed. I've been searching for the right tattoo forever, and now I've found it. My next step was to find a good tattoo shop nearby, so I went into the market and that girl was there again and she said that her friend, some guy named Jasper, works at a place half a mile from here and that he'll be there today at eleven. And then I bought some eggs and bread and coffee."

Alexa steps back from the carving.

"Don't you think you should think about it?" she asks. "This feels kind of fast."

"It doesn't matter that it's fast," Meg says. "It's perfect."

"Maybe you could think about it for the next couple of days, though. You might regret it. This is your body and your body is sacred."

Meg shakes her head as though she is hearing crazy, incomprehensible things.

"But, Alexa," she says, "the beautiful thing about me is that I never regret anything. Ever. If I had gotten your question last night I would have disappointed all of you."

Meg looks at me. She looks at Bev.

"Guys," she says to us. "Help a girl out."

I can see that Alexa's worried, so I feel like an asshole when I say it, but I can't lie.

"I think it's rad," I tell Meg. "I think you should do it."

"Thank you," she says. "Bev?"

Bev leans against the wall and contemplates. I follow her gaze as it moves from Meg to the carving and back to Meg. She takes a slow sip of coffee and swallows.

"Yeah," she says. "It suits you."

"All right!" Meg smiles, triumphant. "It's three against one. Jasper, here I come."

The conversation shifts to the carving itself, and how Meg will need to bring it with her, and how it will probably require stealing—a prospect that in no way excites Meg, who never steals and never lies and believes wholeheartedly in karma. I don't listen that closely, though, because I'm busy watching Bev lean against the counter and sip her coffee, not sure how I feel about this small agreement.

Finally, Alexa stands on her tiptoes to reach the carving, and, sighing, removes it from its hook.

"Done. Okay?" And she shakes her head as if to ask if she really has to do everything for us.

The tattoo parlor is in the upstairs of an old building with high ceilings and shiny white walls. Huge windows open to telephone wires and blue sky. Meg plops down on a couch; Alexa and Bev and I grab binders of tattoo designs; and a skinny kid walks out from the room in the back and says, surprised, "Hey, I know you guys."

He has full-sleeve tattoos and a lip ring and, despite these things, he looks young and wholesome, like a twelve-year-old in a really good Halloween costume.

"I was at your show last night," he adds. "You guys were awesome." He sort of falters when he says the word awesome, and smiles wider to appear more convincing.

"Are you Jasper?" Meg asks.

"Yeah," he says, still smiling and bobbing his head. We all shake hands, and I'm amazed at how good even shaking hands feels now that we're away from home and on our own time and old enough to get tattoos if we want them.

Before Meg disappears into the back room with Jasper, she turns to her little sister and says, "Lex, it'll be okay. People get tattoos all the time."

And maybe it's because Jasper is so chill and approachable, or because his voice doesn't falter at all when he tells us that the *Good Morning, Sunshine* design is going to make "like, the most kickass tattoo ever," or because when sitting on a couch in a tattoo parlor with designs hanging on the wall and cataloged in books, getting a tattoo seems entirely natural—Alexa says, "Oh, I know. I can't wait to see it."

Bev takes Meg's seat on the couch and I sit across from her in a red chair, and for a while we just flip through the binders and listen to the buzzing of the needle and Elliott Smith playing faintly in the back room. Alexa takes a collection of one-act plays from her purse and reads, absent-mindedly twisting her brown feather earring when she isn't turning a page.

I find a stack of calendars on the table, hand-stapled and unevenly cut. Each month features a client's tattoo, obviously shot with some cheap digital camera. Now that my days aren't dictated by school bells and homework, I could really use a calendar.

"Hey, Jasper," I call. "Are these calendars free?"

The buzzing of the needle pauses.

"Yeah, bro, help yourself. January and March are my designs."

Buzzing resumes. I flip to the months. January: a necklace of leaves. March: an owl. Meg got lucky; his work is really good.

Alexa hands me a pen and tells me our plan for the rest of the week. This afternoon we'll drive to Arcata for a show at a bar called The Alibi. Tuesday morning we'll head east to Weaverville for an afternoon café gig. Then we'll make our way north, toward Oregon, and stop somewhere off the highway.

"What should I write for Tuesday night?"

"Hopefully Yreka or something, but I don't know yet. We could end up anywhere."

"I can't write 'anywhere.'"

"Write 'Unknown Motel,'" she says. I do.

From there we'll go to Ashland, where Meg and Alexa's aunt and uncle live, and spend the night with them. And then, we'll drive to Portland for The Disenchantments' last show, and move Meg into her dorm room. We'll drive home after that, in one ten-hour day.

"Then what?" Alexa asks.

"What do you mean?"

"Have you thought about what you're going to do?"

I glance at Bev. She's flipping through the binder pages, pretending not to hear us.

I shake my head. "Not yet," I say.

"Maybe you should teach art lessons to little kids. There are tons of summer camps. I'm sure you could find one."

I don't say anything.

"Not interested?" Alexa asks. "I'll keep thinking."

She crosses the room and peers through the doorway, and I get out my sketchbook and start drawing. Alexa comes back and whispers, "Jasper looks super focused, and Meg gave me thumbs-up, so I think things are going okay."

She looks at my drawing, then over to Bev.

"Bev, you have a pretty neck," she says. "I didn't really notice it until Colby drew it."

I shake my head. My drawing doesn't even compare. But more than that I'm angry at myself for drawing her. Over and over. As if there isn't anything or anyone else that can distract me from her. But Bev just flashes Alexa a brief smile and turns back to the binder—I've been drawing her forever, she's used to it by now—and my face feels hot and I need to think of something else to say.

I'm about to ask Alexa to show me her notebook full of professions when Bev says, "Oh my God, Colby, look at this."

She's staring at a page in one of the binders. She doesn't turn the page toward me, so I slide onto the sofa next to her. Laying the binder across our touching thighs, she says, again, "Look."

I'm not sure I want to sit here, together, but even after everything that's happened it doesn't feel different to be close to her. Her body feels the same.

She points, but she doesn't need to. In the binder is an image I'd recognize anywhere: a bluebird perched on a telephone wire, holding a bouquet of red flowers in its beak. A rain cloud hovers right above the bird, but the raindrops part above its head, leaving the bird dry and content.

"What is it?" Alexa asks.

"Holy shit," I say.

"How could it have gotten here?" Bev asks.

I shake my head. "I have no idea," I say. "This is impossible."

"I know, right?" Bev says.

"What?" Alexa says.

"This is my dad's old album cover. It's exactly like this except that across the top of the tape it said The Rainclouds."

"Someone's obsessed with your dad's band?" Alexa guesses. "Or maybe the picture's been used on other things?"

"I don't think so," Bev says. "Colby's mom painted this just for the cover."

"The painting's hanging in my dining room," I add, and I think of us all sitting at the table, eating dinner together—first my mom and my dad and me and sometimes Uncle Pete, and then all of us and Bev, too, who in eighth grade started to join us at least a few times a week. We spooned countless bowls of carrot ginger soup and ate hundreds of plates worth of grilled vegetables and tofu and rice and spinach salads, and we did it all under the gaze of this fortunate, blue-feathered bird.

I reach into my pocket for my phone, and have to lean into Bev a little to do it. The image of the tattoo appears on the screen of my phone and I snap the picture and send it to my dad.

"Send it to your mom, too," Bev says.

A moment later the phone rings and it's my dad saying, "This is wild!" And as we're talking my mom texts me back with Is THAT A TATTOO!? Alexa takes out a journal and starts writing, probably notes for her play.

Bev sends Mom more details because I can't text and talk to my dad on the same phone, and then Bev takes her own picture of the tattoo and sends it to Uncle Pete, who writes back with, No way! And it's all very fun and chaotic, with several conversations going on at once, but as Dad tells me about the concept for the painting and Mom describes her amazement over the idea of her artwork being permanently on someone's body and Uncle Pete keeps appearing in my call waiting—I'm thinking about how we used to all be together. How after dinner Bev and I would go back to my room to talk and do homework and record ourselves singing while Mom and Dad and Uncle Pete would hang out in the living room with the record player spinning, listening to music from when they were young and trying to hide the marijuana smell by holding their joint out the window. If this were a year or two ago, Bev and I would have put ourselves on speaker phone and talked to the three of them gathered together in one room, and I wouldn't have to avert my eyes when I caught myself watching her, and this conversation would not be in any way lonely.

A little later, Jasper walks into the waiting area.

"Meg's in the bathroom," he tells us, taking the chair I was sitting in before I moved next to Bev. "She did great."

"How does it look?" Alexa asks.

"Check it out for yourself," he says.

Meg emerges from the back with a sunrise and a rainbow on her chest. Her makeup is smeared under her eyes but she's glowing.

We gather around her. Meg: her own piece of art.

"Rad," Bev says.

Alexa smiles. "It's like an affirmation or something. You'll never have another bad morning."

"It looks even better than the original," I say to Jasper.

"The original's on a piece of wood," Jasper says. "This one's on a hot girl. Ready to get bandaged up?"

Meg nods yes.

"So, hey," I say. "How long have you worked here? I have a question about something."

"Sure, come on back," Jasper says. I perch on a stool while he covers Meg's tattoo with gauze and tape.

"See this?" I ask.

He peers over to get a good look at the bird tattoo in the binder and I tell him about where it came from.

"That's crazy," Jasper says. "It's like you guys were, like, destined to come here and find this."

"I completely agree," Alexa says from the doorway, her journal and pen in hand.

"Alexa's really into fate," I say.

Jasper says, "Well, yeah. If this isn't fate then what is, right?"

Jasper explains that he's only technically worked here for a couple years but that he grew up in the shop because his older brother is also a tattoo artist there.

"I started apprenticing when I was fourteen," he says. "They made me practice on myself for a while and then they let me practice on them and then after like a million years

I started to get my own customers." He looks down at the binder and strikes *The Thinker* pose, shoulders hunched, chin on fist and says, "Well, this is one of the oldest binders—way before my time. This is from, like, the early nineties. All I can tell is that it's on a back, and it's a dude's back. My brother might know something about it. I'll try to reach him, but he's at a convention right now. And if he doesn't know then Spider'll definitely know. He's the owner."

He keys my number into his phone and promises a speedy follow-up, and we've said good-bye and are almost out the door to go for lunch, when I say, "Hey, want to come eat with us?"

His whole face lights up when I say it and he jumps off the stool he was sitting on. He rips a light-colored page from a magazine.

"Got something to write with?"

I grab a Sharpie from my messenger bag and he writes *Be back in like an hour or something* and sticks it on the window with black tape.

We walk a few blocks to a burger stand with outdoor benches, place our orders, and pay far less than we should because Jasper knows the girl working.

"Are you sure?" I ask her as I hand over my share of cash.

"They make me wear this hideous hat," she says. "So yeah, I'm sure."

Bev and Jasper and I claim a bench while Alexa and Meg wait for our food to be ready.

Beat-up trucks and old American cars pass on the main road as we wait in the sun. Jasper takes off his hat, runs his hand over his shaggy hair, replaces the cap. Bev's phone vibrates. A text appears on the screen: SWING BY BEFORE U LEAVE. She deletes the text, then finds a name in her contacts and deletes it. I don't even try to hide the fact that I'm watching her do all of this.

"What's the point of getting someone's number if you're just going to erase it the next day?"

"It's awkward not to."

"And it's not awkward to ignore him?"

She shrugs. Jasper's leg bounces up and down, shakes the bench. He looks into the distance as if something has caught his attention.

Bev says, "It's what I always do. It's better for everyone this way."

"You mean it's better for *you*."

Bev sighs like I'm a little kid she has to deal with, and slips her phone into her bag.

"So, Jasper," she says, "do you like living here?"

"No," he says. "You don't have to be polite."

Bev smiles her great smile. Her dimple, her crooked tooth.

"There has to be something good about it," she says.

"Sure. That doesn't make it a good place, though."

Jasper begins listing the many reasons to dislike his hometown, and soon the girls walk over with trays of burgers and fries. Meg sets a basket of fries in front of me. I squeeze ketchup onto the white paper.

I put a fry into my mouth, look up to see Jasper eyeing me.

"Vegetarian?"

I nod.

"You like onions?" he asks.

"Sure," I say.

"Tomatoes?"

"Yeah."

He slides off the bench and returns a few minutes later with a grilled cheese on a hamburger bun. The sandwich has some kind of sauce and lettuce and tomatoes and onions. It isn't bad.

"A girl I used to date was a vegetarian. At least she pretended to be, but then if something looked really good she'd eat it anyway. Like, she would make me take her to certain places because they served salads and then she would take all these little bites of my burger. Like small bites don't count or something. I was like, *Newsflash: a little bit of a cow is still a cow.* She was a drag."

"Sounds like it," Meg says.

Jasper nods. Then, a minute later, he says, "Well, not a total drag. She's a cool girl. It was just that one thing that kind of got under my skin, you know?"

We eat in the sun, telling Jasper about our plans.

"So where are you going?" he asks. "And then where? What's it like there?" And the longer we talk the clearer it becomes that Jasper has never been anywhere except Los Angeles one time for a tattoo convention when he was a kid.

"What you got going on in San Francisco?" he asks us. "I mean, other than the band."

"We just graduated," I say. "All of us but Alexa."

Alexa smiles. "I get to come along because I'm the drummer. And we're moving my sister into the dorms in Portland."

Jasper looks from Meg to Bev, confused, and then we all laugh because we forget sometimes, that people don't understand how Meg and Alexa can be sisters and look so little alike.

"We're both adopted," Meg says, and Jasper rolls his eyes, and jokes, "I was just about to figure that out. I mean, I was *this* close."

He takes a bite of his burger and chews and swallows and then says, "So you graduated. Awesome. Now what?"

"I'm going to Lewis and Clark," Meg says.

"I'm going to RISD."

"Whoa," he says. "RISD. That's major."

Bev blushes, seems proud, and it's the first time I realize that it *is* a pretty big deal. I wonder if, when the college counselor tried to impress upon her the importance of going straight to school, instead of talking to her about tulips, Bev started talking about art school. Or if it came later. If it was her parents who had the idea. Or if all along, this is what she wanted.

"I'm still in high school," Alexa says. "One more year. And then I think I'll probably stay in the city and go to college and get a couple of jobs. There are a lot of things I want to do. I'm going to have to start prioritizing."

"She has this really cool list—Lex, show him—of jobs she wants to have," Meg says.

Alexa takes out her notebook and hands it to Jasper, who flips through it in awe. But Alexa doesn't notice his reaction, because she's intent on Meg.

"You think it's cool?" she asks.

"Of course," Meg says. "It's *so* cool."

"But you always make fun of it."

"Oh my God," Meg says. "Don't take me so seriously."

Alexa beams. When Jasper hands her the notebook back, she holds it like it's a thing of tremendous value. Which it is. It must be great knowing that if something doesn't work out, you have hundreds of backup plans.

Now they're all looking at me—all of them but Bev—because I'm the only one who hasn't answered yet.

I think about telling him that I'm taking a gap year, or something simple and closer to the truth, like, *I don't know.*

Instead I say, "Bev and I were supposed to go to Europe for a year, but instead she decided to go to college without telling me."

"Oh," Jasper says. "Hmm."

I feel bad for making him feel awkward, but I'm not going to pretend that things are fine when they're not. So I go on.

"Yeah," I say. "She told me yesterday. We were supposed to leave next week. She hasn't told me why yet, though."

Bev is staring at the table, not saying a word.

"*Why*, Bev?" I ask.

"*Really?*" she says, looking up at me. "You want me to tell you this *now*?" I can't remember ever hearing her voice sound this way: broken and angry.

"Actually," I say, "I wanted you to tell me yesterday. And a few months ago would have been even better."

"*Jasper,*" Meg says, all loud and dramatic like she's onstage. "What do *you* do? Besides giving spectacular tattoos, of course."

"I have a lot of money saved," Jasper says. "I'm just waiting for the right opportunity to present itself. I heard there's some reality show where a guy travels around the country in an RV and gives random people tattoos. Doing something like that would be cool. To tell you the truth I'd do just about anything to get out of here," he says. "I was thinking about college. For a little while. But no one in my family's been, and I don't know. I had my place waiting for me at the shop. But maybe someday," he says.

Bev picks up her tray and heads to the trash, and soon Alexa is pronouncing it time for us to go, and I'm feeling a little better to be in the company of someone who seems to have his shit together only slightly more than I do, considering that yeah, he has a skill and a job, but he isn't satisfied and doesn't know how to change that.

"San Francisco," he says to me. "At least if you have to change your plans, you'll be doing it there."

"Yeah," I say. "True." Because I know San Francisco's a great place to live and that I'm lucky to have a house to return to and parents to pay the bills and a million shows to choose from on any night of the week and things to sketch everywhere, and it would be a jackass move to turn to someone who doesn't seem to have any of that and say, But I want something *else*. Which is exactly how I feel.

We walk back to the tattoo parlor, to the bus, and say good-bye to Jasper. He says he'll call when he talks to his boss about the bird tattoo.

"I think that something is going to come out of this," Alexa says. "Something important."

"Well, I hope so," Jasper says. "I mean, what are the chances that you guys would end up in Fort *Drag* and decide to get a tattoo and come here and pick up one of the oldest look-books and find a tattoo that one of your moms made?"

"It's a mystery," Meg says.

"Hell yeah, it is. But don't worry, I'm going to figure it out."

Jasper steps back from the bus.

"Meg, take care of that tattoo. No Saran Wrap," he says, and then, to me: "I'll call you later, bro."

Meg wants to drive. Bev climbs into the passenger seat. I sit in the row behind them, off to the side, and Alexa lies down in the back row.

Meg pulls the bus away slowly, and when I glance in the rearview mirror I can see Jasper outside the shop, taking his time walking up the stairs, only reaching the door as the road curves and we leave him behind.

"Maybe we should have invited him to come," Meg says.

No one says anything.

But, yeah, maybe we should have.

We stop at the edge of town to get gas. I jump out and Alexa climbs out after me, takes snack orders for later and accepts our wrinkled bills, disappears into the mini-mart. Bev and Meg stay in the front seat, their windows rolled down, each of them wearing sunglasses that cover half their faces. We talk for a while about how great Meg's tattoo looks, and how much it hurts, and when the tank is full, I start on the windows.

"Sweet ride," says a guy at the pump across from me as I wipe down Melinda's windshield.

"Thanks," I say back. He's leaning against his own VW, a vintage black bug. "Not so bad yourself," I say.

He nods. "Bought it off my neighbor. Fixed it up. Yours?"

"It's my uncle's," I say. "We're borrowing it for a trip."

And then Alexa prances past him. She's holding something behind her back.

"Everybody," she says. "Listen. I have found something amazing."

Meg and Bev stop talking and turn to her from inside the bus. I look. VW bug guy watches, too.

Slowly, with one of the widest grins I've ever seen, Alexa presents us with a CD.

"The Essential Heart!"

I'm pretty sure Meg is rolling her eyes from behind her sunglasses.

"Thanks, Walt," she deadpans, but Alexa is unphased.

"It's a greatest hits album! *Two* discs!"

She rounds to the other side of the bus and soon a power ballad emanates from the speakers. I turn to the VW guy and shrug.

"How'd you end up with all of them?" he asks, amused.

"They're my friends," I say. "And their band's on tour."

"Are you their manager or something?"

"Not really. Maybe. I don't know." Somehow this answer satisfies him enough to move on.

"Where you headed?"

"Arcata."

"No shit, really? That's where I live."

"Yeah?"

"Yeah."

"They're playing somewhere called The Alibi."

He nods in recognition and checks his phone for the time.

"You'll get there with time to hang out first," he says. "There's the main square with stores and bars and places to eat. But actually," he says, eyeing the girls, "I know a better place. There's this café a few blocks off the square that has hot tubs in the back. Clothing optional," he says.

I glance into the van, at Alexa with her eyes closed listening to the music and Meg smirking and Bev watching me, and at first it pisses me off that he's picturing them all naked but really, who could blame him? Certainly not me.

"It's on Fifth and J," he says. I can tell that he's waiting for me to write it down so I open the door for the maps and a pen and write down the directions.

"Thanks, man," I say.

"No problem," he says. "Have fun."

"Meg, will you start the song over?" Alexa asks when I'm back in the bus with the door shut. "I want Colby to hear it."

Meg presses the back button and there it is: epic chords giving way to lyrics about loneliness and love.

I give Alexa a smile and a nod, not sure that I'm all that convincing.

"What was that guy telling you?" Bev asks.

"Not much," I say. "He's from Arcata."

"What did you write down?"

"He just told me about this place."

"You guys, listen," Alexa says. "Here's the chorus; it's so good."

"What place?" Meg asks, shouting over the louder singing and drums of the chorus.

"A café," I say. "With hot tubs."

"I like hot tubs," Meg yells. The song is now at its climax, the singer shouting *"What about love?"* The drums heavy, the guitars chaotic.

"We should go," Bev says. "Sounds fun."

The song fades out.

"You guys didn't listen," Alexa says, sounding hurt.

"Sorry, Lex, but I'm just not into them," Meg says.

"They're really cool. They're these really strong women, and they're sisters, and they've had tragic love lives and a career that's lasted forever. But it's fine. If you guys don't appreciate them you don't have to listen."

She seems so disappointed that I say, "No, they're fine, Lex. We'll listen. Bev, turn this one up, it sounds good."

But the damage is done, and Alexa has unbuckled her seat belt and is now reaching to the front to eject the CD.

"So we all have favorite girl bands now," Meg says, ignoring the sudden absence of music. "Yours is Heart. Mine's the Supremes, obviously. Bev's is Sleater-Kinney. Colby?"

I start to answer but Bev says it first: "Colby's favorite girl band is The Runaways." And there's something about that, the way she says it, that wrecks me. How hearing Bev say a simple fact about me reminds me of who we are to one another. And this—the distance, the anger—all feels so stupid. I want to find something to say that will bring us back, jolt us out of this, but then I catch her in the rearview mirror and the girl I see is a stranger. A stranger and a liar and a crusher of hopes. And my best friend.

"The Runaways," Meg says. "Impressive."

"Not really," I say. "They were just cool. When we started listening to Sleater-Kinney and Le Tigre and all of them, I started thinking about how The Runaways did it first. And Joan and Cherie were super hot, which helps."

Alexa says, "See, this drives me crazy. Colby, I'm not blaming you for this, but it seems like guys only like female musicians that are beautiful. All men need to succeed in the music industry is talent, but women have to be hot. It's infuriating."

"I don't know if that's completely true," I say.

"Believe me," she says. "It's true. Even Anne struggled with it because she wasn't naturally skinny. She used to starve herself and then, when that didn't work, they hardly even showed her in the videos. They just wanted to show Nancy all the time because she was prettier."

It takes me a moment to figure out what she's talking

about, but then I see her staring down at her CD booklet and realize that she's still on the subject of Heart.

"How do you know all of this?"

"Walt told me about it," she says. "He knows all about them."

Meg starts a new playlist, this one also beginning with a Supremes song, and I lean against one window and try to draw what I see through another.

But we pass it all so quickly: the telephone poles and wildflowers and hand-painted billboards for Jesus. The derelict farmhouses, the rusted-out trucks, the signs that tell us how close we're getting to the next small town. Everything I see is fleeting.

So, instead, I draw the back of Bev's neck for the seventh time today, and then I can't look at her any longer.

I dig through my stuff and pull out the calendar. Today and the next six days are filled in, but after that everything is empty. I mark my birthday and my parents' birthdays. I circle Christmas. Still, every blank square is filled with uncertainty. I find the day we'll arrive back home. *Unpack*, I write. *Laundry*. But these things are so simple, really more like items on a to-do list. So, on the next day, I write, *Get over this girl*.

A Sleater-Kinney song comes on and Bev leans forward and turns up the volume. She nods her head with the beat in this way that's kind of nerdy but still gorgeous. I write, *Get over this girl* on the day after, too. And then I keep writing it over and over, until it covers the summer months. Until my plans seem less open.

The bus has fallen quiet. Meg steers us through a turn in the road and, as soon as the curve ends, we are in the middle of a tiny coastal town, with only two short blocks of houses and stores lining each side of the road, most of them old and falling apart. A pink, rusty bike lies in a lot overgrown with dry grass. Next to the bike, four little kids wait at a table, two sitting, two standing, watching the road.

Meg breaks our silence: "Lemonade!"

She pulls the bus over and jumps out. The rest of us follow her into the sun.

"Colby. Bev. We are about to do one of the best things there is to do in life. We are about to buy lemonade from a lemonade stand from grimy little kids who probably didn't wash their hands before squeezing all the lemons and dumping in the sugar. But we aren't going to mind because this is how it is supposed to be. And there is no fighting at a lemonade stand. And no sad looks or awkward silences, because all memories of lemonade stands are and forever must be pure and good and beautiful. Understood?"

We nod.

"All right then."

We cross the grass and gather in front of the table and Meg points to the hand-painted lemonade sign.

"Lemonade sounds sooo good right now!" she says to the kids.

The girl and boy at the table, clearly the leaders, check us out, skepticism in their tan, round faces.

They must be ten years younger than we are. Which makes me, for the first time ever, feel sort of old.

"How much?" Meg asks.

At the same time, the boy says twenty-five cents and the girl says fifty. He blushes. She ignores him, locking eyes with Meg.

"We can swing fifty."

The boy looks relieved, and when he smiles, I see where a new tooth is growing in, larger than the others. But the girl is strictly business.

"Four orders?" she asks.

We all say yes and nod, and she pours pink lemonade from a plastic pitcher into five Dixie cups. She moves carefully, arms shaky with the weight of the pitcher, careful not to spill.

"Two dollars," she says, and then all four of the kids stand with their hands extended to take our change.

We dig through our pockets, try to divvy the change among them. Bev is short a quarter.

"My wallet's in the bus."

Apparently, Meg's speech has made me benevolent, because before I realize what I'm doing I'm telling Bev, "I can cover you," and handing my coins to the girl. She counts them, making sure I haven't cheated her, and as I look down at her wild long hair and her dusty knees and her bike cast off to the side of her, I remember Bev and me when we were little kids, pedaling fast on our bikes through Golden Gate Park, down the trails and across the grass, past the tea garden and through herds of tourists who stepped to the side when they saw us coming.

And I wonder if Bev is thinking the same thing. She has her faraway look. She must be. It makes me want to step closer to her, so I do.

The kids hand us our Dixie cups and we finish the lemonade—really just pink water—in a single sip, crumple the cups, throw them away. I climb into the driver's seat and Bev climbs in shotgun.

"Copilot?" I say, and Bev nods. Alexa hands up the maps and directions.

Bev slips off her sandals and presses her feet against the dashboard, and as I start the bus I try not to look for too long at her ankles, her calves, her knees, the place where her thighs widen to her hips and the frayed hem of her shorts begins.

Nearing Arcata, we pass signs advertising the legend of Bigfoot, a place called Confusion Hill, a drive-through tree.

"Who thinks of these things?" Alexa asks.

"It sounds super fun," Meg says. "I want to go to Confusion Hill."

A little later, off the side of the road, Alexa spots a squat, beige building called the World Famous Exotic Dancing Club.

"Yeah, right," Meg says. *"World famous."*

"Sounds awful," Alexa says.

"Why is it awful?" Bev asks.

Alexa says, "Places like that degrade women."

"How do you know?" Meg asks. "I bet Colby would like it." She reaches forward to rumple my hair.

"Oh, yeah," I say. "The idea of sitting around with a bunch of drunk middle-aged men paying girls to strip for us sounds awesome."

"Maybe the girls like performing," Meg says. "Maybe it turns them on. Bev, you'd be good at it."

Bev turns around to face her. "What are you talking about?"

"The whole look but don't touch thing."

"Look but don't touch?"

"Yeah," Meg says, but she sounds less sure now, like she's regretting what she's saying before she even says it. "Just, you know, you lead people on sometimes."

Alexa tries to take over. "It isn't a bad thing," she says. "You know what you don't want to do, and that's good."

Bev is staring at them in disbelief. "I'd make a good stripper? Look but don't touch? *What* are you talking about?"

"I don't even know why I said anything."

"You've said it, though," Bev says. "So tell me."

Meg sighs. "It's just that you'll make out with people, but everyone knows it won't get past that."

"Why do they say that?"

"Because it never has," Meg says. "At Stewart's house a while ago a bunch of us were standing around and talking about Disenchantments shows, and we realized that apart from Alexa and me, everyone we were hanging out with had made out with you."

Bev turns back around in her seat. I glance at her; she's carving the beginnings of a person.

"Go ahead," she mutters.

"It wasn't that many people," Meg says. "Just Stewart and Amy and Jake."

"And Sara," Alexa says.

"Oh, yeah. That's when Amy and Sara were going out. But they all thought it was funny, you know, that they'd all made out with you but none of them got very far. So that's all that I'm saying about the stripper thing. A lot of people would like to do a lot more with you, but you'd rather have them look but not touch. Or at least not touch that much."

"I thought you had sex with Stewart," I say, and Bev doesn't answer me, doesn't look at Meg when Meg says, "Whoa, *what?*"

She just keeps carving and says, "Can we not talk about this?"

Alexa says, "You guys, it's fine if Bev doesn't want to talk about it. It's personal."

But Meg says, "No way. You had *sex* with Stewart? Why did he say you didn't? And why didn't you tell me?"

Bev offers some weak answer, something about how she can't be held responsible for what Stewart does or doesn't say, but her face is red and I don't think it's because the memory of having sex embarrasses her.

I think it's because she lied to me.

Because really, if Stewart *had* had sex with Bev, everyone would have known. Not because Stewart is an asshole or anything, but because all he would've had to have done is tell a couple people and word would have spread instantly.

The night she told me, we were at a show at this venue on 11th Street where we went a lot, because it's one of the few that admits all ages. It was like any other night we'd go to shows. I'd leave her during the opening act to get us drinks from the bar, excuse myself back through the crowd to her, hand her her drink. Coke, usually. Beer if we got lucky and the bartender was too busy or bored to care. For some reason, though, this night felt different. I think she was dressed up more than usual. Her hair was different. When I told her I'd go get us drinks, it felt, for the first time ever, like we were on a date. Even when I ordered I wondered what the bartender thought as she handed me my sodas, if she expected that I was going to head back to my girlfriend. I caught sight of Bev's long blond hair and made my way back to her, and let myself imagine it—what it would be like, if Bev were my girlfriend. And then I handed her the

Coke and when our hands touched I allowed it to be significant. Through the show I stood next to her, but a little bit behind her. We were surrounded by couples, and they were all leaning into each other or holding hands. I wondered if she felt me standing there the way I felt it. Knew that if she leaned back only a centimeter, her head would be resting on my shoulder.

And then the opening act finished their set and she turned to me and said, "I had sex with Stewart last night."

And I felt all of the air escape the room, but managed to ask, "When?"

"During the party."

"Okay," I said. Which was a stupid response but all I could come up with.

She shrugged. "It was fine," she said. "He wanted to, and I figured why not just do it, right?"

I couldn't figure out when it could have been, because I had seen them making out on the back deck, and then I saw her, just a little while later, with Meg and a few of their other friends, and the time in between seemed too short. But I didn't know. Parties did something to time, I thought. Sped things up. What felt like a few minutes could have been half an hour. And really. The when of it didn't matter. What mattered was the who, and the who wasn't me.

I finished my Coke and she finished hers, too, so I took our empty plastic cups and didn't set them by our feet like I usually did. Instead I made my way through the crowd again over to the side of the stage where the trash cans were. I threw them away. When the band we came to see started playing, I didn't even try to get back to Bev. I found a place to lean against the bar that wasn't taken because of a beam that stood from floor to ceiling and blocked the view of the entire stage. I stayed there for a while, and then, toward the end, made my way back to her. When I found her again I made sure not to stand too close.

All at once, it isn't even a question I'm entertaining. I know that I'm right. Bev never had sex with Stewart. Which means, I think, that she hasn't slept with anyone. So now I'm left with this need to know, again, *why* she would lie to me. About so many things.

Alexa and Meg are still talking about the ethics of the sex industry. They keep the debate going for miles, but Bev and I mostly stay quiet, and that night at the show plays over in my head until she interrupts the memory by asking, "Have you told your mom yet?"

She says this quietly, only for me. It pulls me back from the feeling of that night and the road and the trees out the windows, back into this space with her.

"Told my mom what?" I ask.

I glance in the rearview mirror. Meg's pressing down the edges of her tattoo bandage, she and Alexa still deep in conversation.

"That you aren't going," Bev says.

Signs for highway changes appear in the distance. Bev

holds the directions but she has forgotten to direct us; she doesn't even look at them. Reflected in the windshield glass, her face looks faraway and sad.

"Why would I tell her that?" I ask, turning onto a new highway because its sign says Arcata.

"Are you going anyway?"

I shrug. "I don't know. Maybe." But really I'm just saying this because it's better than saying that I don't want to go by myself, that whenever I thought about traveling I pictured traveling with her.

"I wish I could go with you, just to your mom's. At first I was thinking that I might be able to go and then fly from Paris to Rhode Island, but I don't have enough money."

"We've been saving since freshman year," I remind her.

The highway has turned into a smaller road. I drive past a gas station, a Mexican restaurant, some random piles of lumber, and lots of small houses.

"I know," Bev says. "But I need it for school. My parents are taking out a loan for the tuition but I'm paying for my rent and food." She pauses, then adds, "The dorms are really expensive."

She's saying this all in the quietest voice—I can hear that she's sorry. But still. Picturing her sitting at the table with Mary and Gordon with loan applications and budgeting notes and the shiny RISD catalog, planning her next four years while I was still thinking that we were going away together to have an adventure, to do something different and meaningful, makes my vision blur and my hands clench the wheel so tightly they hurt.

We make our way past shops and restaurants and a theater, no longer in the outskirts of the city.

"Bev, I don't know where to go," I say, and I sound loud and frustrated enough that the whole bus falls silent.

"I know," Bev says. "I'm sorry."

"I mean right now," I shout. "You're holding the fucking directions, I just need you to read them."

She fumbles with the papers, trying to find the right one, to see where we are now, but I pull over and stop fast and grab them from her. I find out where we'll need to turn and pull back onto the road, keeping the directions on my lap.

"I can take it from here," Bev says.

She reaches for the directions but I tell her I got it.

"If I need your help I'll let you know," I say, and we drive the rest of the way in silence.

We drive through a residential neighborhood, past houses with neat fences and colorful gardens positioned next to houses with overgrown yards and boarded-up windows, until we reach the café. When the VW guy said hot tubs I pictured the places around the city that look super sketchy and weird, but this place is cool. It looks like it belongs in a Scandinavian village or something.

We walk in to find a couple guys our age at the counter.

One is steaming milk, the other stands with his back to us, carefully placing lettuce leaves in a bowl.

"Hey," says the barista. He scans the girls' faces, lifts his head at me. "You here for the café or the hot tubs?"

A few seconds later, they are poring over the hot tub price lists and I am ordering an eggplant sandwich, thankful for real food, and setting my backpack down on a table. No one invites me, and I'm not going to presume anything. Anyway: the three of them naked together might be a little more than I could handle.

The girls walk out into the back garden, bleached white towels slung over their arms. I take a seat. I've chosen a corner table, facing an unlit fireplace.

I finish my sandwich and pull out my sketchbook. A tabby cat sits on the table next to me as I draw the old man reading the paper at a table across the room. He doesn't look so hot. His ankles are red and swollen, and the closer I look at him, the more I start to think that he's probably homeless. I work for a while, getting the folds in his paper and the shadows across his shirt. His eyes are downcast and tired. How did he end up this way? I wonder what kind of plans he might have once had, what got in the way. The cat comes closer, and I pet her a few times, and as I pick up my pencil to go back to my drawing I see a red dress and pink hair.

"Come on," Meg says. "I'm buying us half an hour."

She starts packing up my stuff as I try to stop grinning.

I follow her out of the café and into the back, where cobblestones form a trail through flowers and shrubs to several wooden sheds. We find our shed and step in. The air is cooler inside and the light is dim.

"Close your eyes."

I do.

I hear the rustle of Meg's dress.

"No peeking, young man," she says, and I laugh, open my eyes anyway, see her standing in black panties with her arms above her head, her dress covering her face. I shut them before her dress comes off completely and she steps out of her underwear, but after enough time to see her full hips and thighs that are nothing like Bev's but still gorgeous.

I hear her step into the water.

"Shit, this is hot," she says. "Hold on. Okay, we're good."

I open my eyes to see Meg partway in the water, still in her bra with her tattoo safely dry.

She covers her eyes with her hand.

"Your turn," she says.

I undress quickly and step in.

"Don't splash me!"

I ease into the hot water and she lowers her hand. We sit across from each other, smiling, steam rising around us.

"This is the closest I've been to a naked girl," I tell her.

"Liar," she says. "You hooked up with that girl at Bev's party last year."

"Yeah, but we didn't get that far."

"I don't believe you."

"I wasn't really that interested."

"Anyway, I'm not naked. Don't you see this bra? This is the nicest bra I own. I paid forty bucks for it."

"Well worth it," I say.

"I know, right? Check out the lace on the sides."

"Yeah, that's hot."

"It's romantic," she corrects me.

"Okay," I say.

"Just for the record, I'm not hitting on you," Meg says.

"Yeah, I know. I'm not hitting on you, either."

"Oh, *I know*," Meg says, meaningfully, and even though I don't know what's happening with Bev and me, it still feels kind of good for Meg to say that. It makes it feel like there is something between us.

"So, what's going on with her?" Meg asks.

"What do you mean?"

She moves her hand slowly across the surface of the water.

"What kind of secrets is the girl keeping."

"I have no idea," I say.

The ends of her hair are wet now, turning a deeper pink, closer to red.

"I mean, I don't blame her. I've had my darker moments," she says. She changes positions and the surface of the water moves. "But why do you think she's keeping things from us?"

Light shines through slats in the roof. Steam rises. No explanation comes to me.

"I've never understood Bev less than I do right now," I say.

Meg reaches around the back of her neck, gathers her hair in one hand, and brings it around to one shoulder.

"That sounds really simple," I add, "but it isn't."

"It's just weird," Meg says. "I always count on Bev to be blunt about everything. Like during the play last year, she would always say if we made a choice that didn't work for her. I don't know why she wouldn't just tell us."

She wrings the ends of her hair out. Drops of water run down the unadorned side of her chest. She reaches out of the hot tub to grab a hair clip, and it takes all my willpower not to look at her body as she's looking away. It is dark in here, but my eyes have adjusted, and the water is only water, nothing I can't see through. But then Meg is facing me again, and it's enough to look at her breasts rising over her bra as she sighs and clips her hair back.

"What did you mean," I ask her, "that you've had your darker moments?"

"So we're done talking about Bev now?"

"I'm just wondering," I say. "You don't have to tell me."

"No, it's okay. I'll tell you. Short version or long version?"

"Whatever you want." I lean back against the side of

the tub and concentrate on Meg's face as she decides how to begin. She tilts her head, casts down her eyes.

"I went through this hard time in sixth grade," she says. "I started having panic attacks."

"Was something going on?"

She shakes her head, no. "It didn't really have anything to do with what was happening in my life. I mean, there were things that weren't helping. This friend of our parents' was dying. He had always been around and I really loved him, and then he got so sick and weak—he was suddenly old and it scared me to be around him. I started thinking about death all the time. And I had this teacher who I really liked but who kept saying these inappropriate things to me about the way I looked, just like all of these compliments all of the time that I knew were not really okay for him to say even though I kind of liked the attention. Also I was failing math. It didn't matter how hard I studied or how good of a tutor my dads got me, I failed every math test I took. But really, it wasn't about any of that. Anything could set me off. Like this one time, I was spending the night at my friend's house and I wanted to take a shower because we'd been swimming all day and I smelled like chlorine. So I took the shower, and when I got out I couldn't find a towel. So I started freaking out and crying because all I had was my bathing suit and I was too embarrassed to go back out into her house only wearing that."

She laughs, but there's sadness in it. "All I needed to

do was stick my head out and call for her down the hallway and she would have gotten me a towel. But instead I was all shaky and couldn't breathe and stayed in there until her mom knocked on the door and asked if I was okay. So, as you can see, it wasn't about the stuff that was happening. It was about me."

As she tells me all of this, I watch her from across the water: her smooth, pale skin and flushed cheeks, her lips that I've rarely before seen unsmiling. Sometimes it seems impossible to really know anyone. Before this moment I had thought of Meg as always confident, always fun, never nervous or sad or anxious about anything.

"So the panic attacks kept coming and they were so fucking scary. I mean, I was, what, eleven years old? I didn't even know that panic attacks existed. I thought I was dying."

"What did you do?"

"My parents took me to a therapist, and then the therapist referred me to someone who could prescribe meds, because the attacks kept coming."

"And the medicine worked?"

She nods.

"That must have been hard," I say. "To go through all that."

"It was just that before sixth grade everything in my life was good, and then suddenly I learned all of these things.

That I was going to lose someone I loved forever, and that someone I trusted might not have been that great of a person after all, that there were things that I just couldn't do right, no matter how hard I tried and worked at them. It was a lot to take in at once. And maybe most of all it was that I had this problem, you know? That I couldn't handle hard things on my own."

She looks into the black water; her brow furrows. Then she looks up again and smiles. She presses down the edges of her bandage.

"But from now on it's all about sunrises and rainbows."

She says this with such conviction that there is nothing I can say in return. So I lean back and close my eyes, slide farther into the warm water, listen to the sounds of life outside, and try to believe her.

Getting dressed in the shed after Meg has left, I pick up my phone and see that I have a voice mail from Jasper.

"Hey, bro," he says. "So Spider remembers the guy. Dude was the friend of this lady Spider used to date, who is also the mom of a girl I went to high school with. So I just have to get a hold of this chick Sadie and get her mom's number, and we should have a name. I'll get back to you. Oh, and tell Meg that it's time to take the bandage off if she hasn't already. Wash it with her hand and that soap I gave her, and then put on the ointment. And remind her to stay away from Saran Wrap. If I find out she's been suffocating my art in plastic I will be seriously pissed. Make sure to tell her that. All right. Peace, bro."

I set the phone back on the wooden bench and pull on my cutoffs. Then I think I hear Bev's voice.

"Whatever, it's fine," I hear her saying. "I just wanted to look at the downtown area before we have to check into the hotel, and we have to set up at the bar and I need to change my clothes. We have a lot to do and we just didn't have time for you and Colby to hang out in the hot tub for an hour."

"Thirty minutes," I hear Meg say. "And the bar is super close and it's on the same block as the hotel and we have two hours until the show starts."

I stand still and listen for what will come next.

"Obviously," Meg continues, "this is not about schedules."

I push open the door to the shed, and there they stand in the garden. Bev squints through the sun at me, startled.

"Hey," I say. I drop my keys in my pocket, and in the time it takes for me to pull my T-shirt over my head, Meg has walked away, leaving me and Bev alone together.

"I didn't mean to be an asshole in the bus," I tell her.

She nods, looks down at the dust.

"You heard Meg and me, right?"

"Yes."

"I got jealous," she says, and when she looks up at me, there is more openness in her face than I've seen in weeks.

"Why?" I ask. "Jealous of what?"

My heart pounds hard. Maybe this will be the moment.

"Jealous of Meg," she says.

I take a step toward her, but she turns, almost imperceptibly, away from me. My heart keeps pounding, but now for other reasons.

She reaches into her bag for her pack of cigarettes. I watch her light one and try to sound as calm as I can when I say, "What is this about?"

She sucks in smoke, waits for me to explain.

"This," I say, pointing to her cigarettes. "And the not answering the question, and the lying about college, and lying about Stewart, too."

She looks a little lost, a little scared, so unlike herself.

"What's going on?" I ask her.

She shrugs, but not like she doesn't care, like she really doesn't know the answer, or maybe just doesn't know how to tell me.

"I thought we could talk about anything."

I'm trying to stay calm and steady, like I'm coaxing an animal from a hiding place, but I watch as her face hardens. Soon, here it is again: the distance between us.

"I already told you about the application," she says.

"Yeah, but it didn't take twenty minutes. You need recommendation letters. You need to write essays. You need a portfolio. It takes planning."

"I meant the form, the online part."

"You were trying to make it sound like it was this casual, simple thing, but I know that it wasn't."

I watch her face as she searches for some way to defend herself.

I search, too, for new words to ask her to explain.

The light is fading; a breeze picks up. She finishes her cigarette. The cat from inside appears and brushes against my leg. I lean over to pet her for a while. When I stand again, Bev looks at me. I look at her.

We both give up.

We park on the outskirts of the square, in front of an abandoned building. Meg applies her bright red lipstick, Alexa combs her hair. I get out of the bus and lock the driver's door, lean against it and study the brick wall in front of me. Last year I did a research project on graffiti artists and it's cool, now, to look at the tags spread out on the wall and know something about them. Some of them are familiar, from groups of people who tag the same name, and some are new to me.

I follow a few tags across the wall, up to an expanse of whitewashed brick.

"Hey, you know what would be so cool?" I say. They've all gotten out of the bus now and come around to my side, looking where I'm looking. "If we graffitied The Disenchantments picture up here."

"Oh my God," Meg says. "That would be awesome."

We envision it, where each eye would go, how the tear would settle into an area of the wall where a few bricks are missing in a shape that's already almost tearlike, how we would paint the letters of the band name across the top.

"We should do it," Bev says.

Alexa nods.

"All we need is spray paint," I say. "I could stand on top of Melinda and you guys could stand on both sides of the block to let me know if anyone's coming. It would probably take around an hour," I say.

"Let's do it after the show," Meg says, and we all agree.

The square is pretty cool—grass and park benches, a few trees, old-fashioned streetlamps—and the buildings that surround it look like they're out of a Western. An American flag flaps above us.

Meg points out a record store. "Let's go in," she says.

"Sure," I say, but Bev wants to sit in the grass and carve, and Alexa sees a shop that sells hemp clothing and incense and tells us she'll meet up with us in a minute.

A bell on the door chimes as we walk in. I start at some Bob Dylan records, and recognize a few of them from my parents' collection.

"Colby, look at this." Meg holds up a Supremes record. "*Look* at Diana Ross's eyeliner."

I nod. "Cool."

She widens her eyes as if I'm crazy and pushes the record closer to my face, so I peer at it and say, "Oh my God, you're right. The way it starts all thin and then gets thicker. And, *whoa*," I grab at my heart. "That slight curve up in the corner . . . How will I ever draw again after seeing a line like this!"

"That's more like it." Meg puts the record back in the rack and flips to the next.

"You like The Supremes?" The girl who works there leans over the counter, closer to us. She's dressed similarly to Meg in a short strawberry-printed dress. She has long bangs swept to the side of her face and bright pink lipstick, and looks just a few years older than we are.

"They're my favorite," Meg says. "I just made ten playlists and every one starts with a Supremes song."

"*Every* one?" I ask.

The record store girl laughs. "That's so cool," she says. "Have you heard The Chiffons?"

Meg shakes her head, no.

The girl strides over to the *C* section and flips through a few records.

"I like your dress," Meg says.

"Yours, too," says the girl. "Oh, too bad. I guess someone bought them out since my last shift. They were recording at the same time as The Supremes, but they were on V-tone instead of—"

"Motown," Meg says, grinning. "How about The Marvelettes?"

"Love them," the girl says. She leads us to the *M*s and selects an album: *Please Mr. Postman.*

"I know that song," I say.

"It's sooo good," Meg says.

The girl nods. "Yeah, this whole album is fantastic. They came first, you know. Even before The Supremes and Martha and the Vandellas. I love Gladys Horton's voice."

Meg is so excited that her head moves like a bobble-head doll's. "I know, me too! It's like a little smokier than Diana Ross's, right?"

"Yeah. It's *so* sexy. So are you guys just passing through?"

"We're in a band," Meg says. "Well, I am, not Colby. It's a girl band. We're playing a show at The Alibi tonight."

"You should come," I say.

"Yeah!" Meg says. "You should *so* come."

"I wish I could," the girl says. "But my baby is with the sitter and I have to go straight home when my shift is over."

"That sucks." Meg looks away from the girl, crestfallen, but then her eyes focus on the record in her hand and she gets a little brighter. "I'm going to buy this," she says, and sets The Marvelettes record on to the counter.

"You'll love it. I have all of their albums. The Supremes', too. I even have all the EPs."

"Wow, really?"

She nods. "And some other groups."

"So you're a collector?" I ask, flipping through a stack of postcards as the girl rings Meg up.

She nods. "Yeah. It's why I got the job here. I needed the store discount. Plus sometimes it's hard to track down the rare recordings, so it helps to know all the distributors."

"So do you keep your collection at your house?" Meg asks.

"Yeah."

"Do you live close?" Meg tries to act casual, but it's clear she's looking for an invitation.

"Yeah," the girl says again. "Just a few blocks away. Are you sticking around for a couple days?"

Meg and I shake our heads. "We have a gig tomorrow," I say. "In Weaverville. An afternoon show."

I choose a postcard to send to Dad and Uncle Pete, a photo montage comprised of a bald eagle, an American flag, and a forest. It's so random and dramatic—I know they'll love it. I get out my wallet but the girl tells me not to worry about it, so I slip it in my backpack.

"God, I would love to see those records," Meg says. "They're, like, the original albums? From the sixties? Do you have *Meet the Supremes*?"

"Yeah, I have all of them."

"*Where Did Our Love Go?*"

She nods. "I have two. One of them is autographed."

Meg's eyes get wide. "Who signed it?"

The girl smiles.

"Florence?"

She shakes her head, no.

"Mary?"

No, again.

Meg looks like she's about to pass out. She opens her mouth, but it's like she can't even bring herself to say the name.

I help her out: "Diana?"

"Yeah," the girl says. "I had to save for months. Here you go."

She holds Meg's record out to her, now packaged in a flat, square paper bag. Meg says thanks and reaches for it, and for a moment they are both holding the record at the same time without letting go.

Then the girl releases the bag and steps back.

She nods and her eyes get far away. I can tell she's considering something, probably counting hours and reviewing her work schedule and wondering if she really wants to have us over.

Finally, she says, "It's great to meet someone else who loves The Supremes. Don't forget to look up The Chiffons, too. They're a really good group."

"Okay," Meg says. In spite of her attempts at nonchalance, she shrugs like she's a little pissed off. She manages a smile, and pauses in the doorway.

"'Come See About Me' is my favorite."

"Really?" the girl asks. "It's mine, too."

Meg waves good-bye, and we walk out into the late afternoon sunshine. Alexa has joined Bev already, so we go sit with them on the grass. Meg tells them the whole story.

"It's so disappointing," she says.

"Yeah," I say.

"I mean, how often do you meet someone who not only has the exact same favorite group as you but also the exact same favorite song by that group?"

"Yeah."

"And it was so obvious that she wanted to invite us over and I clearly wanted to see her record collection. I've never met anyone, except your parents and their weird friends—"

"What are you talking about? Our friends are great."

"—who even has a record collection at all. I even bought this record from her and I don't have a record player."

"It seems like it was almost a spiritual connection," Alexa says.

Meg scowls. "I don't know if I'd go *that* far."

Bev takes a break from carving to look up and ask, "Why'd you buy a record if you don't have any way to play it?"

"Because," Meg says, "that's what you do when someone tells you something is great. You take that risk."

"And at least now you'll have something to put on if you do get a record player someday," I add.

Bev nods like I've made a valid point, and turns back to her work. Her hand is covering most of the figure, but the size and wild hair makes me pretty sure it's Walt.

The show is in a bar called The Alibi, which is next door to another bar, The Serenader, and next door to that is our hotel. We check in, carry our bags up three fights of wide, red-carpeted stairs, and then try to enter the bar. Alexa explains to the bouncer that we are the band. She's already told us that, according to California law, you have to be eighteen or older to perform in a bar that does not also serve food, so we pull out our IDs. Mine, Bev's, and Meg's are real. Alexa's once belonged to Jessica Perez, who graduated a year ahead of us.

He lets us in and we carry all of the equipment past a group of guys and girls who barely look older than us, dressed in corduroys and flowy skirts and sandals, and then past older people with bad teeth and loud voices, until we reach the stage in back.

For a while, the girls just move around on the stage, taking instruments out of cases, plugging things in. I take a seat at the bar and Meg strums a low note; Alexa pounds a beat on her drums. Bev sings a phrase into the microphone, then steps back, picks up her guitar, and tunes it with her ear to the wood. A huge, porcelain mermaid looks over the stage with seaweed hair and a gold tail and glossy, white skin. I start to sketch the stage and the mermaid, but before long I'm just sketching Bev as she leans against a wall and waits for the rest of them to finish setting up. All the men in the bar are watching the three of them move. There is the promise of something good.

They start to play, and the bartender remains impassive.

Bev shouts the opening lines to their first song. A balding guy with a ponytail thrashes his head to what should be a beat. "Yeah!" he yells with what I think is complete sincerity. He continues to thrash for so long that I wonder if he might be hard of hearing, but a little after the second song begins—*"Silence on my mind, silence on my mind/You interrupt me, all the time, all the time"*—he gives up and returns to his drink.

We stay at the bar for a while after the show. I sit with Alexa and watch Bev from across the room as she talks to a girl with long red hair. The redhead throws back her head when she laughs, and she laughs often. She is the kind of girl that I would think was hot if she weren't hanging on Bev like an accessory. If the sight of her hand on Bev's waist didn't make my stomach hurt. Bev leans over the pool table and moves the cue back and forth between her fingers. I think of this song they keep playing in the car about a girl who watches constellations change with the pool balls, and the redhead leans over to whisper something in Bev's ear, and I feel so ready for something new.

So I leave Alexa and sit up at the bar and talk shit with the bartender. I'm such a cliché except for the fact that he's pouring me soda waters instead of shots and doesn't seem all that sympathetic to what I'm going through.

"Just one drink," I plead.

"The only drink you're getting from me is one I'd give to my five-year-old." He slices a lime and sticks it on the lip of my glass. A consolation prize.

"You're with the band?" he asks.

"Yeah."

"Just you and those girls?"

"Yeah."

"How'd you score that?"

"I wouldn't say any scoring took place."

I squeeze the lime into my drink. Sip. It does nothing for me.

"Just one," I say again. "Then I'll leave you alone, I swear."

He leans on the counter, close to me.

"Compel me."

This guy has huge shoulders and arms and a tight motorcycle shirt. His thick neck is covered in skull tattoos, but there is something in his face. Openness, maybe. Or just something kind. So I lean forward on the bar stool until our faces are close and I don't have to shout, and I say, "I just graduated from high school. I don't have a job or a car or an apartment. I'm not going to college. And I have no idea what I'm doing with my life."

He shakes his head with sympathy.

"That's part of it," I say.

"What's the other part?"

I turn to look for Bev, who is now making out with the redhead in the corner, point, and say, "I'm in love with that girl."

He squints to see better.

"Shit," he says.

I nod.

The bartender shakes his head again, says, "Kid, you're killing me," and pours me the biggest shot of whiskey I've seen in my eighteen years on Earth.

I drink my shot fast enough that he must feel confident in the fact that I have already been corrupted, because a few minutes later when he's finished with some customers at the other end of the bar, he comes back and, without a word, refills my glass.

He leans over the counter and scans the crowd.

"You guys know Sophie?" he asks.

"What?"

He points and I turn to see the girl from the record shop

talking to Meg. They are both beaming, and then Meg starts jumping up and down.

"We met her earlier," I say. "We invited her to the show."

Soon Meg has pried Bev from her redhead and rescued Alexa from a group of college guys, and she's up at the bar telling me that we have places to go.

"And by places," she says, "I mean Sophie's apartment. We are going to have a dance party."

"A dance party? Are you joking?"

"I wouldn't joke about something like this," Meg says, so excited that she looks almost deranged. She grabs me around the waist and pulls me off the bar stool. When I unfold my wallet the bartender shakes his head.

"I don't take money from children," he says.

"Do you mind taking your shoes off?" Sophie says at the door. "My baby just started crawling, so I want to keep the carpet clean for her."

The carpet is bright red shag. It matches the pattern of her dress so perfectly that I wonder if it came that way or if she chose the color. The girls all kick off their sandals, and I bend over to untie my laces. Blood rushes to my head; I almost stumble over. I catch myself, though, and soon I'm following the rest of them into Sophie's living room, which is decorated all retro with a yellow sofa and a beanbag chair, and tin signs decorating the walls, and a small, banged-up, but still cool, dinette set in the corner with red-and-white striped vinyl chairs.

A woman turns off the television and gets up from the couch. She smiles a simultaneous hello and good-bye, and slips out.

Meg is already across the room, gazing at the framed Supremes album cover. I make my way over to her.

Scrawled in black pen over the olive-green background is, *Dear Steve. With love, Diana.*

"Who's Steve?" Meg asks.

"I have no idea," Sophie answers.

Meg reaches out and traces *Diana* with her finger, and Sophie crosses the carpet to the record player. She finds a record, puts it on.

"This is the album I sold you earlier," she says. The record crackles and then the simple guitar chords and piano begin, and a woman sings, honestly, plainly, giving someone permission to break her heart.

"This is so good," I say.

But old songs are so short, and it's over almost immediately. When Meg manages to part from the framed record, Sophie asks us, "Do you want to see my baby?"

We all nod, even Bev, and Sophie makes us promise to be silent as the five of us tiptoe, barefoot, down the carpeted hallway. Sophie twists the knob and pushes open the door. We follow her in.

The crib is in the center of the room, with padding on the sides so we can't see through the wooden bars. We gather around it.

There she is.

One foot sticks out of the blanket, covered by little pink footie pajamas. Sophie covers the foot with the lightweight yellow blanket and the baby breathes in and then sighs. Sophie smiles and rests her hand on the baby's belly and we stand for a moment like this, together, watching her hand rise and fall with each breath.

"Sometimes," Sophie whispers, "I wake her up just to hold her. I can't help myself."

I look up at Sophie's face and watch as she watches the baby. Sophie's so young, it's crazy. I can't even fathom it—being responsible for a tiny person's life in just a couple of years. Paying rent not just for a room in a shared apartment, but for the entire apartment. In a way, though, it might ease the burden of decision making. The future wouldn't be so open; the list of possibilities would shorten. All the vast and terrifying questions—*Where should I go? Who should I be?*—would be replaced with absolutes. Rent an apartment. Find a job. Be a parent. Soon I'm seeing it. Bev and me back in the city, moving into a tiny two-bedroom. I'm working in an art supply store and she's waitressing at some cool new neighborhood restaurant, and we're tied to each other not only by love but also by this baby who we have to feed and dress and rock to sleep. And okay, maybe the whiskey is fucking with my head, but thinking about it fills me with longing for Bev again. Not anger, not even confusion. Just love. And hope. That one day we might have something like that.

"She's so tiny," Alexa whispers.

"Can I draw her?" I ask, before even thinking about asking.

Sophie cocks her head, looks at me curiously, but says, "Sure," and I'm relieved because I have to do something with this feeling.

So I go back out to the living room and grab my stetch-book and pencil, and then I return to the side of the crib and start to lay it out on the page. Soon Bev leaves, followed by Alexa. Then it's just Sophie and Meg and the baby and me.

"What happened with her dad?" Meg asks.

"We were never that serious."

"So he left?"

"Not exactly," Sophie says. "He offered to stay. I decided that I'd rather do it on my own. It's difficult, but it's better this way. To be just two."

"Was he a crappy guy?"

"No," she says. "But I didn't love him."

They stand with me for a while longer. I'm working on the folds of the blanket, the shape of the baby's body beneath it. Soon I get to her face. Her eyelashes, her full cheeks, her tiny, pouty lips, and her little chin, and Meg declares it time to get back to the records and Sophie tells me to take my time. She leaves the door open and light floods in from the hall. I sketch the baby's delicate fingers, her thin curls. Then her eyelids flicker and she sighs and moves a little bit, and I'm afraid that she's going to wake up. I put my hand down on her belly, the way Sophie did, and she breathes deep again and then quiets. She is so small and so warm.

Back out in the living room, the record louder now, an upbeat song playing, Sophie asks to see my drawing. I show her.

"This is incredible," she says, and though that might be an overstatement, it did turn out pretty well.

"Look at her little earlobe," she gasps. "It's perfect. It's exactly like her."

"Here," I say, tearing the page out of the book. "You keep it."

"Really?" she asks.

"Yeah," I say. "Of course."

Her face brightens and she darts up from the couch and over to a chest which she opens and rummages through.

"I got this at a garage sale a few weeks ago." She lifts out an old frame that's tarnished in a cool way. "I think it'll fit."

She makes me sign the drawing and then she puts it in the frame, and places the frame on a shelf near the signed record.

"I love this," she says. "*Love* it. How do you draw like that?"

I laugh. "I don't know," I say. "It's what I do."

I know that I'm good at drawing, but I've been doing it for so long that I don't even think about it that much. But she's standing here, surveying me like I've just performed magic. I start to get uncomfortable, so I laugh and say, "Hey, I thought this was a dance party," and soon everyone is dancing. Everyone except for Bev, who takes a seat on the beanbag chair and gets out her sculpting tools.

Meg and Sophie take turns at the record player, changing the tracks from one upbeat song to the next. We dance by ourselves, all together, in pairs. I'm tired and the alcohol hits me in waves. One moment I don't feel anything, and then the next I'm reeling.

A new song starts and Sophie grabs my hand.

"Most guys look so awkward when they dance," she says. "Not you."

"There's a reason for that," I tell her.

"Oh, yeah?" She arches an eyebrow.

"It's because I don't give a shit," I say. And when I say it, I believe it. Because really, it doesn't matter: Bev can make out with a girl in a bar, and I can go home and live with my dad, and my mom can live in Paris forever, and we might all still be okay. In just a little while we will forget all the things we used to want and adjust to the lives that we're given.

But Sophie laughs. She reaches out, grabs me around the waist, pulls me close. I stumble into her soft arms and feel her body against my chest.

"That's not why," she says into my ear.

Bev watches me from across the room where she sits, carving a drum kit. When she catches me looking back, she turns to her piece of wood.

I close my eyes.

The room spins and Sophie and I spin with it. Her eyelashes brush my forehead every time she blinks.

"Why is it then?" I ask, my mouth close to her ear this time.

"It's because you feel it so much," she says. I smile wide without pulling away because, of course, she's right. Before the song fades out, Meg starts a new one. Fast, showy piano, drums, and harmonizing women crackle through the speakers, and then a woman sings, *One fine day* . . . She sounds so happy even though she's singing about being dumped, and I can't tell if she actually believes that the guy she's singing to will ever love her, but it hardly matters because Sophie and I are moving faster to keep up with the tempo, and Meg is jumping and spinning around the room, pink hair everywhere, and Alexa dances like a hippie, all blissed out with her arms snaking above her.

I spin Sophie and when she comes back to me, I say, "You're right. I love this."

"It's The Chiffons," she says. "You have to love it."

But I don't just mean the music. I mean all of this, everything, the desperation of the song and the imprints of our feet on the red shag rug, Sophie's strawberry-print dress, the record player and every single record. The baby, sleeping through everything, sleeping through us. Meg and Alexa and Bev and Sophie. I'm in love with all of them.

The song ends before Meg has chosen another record, and as the room gets quiet I take a step away from Sophie. The floor tilts; I catch my breath.

"I'm in love with all of you," I say.

Alexa beams and Meg says, "Love you back." Sophie steps forward and rumples my hair, and Bev glares at me but the glare hardly matters because all I see are her gorgeous shoulders and her neck and her mouth that I've been wanting to kiss forever.

"Don't look so mad," I say to her. "Especially you."

Meg's slipping a new record out of its sleeve. "But Meg is the first girl I ever saw naked. See, Meg, I didn't forget."

"It happened approximately six hours ago. I *hope* you still remember."

Another song begins and I walk over to Bev. She's carving the crash cymbal. She doesn't look up at me.

"That's the cutest drum kit I've ever seen," I say, softer, just to her.

I extend my arm toward her. She still doesn't look.

"Dance with me."

"I'm carving," she says.

I don't say anything; I just keep holding my hand out to her.

"I wouldn't want to keep you from the unwed mother," she mutters.

"The *unwed mother?*" I say. "You can't be serious."

She pretends to carve but I can see that she isn't really doing anything. Finally, she puts the drum kit and the knife down on the chair and looks up at me. She's trying not to smile.

She grabs my hand and I hoist her up, and then she's here, I'm holding her close, and we're dancing to The Supremes singing "Come See About Me." Diana Ross croons, *"No matter what you do or say/I'm gonna love you anyway."*

"Do you think Meg chose this song for me?"

Bev manages to dance and shrug at the same time.

I sing louder over the next verse: *"You make out with a girl in a bar/But to me you're still a superstar."*

Bev blushes and laughs, and I stop dancing and say, "What's up with that anyway? Why do you always do that in front of me?"

But she shakes her head and grabs my hand and says, "Let's just not think about anything."

"That sounds like a good trick," I say.

"Shh," she says.

"Sounds like a good trick!" I whisper, and she laughs and covers my mouth with her hand.

Her palm is soft and smells like lotion and wood. I breathe her in. Try to think about nothing but right now.

———

Back at the hotel, after only an hour of sleep, I wake up with a start. Then I can't fall back. A crack runs from one corner of the ceiling to the other, where it is joined by two other cracks.

I shut my eyes and try counting.

Maybe I should go to art school. Maybe I should drive, alone, across the country. Maybe I should get a job at a restaurant and move into a room in the Mission.

I can hear Meg breathing. Bev has kicked the blanket off; light from a passing car casts over her.

I stop checking the time.

Dust and cobwebs coat the chandelier.

Maybe I should work on a series of drawings and try to get a café show. Maybe my mother will come back home.

Later, the squeak of bedsprings: movement. I sit up and look. Alexa is easing off her bed, stepping carefully across the room, still night-blind.

"Lex," I say.

She jumps a little.

"Oh, sorry," she says. "I was trying to be quiet."

"No, it's fine, I was up. I was thinking—Do you really think you can find a job in your notebook for me?"

I move to the edge of the couch, closer to her.

She nods. "I have over seven hundred jobs listed."

"That's great," I say. "So what do you think? Do any of them stand out?"

"Yeah, we can find something."

"Want to go out in the hall and look?"

She doesn't answer.

"Now?" she finally whispers.

"Yeah."

"I'm actually really tired right now. I was just getting up to pee."

"But it could be super fun. There's tea and hot water down in the lobby. I could go grab us some and we could sit out in the hall and look."

"I don't know. I'm really tired," she says. "I think I need to sleep."

I check my phone. It's 5:00 A.M. Of course she's tired.

"Okay, yeah, no problem," I say.

"We can look in the morning," she says. "You should sleep, too."

"Yeah," I say. "I know."

When she shuts the door to the bathroom, I slip off the couch and go out into the hall. I head toward a window but what I see only makes me feel worse: a few skinny, jumpy people, hunched over together in the park. I lower myself onto the worn carpet, look down the hall at the long rows of doors, and wonder how many of the rooms are occupied, and who is sleeping, and if anyone else is awake.

After a little while, when the first hints of the sun appear in the window, I walk the three flights of stairs down to the lobby. I say good morning to the woman at the hotel desk. I make myself tea.

Tuesday

"Okay, this question is for me," Meg says. "'Meg, do you believe that people can stay in love?' Ooh, good one."

"Colby?" Bev calls. It's startling to hear my name following the question I wrote. At first I was going to avoid real questions again, but then I gave in. If we're going to spend the car ride doing this, I might as well ask about things I want to know.

"Yeah?" I call up to Bev.

Bev is taking her first driving shift of the trip. She drives more smoothly than Meg, who tends to accelerate every time she gets excited about something and slow down every time she spaces out.

"Can I wear these?" She points to my aviator sunglasses,

hanging over the curtains on the window. "Mine are buried in my stuff somewhere."

When we first got on 101 this morning, we were surrounded by bright mist that wove around the trees and the bus, but now the fog is dispersing and the sunlight is so intense it's almost painful.

"Sure," I say, knowing that usually she wouldn't ask for permission, she would just put them on. She's been acting polite and careful around me all morning.

"You bought them for me," I add. "So I think that means you get to wear them whenever you want to."

"Thanks."

"Sure."

Meg gives me an *Oh, please* look before resuming the game.

"My answer is yes," she says. "Completely. I *so* think that people can stay in love."

"Our parents are in love," Alexa says.

"Exactly," Meg agrees. "And Aunt Reese and Uncle Theo."

"Oh my gosh, I can't wait to see them tomorrow night!"

"Me too. You guys are gonna love them. And Colby, your parents are in love, and Bev, yours, too."

"Staying married is not the same thing as being in love," Bev says to Meg.

"I never said it was."

"Yeah, but you just assumed that my parents were in love because they're married."

"No. I said they were in love because they always seem happy when I see them together. For a long time, my parents couldn't even get married. Marriage has nothing to do with it."

Bev doesn't respond, just watches the road. I search for her reflection in the windshield but my glasses cover half her face. It's never crossed my mind that Mary and Gordon might not be happy together, and suddenly, even after Meg's emphatic yes, doubt creeps in. Maybe Mary and Gordon aren't in love; maybe my mother isn't coming home; maybe Bev will never change her mind.

After a few miles, Bev pulls over to a parking lot on the side of the highway so that we can hike down to the river. We wade in the cold water, and I stay a little longer, wander off from the rest of them. I call back all of these memories of my parents and me, taking day trips, cooking dinners, watching movies, making music. Ma laughing, Dad putting his arm around her. We were happy, all three of us.

I am almost sure.

When I get back to the van to take my seat, I see that Alexa has taken all the strips of paper and grouped them by handwriting. There are Bev's, about specific moments and events; Alexa's, about experiences and life; Meg's, about impulses and fantasies.

And then there are mine, glaring up at me. Saying, *You don't know anything about anyone. Not even yourself.*

The Disenchantments' only afternoon show is in a town called Weaverville, at this bright café on a block of Gold Rush—era buildings. Posters and pamphlets for upcoming events along with community announcements hang in the window: dog walker for hire, meeting about a new traffic light, a show from San Francisco band The Disenchanters.

"Hey," I say. "Look—they got the name wrong."

"Oh, no," Alexa says. "The Disenchant*ers*? That's not what we are at all."

"I kinda like it," Meg says. "We sound like a heavy metal band or something. *All the way from San Francisco, here to crush your hopes and spit on your dreams, I bring you, The Disenchanters! Let's give them a hand!*"

Bev just laughs. "That's awesome," she says. "We should make sure to get a poster to take home with us."

Inside, the tables and chairs are mismatched and colorful amateur paintings hang on the brick walls. We introduce ourselves to the kids working there—a short round guy named Mark and a girl with a brown ponytail—and Alexa tells them what the band's actual name is and they apologize over and over. Alexa borrows my Sharpie and crosses out the name on the poster in the window and rewrites it correctly, and then asks for a sheet of paper from my sketchbook so that she can make the set list even though they only know seven songs and they play them in the same order every time.

Mark and the girl give us free smoothies. They say hi to the customers, call them by their names. Everyone I see seems open and friendly.

Maybe I could live in a town like this.

I imagine myself waking up in a rented room in one of the oldest houses in California, riding my bike to this café, saying hey to the guy and girl working here, and talking about some random event from the night before—in a town this small everyone of a certain age must be friends with one another—and then moving to a table by the window and reading the newspaper. I try to think of what might come next, but I can't think of anything beyond the morning.

"Colby," Meg says. "You aren't listening."

As soon as I turn back to their faces, the illusion of life here vanishes.

"I was asking if you'd heard from Jasper yet," Alexa says.

"Not since yesterday."

"Maybe the tattooed guy is an old friend of your dad's, or Pete's," Bev says.

"But wouldn't they have known about it if the guy was their friend?" I ask.

"Yeah, that's true."

"I bet it has more to do with the image," Alexa says.

"Maybe someone just saw the bird on the tape cover and liked it."

Meg says, "Maybe he's a weatherman."

"What?" I laugh. "A weatherman?"

"Yeah," Meg says, as though this is an obvious possibility. "The rain cloud? Remember?"

"I remember," I say. "But raindrops parting for a bluebird doesn't exactly say 'weatherman' to me."

"Well, I think it's the most logical guess so far," she says. "In fact, the mystery is solved as far as I'm concerned."

She grins, stands up.

"Showtime?" she asks, and the rest of them get up with her.

I stay at the table for a little while and flip through Alexa's notebook.

1. Mailman

46. Lawyer

79. Art director

The café fills up with locals and the girl working walks up onstage to introduce the band.

"Hi, everyone," she says, a little shyly.

"Hey, Lily!" a few people say back to her.

"We're really excited to have The Disenchantments here to play for us this afternoon. They're touring from San Francisco to Portland. Let's welcome them to Weaverville!"

Lily claps, her ponytail swinging side to side. The customers set down their mugs to join in, and then the music begins.

108. Secretary

212. Literary agent

289. Movie actor

305. Florist

Meg plucks a particularly off note and I glance up to see Lily and Mark exchange a look. She smiles and he widens his eyes, both of them amused.

523. Sociologist

682. Tightrope walker

Halfway into The Disenchantments' set, I leave Alexa's notebook and my calendar on the table and go up to the counter for water. As I'm pouring, trying hard to block out the amp feedback, Mark appears next to me with a rag to wipe off the stray sugar granules and puddles of spilled coffee.

"They make quite the band," he says.

"That's a nice way to put it."

"At first I thought they might just need a minute to warm up."

"No," I say. "This is what they sound like."

Mark turns to look at them. Meg is jumping around the stage, forgetting to even play her instrument.

"Last summer the house next to me was under construction," Mark says. "It kinda sounded like this."

I wander outside with my water and my phone and sit on the steps leading up to the café door, the air so dusty and hot that breathing requires effort.

I've been meaning to check in with my dad.

As I pull up his cell number, I can feel my mouth getting dry, my heart pounding harder, neither of which has ever happened to me before talking to one of my parents. Even when I told them that Bev and I were going to travel before going to college, I didn't feel nervous. They sat side by side on the living room couch and I sat in the worn, green easy chair and they watched me closely and listened to the things that I said. I knew that they would understand, and they did.

But for some reason it's harder to tell him that I'm not going. I've never kept anything this big from him, but I can't tell him yet. First, I need to know what I'm doing instead.

So I lift the phone to my ear and tell myself that everything's fine, that I'm not going to talk about Europe yet, and I don't have to ask him anything about Mom if I don't want to. This can be an easy conversation the way all of our conversations are.

"I'm glad you caught me," he says when he answers. "I've been screening my calls. It's hard to be this famous."

"What are you talking about?"

"The tattoo!"

"Oh," I laugh. "Right."

"I talked to Pete about it. He found a business card from a show we played at a brewery in Ukiah. He says he remembers us having some real dedicated fans in the audience who drove from Fort Bragg to come to the show, but I'm not so sure. Between you and me, I think Pete might be manufacturing some memories."

I tell my dad about Jasper and how he's investigating for us, about the heat and the shows and the places we've gone so far. He laughs forever about Walt.

"Don't tell your mother that story," he says. "She'd never sleep again, knowing you walked into a strange man's basement."

"Yeah, I'll leave out that part." I pause for a moment, decide to keep going. "How's Ma doing?"

"Great, I think. She's learning fast."

"When does her class end again?"

"There are different levels and different sessions," he says. "As soon as one ends she's evaluated and then the next session starts. She has the option to keep going until she's finished with the highest level, but I don't know how long it will take her to reach it, or if she'll want to stay all the way through."

"Sounds complicated," I say.

"Yes, but it's her dream."

"Yeah," I say. "I know."

"She can't wait to see you."

My heart speeds up. I change the subject.

After the show has finished and we've packed the bus, I consult my calendar and I climb into the driver's seat.

"Off to the Unknown Motel," I say. "Hopefully in Yreka."

"Exactly." Alexa nods and tells me to pull out and make a U-turn and get on Highway 3.

We drive past a lumberyard, full of a forest's worth of felled trees. I slow as we pass it. It's almost too big to comprehend.

But soon we are actually in the forest, in the shade, and I stop worrying about the bus overheating and decide we need some mellow music. Alexa scrolls through my choices, and soon Bon Iver is booming through the speakers—melodic, insistent, all about heartbreak—as I navigate winding, green roads.

About an hour later we reach an unmarked divide in the road. I stop. Alexa checks her directions. She frowns. She unfolds the map, turns it over, searching for a closer view.

Meg and Bev have been quiet in the back, sleeping or reading or just being still. Now I can hear them moving on the seats.

"Meg?" Alexa says. "I think we need your phone. I can't figure this out."

"Sure," Meg murmurs, and hands her phone to Alexa in front.

Alexa stares at the screen. "No service," she says.

I grab the map and take a look, but Alexa's right: wherever we are, it is too remote to show up. I look at her. She looks back. And then, her face goes from puzzled to confident: "The Magic Eight Ball! Meg! Pass it up here."

"I think we should go left," I say.

"That would make sense." Alexa nods. "Because we *were* going east and eventually we need to go north. But it's also possible that we aren't supposed to turn yet—the roads curve around so much—maybe our turn comes later.

"This way we can rely on a power greater than ourselves," Alexa says, taking the black-and-white ball from Meg.

Bev's laughter comes from the far back. It's been days since I've heard her laugh like this.

Alexa takes a deep breath and asks her question loudly and clearly, slowly enough for the Magic 8 Ball gods to hear and understand her: "We are going to Yreka. Should we go straight at this divide in the road?"

We all watch as she shakes the ball, lean forward as the triangle floats up through the bubbles in the cloudy water.

IT IS DECIDEDLY SO.

"There," she says, smiling. "It's decided."

"I think we should go left," I say.

"The Magic Eight Ball has spoken."

"The Magic Eight Ball is wrong."

"It's fifty-fifty anyway," Meg says. "None of us knows for sure."

"Lex?" I ask.

She points straight ahead.

I glance back at Bev. Amusement flashes across her face.

"Okay," I say and, against my better judgment, go straight.

Everyone is wide awake now, looking out the window, waiting for a sign. The road narrows, curves to the right. The forest thickens. Branches reach over us and a million bright spots of light mark the road where the sun shines through the leaves. Once in a while: patches of brilliant purple flowers.

In my rearview mirror, I can see Bev's hand where it rests on the windowpane, her long, slender fingers. It's been too long since I've drawn her hands.

"This is so beautiful," Alexa says.

Bev should be next to me. Her hand should rest on my body somewhere. We should be thinking some simultaneous thought, and I should be full of awe instead of aching.

"Yeah," I say finally. "It's pretty. But it doesn't feel right."

Alexa leans so close to me that her feather earring grazes my cheek.

"The Magic Eight Ball told us. Unequivocally."

———

We drive two more hours down the same road before the trees open to a small town. When we get out at the tiny gas station and ask an old, mostly toothless man where we are, he points to a spot on the map that is considerably southwest of where we were this afternoon. I don't react because I knew this would happen.

Alexa blushes, too embarrassed to say anything.

"Whatever," I say. "It was pretty."

Meg and the old man plan our route back north and I pump the gas, and Alexa asks, "Why would it lead us in the wrong direction?"

"Because it's a toy," I say. "It's manufactured by, like, Mattel or something. It's made out of plastic and water."

Alexa sighs. Looking across the street at a fruit stand with hand-painted signs declaring DELICIOUS! PISTACHIOS! CHERRIES!, "I'll go get us some snacks," she says. "Who knows how long it will take us to get back on our route."

She shuffles away, her feather earrings barely fluttering.

I lean against the bus and scan the station for Bev. Apparently we have cell service back. She's out on the road, walking in slow, dreamy circles, probably talking to that red-haired girl who she reached at a number she will not erase from her phone anytime soon.

This is not good. Now we have to backtrack for over two hours, and Alexa is sad, and Bev doesn't love me, and we will probably not make it to the Unknown Motel in

Yreka. Not all of these are problems I can fix, so when Meg comes back to the van I tell her that something needs to be done about her sister.

She laughs. "It was for the best. Something had to snap her out of this fate bullshit."

"People are allowed to believe in fate," I say.

"Yeah," Meg says. "But it's stupid. And Lex doesn't even believe in it. She's organized and practical and always in control. She shouldn't try to pretend she's someone she's not."

Meg's probably right, but I just shrug and say, "I don't think it's stupid."

Because I understand why Alexa would want to believe in this stuff. What if all of the disappointments and letdowns aren't meaningless or random? What if they're something more than that? It's better to think that fate is the reason my plans have been ruined—that it might be because there's something better for me out there, or something that I'm meant to do—than how I've been thinking about it for the last couple days.

But I don't get into that now. Instead, I devise a plan to make Alexa happy again, and Meg rolls her eyes but says "okay," and when Bev hangs up and joins us again she smiles her amazing smile and says it's a great idea.

I climb into the backseat and Meg takes the front, and we wait until Alexa shuffles to the bus.

"I need you to copilot," Meg says.

Alexa stands outside the shut passenger door for a moment, and then climbs in. She eyes the Magic 8 Ball as if it's betrayed her and then she moves it to the backseat.

Bev and I wait until we've turned onto the road, and then we shout, *"One, two, three!"* and Meg turns on the stereo, which is up full blast, and Heart pours out of the speakers. Bev and I have the lyrics held between the middle row where Bev's sitting and the back row where I am, and we sing along together, loudly with the opening lines.

"You guys," Alexa says, defensively, as though we're still making fun of her.

But we keep singing, and the music builds to the chorus and Bev, Meg, and I all belt, *"What about love!/Don't you want someone to care about you? . . ."* And soon Alexa is smiling, and by the time the next chorus comes she joins us and then the bus is full of Heart and of us, and we're all hoarse and laughing by the time the song ends.

We drive a few more miles and everything seems to be going okay. Meg and Alexa are talking in the front with Heart still playing, softer now, and I lie down, ready to sleep through the next hundred miles. I close my eyes and I'm so tired that I've already started drifting off. In my black, near-sleep state, I smell Bev's cigarette-scented clothes and feel my seat give as the smell becomes stronger. Then Bev's breath is warm on my ear, whispering, "We should have listened to you."

And this is not a fantasy. This is real.

I keep my eyes shut, hardly breathe. I've never had

to treat Bev so gently before, but now I'm afraid that any wrong move will send her away from me again. I wait for the springs to bounce back as she gets up to move back to her row, but instead I only feel her shifting. I think she's taking off her shoes now. And then I feel her against me, lowering her face onto my leg and settling there.

And I am wide awake now, motionless, for all of the miles and minutes that Bev sleeps.

Redding greets us with wide, newly paved suburban streets and a shiny, bright gas station. Bev and I sit up for the first time in hours.

She runs her hand over her hair. It's sticking up on one side, all blond and messy. My body aches from holding one position for so long.

"What time is it?" Bev murmurs.

"Almost nine," Meg says. Outside, the sky is darkening. Patches of bright blue light surround the streetlamps' yellow glow.

I ask if we're going to stay here tonight and they say yes, and soon Alexa returns from talking to the station attendant, and guides us to a part of the city where we should be able to find a room. Soon, ahead of us, motels line up, one after another, all advertising gloriously cheap nightly rates.

We choose the Starlight Motel for its name and its red, fifties-era sign.

"Sophie would love this," Meg says, and I say, "Yeah, she would," and Alexa says, "I think I might write my play about Sophie."

"What about my dad and Uncle Pete?"

"I love the idea of musicians, but really my strongest actors are girls. That junior Gabe could have a leading role, but Sara's really the best in the program, so I feel like I should write her a good part."

"What would you do for a baby?" Bev asks from next to me.

"I don't know," Alexa says. "That might be tricky."

As we pull into the parking lot, I remember a collage we studied in school of this almost-naked couple in their living room. I don't remember much about it, except that it's credited with starting Pop Art, and the ceiling in the couple's house is not actually a ceiling but the moon.

"What was the name of that collage Ms. Jacobs taught us about," I say, "the one with the moon for the ceiling?"

"*Just What Is It That Makes Today's Homes So Different, So Appealing?*" Meg says. "I love that piece! With the 'Young Romance' poster and the wife doing some weird erotic swoon. So fabulous."

"Pop Art seems so shallow," Alexa says.

"That's the point," Meg snaps. "That's what makes it Pop Art. Sometimes it's okay for art to be fun."

Alexa is right, I know. The trouble is that sometimes I read too much into things. Like, okay, I understand it's a joke: the thing that makes "today's homes so different" is that there's a moon where a ceiling should be. Ha. But I remember the moon striking me as important and dangerous, like the man and the woman were trapped, like it was the beginning of the end of the world.

I'm still thinking about the collage as we traipse into the lobby. Once inside, though, it becomes apparent that the decor is more family room than it is Pop Art. Faded black-and-white photographic portraits cover the walls, mostly stiff studio shots, but some more casual photos of kids in backyards and men with slicked-back hair standing next to shiny vintage cars.

No one is at the counter at first so we have time to get a good look at the pictures. There are class photos and prom photos, girls with cat's-eye glasses and guys with Elvis hair.

"I would kill for this dress," Meg says, pointing to a photo in the corner.

I'm headed over to see when a voice behind me drones, "You here for a room or what?"

I turn around. A scraggly-haired man in rumpled clothes stares at us with an expression of complete boredom.

"Yeah," I say. "Just for the night."

At the counter, I catch a glimpse of his name tag: MELVIN.

When I tell him that we only want one room, his expression approaches disapproval but never quite gets past boredom, and as he fills out the paperwork I ask, "What's up with all the pictures, Melvin?"

"Family who used to own the place left 'em behind. How many keys you need?"

"Two's fine. So they sold the motel and just left all their photos?"

Melvin looks up from the paperwork to me with hooded, watery eyes.

"Appears that way," he says. "Doesn't it."

I am deciding whether to continue this conversation with Melvin, who apparently thinks that I'm either a little slow or trying to make trouble, when Alexa appears next to me, bright blue earrings peeking through her long black hair.

"How could they do that?" she asks.

"I know, right?" I say. "It's crazy."

"Look at all of these," she says, and we wander back to one of the walls as Melvin continues filling out his forms. "Look at how happy they are here."

In the photograph we're looking at, a young, smiling mother and father stand together on a front lawn. The mother holds a little boy's hand, the father has a baby under his arm.

Alexa shakes her head. "What would happen to make a family just leave all of this?"

We stand together, searching their tiny faces. Were they living the lives they wanted? They look strong and healthy; they have perfect photographic smiles. Still, it's impossible to know.

"I need your signature," Melvin says.

I head back to the counter, and Meg prances up, too, cocks her head, and asks, "Is there anywhere nearby that's still open for dinner?"

As bored as Melvin has been with me, he appears equally unimpressed with Meg. His eyes scan her pink hair, her tattoo, her short dress, before turning to take the keys from a Peg-Board.

"Around the corner. River Bar and Grill."

"Is there a river near here?" Alexa asks, excited.

Melvin points to me to sign the receipt, hands me the keys, and says, "No."

The River Bar and Grill has a veggie burger on the menu. I turn to Bev, show her. She thanks the universe on my behalf.

We are sitting at a table in the center of the dim room, with ice water in smudged glasses and the promise of nourishment and a lady with too much makeup on a stage singing karaoke. Soon our orders have been taken and our food has arrived, and my veggie burger is the best thing I've ever tasted. Bev and I see a man eating in a corner who reminds us of a guy we once met on Muni who talked to us the whole ride home about sadness. He told us that we were too young to understand but that soon we would be old enough.

"What did you say?" Alexa asks.

"Colby tried to be polite. Like, 'Well, maybe we don't

know exactly what you're talking about but we do know what sadness is.'"

"Yeah," I say. "And you just told him he was being ridiculous."

"It *was* ridiculous," Bev says. "I mean, really? Everyone knows what it's like to be sad. It's a universal feeling. Adults are always telling kids that they won't understand till they're older, and yeah, maybe that's true with some things, but I wasn't going to let him get away with that one."

"Was he crazy?" Meg asks.

Bev looks at me and smiles her amazing smile and says, "We couldn't tell, right?"

"Yeah," I say. "I mean, he seemed, like, distressed. Like it was a really terrible day. But I don't think he was crazy. I didn't get that feeling from him."

Still watching me, Bev nods up and down, very slowly. I could talk with Bev about sadness forever if only she would keep looking at me this way.

"I felt the same," she says. "I think he might have been having some kind of crisis, but he wasn't crazy."

"Well, check out his doppelgänger," Meg says. "I think he might be in crisis land, too."

I don't look until Bev turns her face away from mine.

And then I do, making us a table of four nosy, staring teenagers in a restaurant full of older locals who are talking to the karaoke host, finishing their dinners, and making their way to the dance floor.

The man is polishing off the third pint of beer he's had since we became aware of him. He is alone, his dinner is untouched, and now he is carving into the table with a pocketknife.

"Poor guy," Alexa says. "Where are his friends?"

Meg shrugs. "Maybe he doesn't have any."

"No." Alexa shakes her head. "He has friends."

We watch him for so long that he senses something, glances up. We all look away quickly except for Alexa, who smiles and waves.

"Alexa," Meg hisses.

"What? I'm just trying to be nice."

The waitress comes by our table with the check and we pull out our wallets and divide the total, leaving her many small, crumpled bills and a nice tip. I head toward the door, combing through childhood memories, ready to remind Bev of something great that she's forgotten about when we get back to the Starlight. I imagine us staying up late and talking far past the time everyone else has fallen asleep. *Remember that?* I'll ask, and she'll say, *Oh my God, I haven't thought of that in forever!* And when we finally do drift off to sleep we won't move from where we were, and she will lean against me like she did in the car, and by the time she wakes up she'll have changed her mind.

But Meg shouts, "Colby, where are you going?" and I turn to see them at the karaoke machine, sifting through the song choices.

"The Runaways!" Meg is saying when I make my way back to them. "Colby, I'm so being Joan Jett tonight." She writes her name on the list, followed by "School Days."

"Want to sing a duet with me?" slurs a voice behind us. We turn to see the Muni guy's doppelgänger with his eyes fixed on Alexa.

"Oh," she stammers. "Um . . ."

"Nope, sorry," says Meg. "This one needs the spotlight all to herself."

He narrows his eyes at Meg and then returns his attention to Alexa.

"Lemme know if you change your mind."

She nods.

When he leaves, she says, "Maybe I should just do it."

We all shake our heads no.

"It's only singing. He seems so lonely."

"You look miserable just thinking about it," Meg says. "And his loneliness has nothing to do with you."

"I feel so mean."

Meg says, "Forget him. I think I saw Joni Mitchell in here."

"Really?" Alexa's face turns hopeful. "I love Joni."

"I know you do," Meg says. "Look, here she is."

Alexa chooses her song. We suffer through a couple of strangers singing country, and then Meg's name is called and she pulls Bev up with her. They beckon for Alexa but she says no.

"Let's go watch from over there," she says, pointing to a less crowded part of the room, and we head over as the opening bars blast from the speakers.

"Here, sit here," Alexa says. "Now I'm going to lean against your back and you can lean against mine."

We sit, back-to-back, heads turned to the side, and listen to Meg shouting out the lyrics, *"School days, school days / I'm older, now what will I find,"* and watch the two of them jumping around, one teenage girl band imitating a much better predecessor.

When their song is finished, Alexa and I stand up and watch a man sing a rock ballad. Alexa sways to the music, offers me a pistachio from her bag, smiles. A green feather in her black hair, peace signs painted in blue on her hands. She is okay now: the drunk guy has vanished, the Magic 8 Ball disappointment and the pains of being coldhearted are behind her. Soon the host calls her name again and the music for Joni Mitchell's "Help Me" begins, and she turns and walks onstage.

She starts singing, almost in time with the music. Bev and Meg appear next to me, and with a little cheering from us, Alexa slips off her sandals and prances around, doing her best Joni impression, all high and sweet and fluttery.

Then she drops the line and winces, reaches down to her foot.

"Uh-oh," Meg says.

Alexa picks up the next line and finishes the song, trying

to smile, dancing more cautiously. When the song is finished she limps to the side of the stage as a gray-haired woman in leather pants takes over to sing "Satisfaction."

"Splinter?" I ask Alexa. She nods. Her feet dangle over the side of the stage. We're in a corner, well out of the spotlight.

"I think I have tweezers," Meg says, and hands me her makeup bag.

"You were great. Everyone loved you," I say as I unzip Meg's little case and sift through all the girl things to find the silver tweezers. I climb onto the stage and hold her foot up to the light.

"Okay," I say. "I see it."

She frowns.

Holding the soft arch of her foot, pressing in with the tips of the tweezers, I get the splinter out easily. I hand her the thick, sharp piece of wood and she holds it to the light. Her eyes are sad.

She says, "The world is against me."

Bev and Meg walk across the street to the liquor store, and return ten minutes later. It's so perfect that I have to beg all night if I want a single drink and they, out of nowhere, have two six-packs of beer, like, *We're girls and we're pretty, so look!—anything we want.*

My phone buzzes in my pocket. Jasper.

"Not much to report," he says. "I've left that lady a couple messages but she hasn't called me back. I'm gonna ask Spider if he'll call. Maybe since they used to be a thing or whatever she'll answer."

"Hey, man, are you okay?" I ask, because his voice lacks its usual buoyancy.

"Uh," he says. "I don't know. You know, hanging in there I guess."

"Is something going on?"

"It's cool," he says.

It sounds for a moment like he's going to say something else, and I wait, let the quiet last, because a heart-to-heart with Jasper sounds pretty fucking great.

"But anyway, I just wanted to let you know. Thought I'd have more by now but I'm working on it."

"No worries," I say.

Across the room, the girls are getting changed into more comfortable clothing, suddenly unconcerned by my presence, braless and bare-legged, stepping out of jeans and into boxer shorts or cutoff sweats.

I contemplate saying good-bye and hanging up, but then I say, "Okay, but really. What's going on?"

"Honestly?" Jasper says. "I just have to get the fuck out of this town. I get depressed just walking out the front door every morning."

"You should leave," I say.

"Yeah," he says. "When the time is right. But I got a mystery to solve first. A guy I work with has this complicated theory about, like, stolen identity. He was going on this afternoon about how maybe the guy got the tattoo to convince people that he was in your dad's band."

"Why would he want to do that?"

"To impress people. To seem important. Shit, I don't know."

We talk a little longer, and he sounds better by the time we hang up, but I'm pretty sure he's faking it.

I set my phone down on an end table next to a closet that Bev is exploring.

"We should put stuff in here," she says.

"Why?"

"Whenever I take trips with my parents they always unpack. They hang up their jackets and put their clothes in the drawers like they're going to stay awhile."

"But we aren't staying awhile," Meg says. "We're staying, like, ten hours."

"Yeah, I know. But we have this whole closet. We should use it."

"We're supposed to be rock stars," Meg says. "We're supposed to trash hotel rooms, not get all domestic."

Even though it was only karaoke, Bev has her post-show glow, and watching her now with her messy hair and strong, wiry arms, black eyeliner, and jeans tight and low on her waist, I can see Meg's point. Bev doesn't look like the kind of girl who stays anywhere long enough to unpack. But I can also see that, for some reason, this matters to Bev. She has her bag unzipped and all of her clothes are neatly folded. I look around, pick up an amp, and say, "Here."

"I'm not sure that's a good idea." Alexa is watching from across the room. "What if we forget it?"

But Bev takes the amp from me, sets it down on the closet floor, and shuts the door.

"I won't forget," she says, ripping a strip of paper off a Starlight Motel brochure. *Remember amp*, she writes, and drops the note into her bag.

She looks satisfied, and I decide that this is a good time to bring up the first memory.

"Hey, Bev, remember that time we got caught cheating on the vocab test in seventh grade?"

"Yeah?"

"We told Mr. Hastings that we weren't cheating, we were collaborating."

"Yeah?" she says again, giving me this *So what's your point?* look.

"We were such con artists."

"Not really," she says. "That was a pretty lame excuse."

She walks away from me to the other side of the room, and with her goes all of the good from earlier today. She joins Meg and Alexa, who are getting out pens for round one thousand of their question game. And I want to say something to Bev, I want to ask what the fuck her problem is, because I know that she remembers us standing in the principal's office together, when I was still shorter than she was and she was still called Beverly, defending ourselves and one another, believing we were smart and mature and able to talk our way out of anything. I know that girl better than I know this one. I can't believe she would pretend that who we were then doesn't matter.

"Who has paper?" Meg asks.

I say, "We don't need paper. It's completely obvious who wants to know what, and even if it wasn't, we all know each other's handwriting."

Meg shrugs. "Fine with me. So who wants to start?"

"Bev, tell us the saddest moment of your life." My words come out loud, forceful, and I walk to their side of the room and look down at her.

Bev turns to the window.

Alexa's eyebrows furrow in concern. "We asked her that already."

"She didn't answer."

Meg opens her mouth to say something, but thinks better of it. Bev looks up at me. Her eyes are challenging like they used to be when we were kids wrapped up in games. She always cared more about winning than I ever did.

"Okay, Colby. The saddest moment of my life. Do you

remember the science fair at the end of eighth grade, when we did that experiment on magnets and electricity and we left the wire at my place?"

"Yeah."

"Remember that I ran home to get it before the judges got to our station?"

I nod. She doesn't look at anyone else, and I understand that this is a story that's only for me.

"So I got to my house, and I went in the front door, and there was this pair of boots in the living room. They were green, scuffed-up cowboy boots that I had never seen before. Everything was quiet, so at first I was afraid that some man was robbing the house, but then I realized that was stupid—why would the guy take off his shoes?—so I walked through the house, to the end of the hall by my parents' room, and then I started to hear things."

"What things?" Meg asks.

And it's the most awkward feeling, like when a room full of people quiets all at once, and nobody wants to be the person who breaks the silence.

"They were fucking, obviously," Bev says.

Alexa moves closer to Bev, puts her arm around her shoulders. Bev doesn't pull away.

"What did you do?" she asks.

"Nothing. I got the wire and then I ran back to school."

"You never told me that," I say.

Bev takes a swig of her beer.

"Bev," I say. "That's really fucking huge, and you never told me."

"I never told anyone," she says, shrugging off Alexa's arm.

"But I'm not *anyone*," I say. *"Fuck."*

And my hands fly up to my face and I stand there like a pathetic asshole and say, "I'm your best friend, remember? I'm not *anyone*."

Alexa starts to say something calm and reasonable, but I don't want to hear it. Bev's been keeping things from me for too long. *Since eighth grade?* And then it all starts to come together—the summer we were fourteen. The song she listened to on repeat, about a life that used to seem perfect. The way she started to get quiet and distant, and I mistook it for an affect, or a natural part of growing older. But most of all, the fact that the science fair was near the end of the school year, and only a couple weeks after that was when we watched all of my parents' Godard films, and Bev said, *Let's go the second that we're free.*

It was years ago, but I hear her voice so clearly, can remember exactly how she said it. I repeat it to her now: *"Let's go the second that we're free?"* And the truth is so terrible that I have to laugh. "I get it now," I tell her. "I thought you wanted us to do something great. Together. But really you just wanted to run away."

She starts to respond but I don't want to hear her, so I grab my wallet, unlock the door, and head to the motel office. I ring the little bell on the counter over and over until Melvin stumbles out of the back.

"Something wrong with the room?"

"No. I just need another one."

He grumbles something incoherent and takes my credit card.

A few minutes later, I'm letting myself into a new room. It smells like cigarettes and stale perfume, but it's quiet and it's a corridor away from her. The lamp on the table flickers and buzzes when I switch it on, but eventually it casts light over a grimy carpet and a stained green bedspread. I switch it off again.

I pull down the bedspread and collapse onto the sheets. I lie there for a long time, wishing I could call someone at home. I consider trying Uncle Pete. But what if he's finally drifted off after hours of infomercials and magazine perusal? All I know is that I don't want to give anyone a heart attack by calling at 2:00 A.M. I close my eyes, and then I remember my mother.

It is eleven in the morning in Paris, and she answers with a singsong *"Bonjour!"*

"Hey, Ma."

"Colby, *mon chéri! Ça fait tellement plaisir d'entendre ta voix, mon petit aventurier."*

"Ma," I say. "It's the middle of the night. Can we speak English? Please?"

"Bien sûr, honey," she says. "Of course. I might be a

little rusty, though. I speak French all the time now. Two nights ago, I even dreamed in French."

"What was the dream about?" I ask, but I don't really care about the dream. I just want to hear her voice.

"I was walking along the Seine, like I do every day, and I looked up and all of my favorite French words were drifting across the sky on kites."

"That sounds beautiful."

"Oh, it was. It was so beautiful. I can't wait to show you everything."

Just then I hear knocking. I stand up and drag the phone with me to the door. My mother is telling me about the park a block away from her apartment, about the different trees and the vines that climb the wrought-iron gates, and I peer through the peephole to find Bev, rubbing her arms for warmth, small and distorted through the fish-eye glass.

"Hey, Ma?" I say. "I'm sorry. I gotta go now. But it sounds really amazing. I really can't wait to see you."

"Okay, *mon chére. Bonne nuit.*"

I open the door as wide as the chain lock will allow, which is not wide at all.

"Hey," Bev says.

"Hey," I say.

"Let me in," she says. "I need to talk to you."

I shut the door. Lean my forehead against the cracked paint. Slide the chain free.

Let her in.

But she doesn't talk.

Instead, she locks the door behind her, turns around, and touches my face. Anger dissipates, gratitude rushes over me. I want to say thank you but then her mouth is on mine.

I'm not thinking about the redhead or the guy from Fort Bragg or any of the others. I'm not thinking about the way that she's lied to me. Maybe those were just moments meant to lead to this one. To touching the skin of Bev's back beneath her bra clasp, to the clasp unfastening, to the place on her rib cage where my hand rests for a moment as we kiss deeper.

And, okay, the reason I've never had sex is not a mystery to me. It isn't that I haven't wanted to, it's just that I've been waiting for this:

For Bev to bury her fingers in my hair and pull my face to hers. To kiss her this way: not too hard, but not gently.

Bev takes a step back and lifts her shirt over her head. She lets her bra slip off her shoulders. And even though I've imagined her like this a million times, she is so beautiful my chest aches. Not only my heart, but muscles and tendons and bones, even the air in my lungs. Everything hurts but I would hurt this way forever if we could just stay. Bev and me in this dimly lit room in this shitty motel in a town that lies between better destinations. Bev unzipping my jeans and unzipping her own. Bev in nothing but blue-green underwear, and then in nothing at all.

I pull the comforter off the bed. The sheets smell like bleach. A small foil square has appeared in Bev's hand, something I didn't have because I wasn't prepared for this, and she kisses my neck with lips that are softer than I could have imagined in a million more fantasies of her. Before she turns out the light, she looks into my face, eyes clear the way they were when we were years younger and she had nothing to keep from me. Not for long but for long enough that I understand this is what was supposed to happen all this time. It was always supposed to be me and Bev.

Like this.

Together.

Wednesday

The sheets are cooler than they should be. When I open my eyes, I see Bev smoking at the foot of the bed, in my white T-shirt and her underwear.

I sit up, reaching for her.

"Good morning," I say, and when I think of her last night, moving above me, it's as if we're floating for a moment, weightless, alone in a place where gravity doesn't apply.

She sucks in. Exhales a cloud of smoke. She doesn't turn around, and I plunge back to earth. There is a tightening in my stomach, a message there: something has changed.

"Was last night what you wanted?" she asks.

Her smoke hovers in the air between us.

"Yeah," I say. "I mean, it was part of it."

She stands, her back to me. A girl in a dingy motel room, almost naked with sunlight glinting above shabby curtains.

She checks the watch I gave her. "We need to leave," she says.

"Bev," I say.

"What?"

Then I say, "Beverly."

All three syllables.

It is only her name but what I mean is, *Come back to me.*

Still facing away, she opens the curtains and lets in light. She is surrounded by brightness. Her hip bones, her long legs. The outline of her back and shoulders through the thin white cotton.

I try again: "Beverly."

Come back as the girl I used to know, the one who did math problems in her head and laughed hard and rode her bike faster than anyone.

She turns and stubs her cigarette on the bedside table-top, already scarred by dozens of cigarettes. She pulls my shirt over her head and stands in front of me, and even though only a few hours ago I wanted to thank her, now I look away. She might as well be wearing a coat of armor. My shirt lands by my foot.

"Five minutes, okay?" she says, and then she disappears into the bathroom.

———

Everyone's quiet in the van. Meg was in the driver's seat when I got out there, but I told her I felt like driving so she moved to the back. Bev was ready a few minutes before I was, and I don't know what she told them. It could have been everything. It could have been nothing. I don't know.

Yesterday's forests have given way to a straight, wide expanse of highway. No shade, no wildflowers, just concrete and hot sun and the occasional billboard. At one point, to compensate for the absence of anything good out the window and inspired by last night's performance, Meg puts on The Runaways. She sings and Alexa sings along but the enthusiasm is lost by the end of the first verse, and after they stop singing, Joan and Cherie just sound loud and stupid, and Meg turns the volume down, little by little, until we can barely hear them.

Through all of this, Bev listens to her Walkman. Every time I catch her reflection I feel as though I've been shocked: first the electricity, then the emptiness. The presence, then the absence, of light. I want to pull over and hold her. I want her to look at me the way she did last night.

Later, at a gas station, when I am standing at the pump and Bev is smoking around the back of the building, Meg climbs out and stands with me.

"The tension in there is almost unbearable," she says. "But considering that Bev didn't come back to our room last night, I think a high five might be in order."

She holds up her hand. She smiles a little, but her eyes are concerned. I raise my hand. It meets hers with the quietest of slaps. Neither of us lowers our arms, so we stand still, together, hands touching above our heads.

A little later, we pull off the highway in Weed to use the bathrooms and stretch our legs. Alexa calls her aunt to let her know where we are and when she thinks we'll arrive. Soon Meg prances out of the gas station store wearing a trucker hat. As she gets closer, I can make out the design. It's one of those sexy girl silhouettes that semis have on their mud flaps or license plates. In red script above the girl: *God Bless American Women*.

"Dare you to wear this," she says to me.

"You *dare* me?"

"Yeah."

I grab the cap off her head and put it on mine, skewing it to the side. No big deal. Alexa and Meg are smiling at me. Bev is looking at the concrete.

"So?" I ask.

"I'd date you," Meg says.

Alexa giggles. "You have to take that off before we get to our aunt and uncle's."

"I thought I'd class it up a little," I say, faking incredulity. "I want to make a good impression. I just can't believe I left my Confederate flag shirt at home."

The sisters laugh and Bev forces a smile, and then we all just lean against the bus for a minute, watching the semi trucks pass in a row, an orange truck followed by a blue one followed by one with silver dolphin decals and chipped gold paint.

Alexa finds the snacks from yesterday's fruit stand.

"Cherry?" she offers us. "Pistachio?"

Bev says yes and digs through her purse. She finds a scrap of paper and takes out her gum, but then she freezes.

"Shit," she says.

"What?" we all ask.

Then I look at the scrap of paper. *Starlight Motel.* A reminder, too late.

"The amp," Bev says.

Meg stares at Bev. She blinks. "Oh, fuck," she says.

Slowly, we all turn to Alexa, knowing that though this will throw all of us off, she'll be the one to take it the hardest. Her eyes are open wider than I've ever seen them, a cherry suspended in midair between herself and Bev.

"I told you not to put the amp in the closet," she says.

"I know," Bev says. She looks awful, mascara smeared below her eyes, hair in need of washing. Her white tank top is smudged with something blue—maybe Alexa's hand paint—and across her face is utter hopelessness.

Bev blinks back tears but Alexa either doesn't notice or doesn't care. All signs of gentleness fade away.

"They're expecting us in an hour. They're making dinner. She was setting the table for us when we called her."

"Fate?" Meg jokes, but Alexa ignores her.

"I *reserve* our places to stay and I *book* us our shows and I *try* to get us where we need to go but I *can't* do *everything*. And we can't have a show without an amp."

No one knows what to say. We are at a standstill. We can't afford to buy a new amp, and that one is on loan from my parents' friend, so even if we could scrape together the money I wouldn't want to come home without it. But Alexa and Meg's family is waiting for us, and it's clear that Alexa needs some off time.

"I'll go back by myself," I say.

"How?" Alexa asks.

"We'll find a bus station. There has to be one in this town."

"I just really want to see my aunt," she says, her voice hopeful.

"You can," I tell her. "You can see your aunt. We just have to find a bus station. You guys take Melinda and I'll bus back to Redding. Then I'll get as close as I can to your aunt's house tonight and one of you can come pick me up."

"You sure?" Meg asks.

"Yeah, it's no problem."

Alexa breathes deep, squeezes my arm.

"Thank you," she says.

The gas station attendant directs us to the Greyhound station in Weed, a shabby brown building set back from a residential road. I grab my bag and tell Meg that I'll call her phone when I board the bus for the trip back, and I'm almost out the door when Bev says, "Wait. I'm going, too."

I shake my head. "I'm fine. You should go with them."

"No. I'm the one who forgot the amp."

"You don't have to."

"I know I don't have to," she says. "But I am," and she steps out after me, messenger bag slung over her shoulder.

"Take good care of Melinda," I say.

Meg crosses her heart, waves good-bye. I watch Melinda until it disappears, and then I join Bev inside. She stands at a Coke machine, feeding it a crumpled dollar that it keeps spitting back at her. The woman at the ticket counter shows me the Redding station on the map, and I'm relieved to see that it isn't too far from the Starlight. When it's time to pay, Bev appears next to me, holding more crumpled bills. I hand the woman my credit card.

We have to wait over an hour for our bus to arrive, so when a boisterous woman in cargo pants and an American flag T-shirt sits next to us, I am more than happy to hold up my end of the conversation.

When she really looks at me for the first time, I remember that I'm still wearing the mud-flap girl hat, but the woman doesn't seem to care. I wonder if she knows I'm being ironic. Or maybe she takes it as a compliment—I mean, she *is* an American woman.

She tells me that she's returning home from three weeks on the road, shows me a photograph of her daughter. I ask her what it's like to drive a truck and she tells me that it's lonely.

"It gets in your blood, though," she says. "If I go more than a few weeks between jobs I get restless."

Bev puts on her Walkman.

"And there's always the CB," the woman says. "I got friends I've never met in person, but we know each other through the radios."

The trucker is going north; her bus arrives before ours does.

As soon as she walks away, Bev takes off her headphones.

"Don't try to tell me you're thinking of breaking into the trucking profession."

"As you might remember," I say, "I'm kind of at loose ends right now."

She puts her headphones back on and I lean forward with my head in my hands. It would be so much easier if she had chosen to go with Meg and Alexa, if I were here by myself and not thinking of last night every other moment, and wondering—always—how Bev and I got to where we are now. So unlike how we used to be.

Gently, I take Bev's headphones off her head. I make my voice even and kind. I try again.

"I was asking for Alexa," I say. "I don't remember seeing 'trucker' on her list."

Bev nods.

I say, "We're alone now. The trip's almost over."

She presses the stop button on her Walkman.

I say, "Maybe you could try to tell me why. I get it now, why you would have brought up going after eighth grade. But we spent four years after that planning. Why didn't you tell me that you changed your mind?"

I watch her face. She blinks a couple times. She swallows. She takes a breath, and says, "I keep trying to think of how to explain it—" and then a voice booms over the intercom.

Our bus has arrived.

We pick up our things and walk outside and stand in a line we probably should have been in before. By the time we board, there aren't any seats next to each other, so Bev takes one near the front as I continue down the aisle, away from her.

There is only one car in the Starlight parking lot.

"Looks like another slow night."

"Yeah," Bev says.

In the lobby again, Melvin regards us from across the counter as though we are complete strangers.

"Hey," I say. "We checked out this morning? Remember?"

His expression doesn't change. Eventually, he lifts an eyebrow.

"Okay. And now you're back."

"We forgot something," Bev says. "It's in the room we were in last night. Two-o-six."

Slowly, he turns on his stool and takes the key from the Peg-Board behind him.

"Or it might be in the room I was in," I say. "One eleven."

Bev turns to me but I pretend I don't notice.

Melvin's hand moves across the Peg-Board. His face is skeptical, but he hands me the key.

"Meet you back here in a few minutes," I say to Bev, and slip out the door before she can respond.

The room has been cleaned. The carpet vacuumed, the bed made. For some reason, I expected it to be untouched since we left. Why clean a room in a motel where no one stays? You would think Melvin could give the maid a day off, but the room looks just like it did when I first walked in last night.

Still, even though the room is absent of any trace of us, I can get back some of the feeling of last night. We were right here. Her hair smelled like oranges and smoke. She was arching her back, breathing hard, watching my face. Every time she touched me I wanted to thank her, but it was only the beginning of us. I thought I had the rest of my life to say thank you, to tell her all of the things I was thinking, so I just kissed her everywhere I had fantasized about kissing her, and on other places, too—the inside of her elbow, the bottom of her rib cage—places I hadn't yet discovered in the thousands of times I had imagined being with her like that.

We were right here.

The comforter stretches taut over the bed. Our footsteps have vanished from the carpet. I can't believe that we could be so impermanent. I can't even smell the smoke from Bev's cigarette.

I need to leave something behind here. Something that will stay. This room should be a historical landmark, the site of the beginning and end of Colby and Bev. Several minutes have passed, and I know that if I wait too long there will be a knock on the door and I'll have to go, but I need to leave a mark. It has to be significant enough to last, but subtle enough that the maid won't notice and wash it away.

As I'm looking around, I realize that I never noticed the print above the bed. It's another in the family series—a faded wedding portrait. Groom in tux. Bride with pearls.

It comes off the wall easily.

I set the print on the bedspread and wipe away the dust on the wall with the sleeve of my hoodie. I take out a Sharpie from my bag. The wall has yellowed to create a perfect rectangle where the photograph must have been hanging, unmoved, for years.

I fill the whiter space with this: *I never got to tell you how beautiful you are.*

And then I return the frame to its place on the wall and go back out into the night.

We walk back to the Greyhound station in silence, each holding on to a handle of the amp to share its weight. Bev doesn't ask me why I went to the room, and I don't tell her what I did there. People are scattered throughout the station, waiting for our bus, but I don't start conversations with any of them. Everyone looks tired, and I imagine that we are all on the edge of something terrible. We're all broke and unemployed and desperate for something. This overweight, middle-aged man with sweat marks on his shirt sits near us, looking out the window. I watch his sad reflection and feel a sense of camaraderie. *Yes,* I say to him in my head. *Our lives are changing, and not for the better.*

Soon the bus arrives. It smells like mothballs and it's so hot I can hardly breathe, so as soon as we find a seat in the middle I slide in first and open the window to the cooler night air. Bev sits next to me. When I avoid looking at her face, I end up looking at her bare thighs and knees.

I turn to the men and women filing in, most of them

alone. The overweight guy doesn't get on. He must be waiting for a different bus to take him somewhere else. When the bus pulls out I catch a last glimpse of him as we drive away. He's sitting inside the bright station next to a Coca-Cola vending machine, looking out at us. But he actually doesn't look sad. He looks peaceful and maybe even content, so I change the story and decide that his life isn't changing at all. He just works really hard every day and then rides the bus home to someone who finds him funny or smart.

The bus turns onto the freeway and gains speed. Bev shifts on the seat and takes a breath. I think, *Okay: we're going to talk about us now.*

"I can tell you more about that day," she says. "About the boots and my mom and everything."

I turn to the window: darkness moving fast, headlights on a rough road.

I nod, but I don't know if she's looking at me.

"So what happened is that a couple weeks later, I saw the boots again. I'd probably seen them a million times before the science fair day but I didn't notice them because they hadn't meant anything to me. You know what I mean?"

I nod.

"They were Steve's," she says.

Steve and his wife, Joanne, are Bev's parents' closest friends. They're the people Bev's family spends Thanksgiving and the Fourth of July with. When we were kids, she called them aunt and uncle.

"They came over for dinner," she says. "Like they did all the time, and he walked in and he picked me up and hugged me. And when he set me down I saw them."

"You're sure they were the same ones?"

"They're cowboy boots and they're *green*."

"Yeah," I say. "Okay."

"And then I had to sit there all night, watching my dad with his arm around my mom's shoulders, smiling at her, refilling her wineglass." She gets quiet and shakes her head over and over.

"My dad really loves my mom," she says. Her voice is so low I can barely hear what she's saying. "I mean he really loves her."

She says this like love is the saddest thing.

Maybe it is.

"He thinks they're happy. He has no idea. But every time it's her birthday and he plans what to get her, every time she kisses him or holds his hand in front of me, every time my dad hangs out with Steve, or Joanne comes over to do some home decorating bullshit with my mom, whenever they do anything at all, I feel sick. Everything about us is fake and my dad doesn't know. My mom tells me she loves me and my stomach hurts, because we're living this fake perfect family life. And then I'm mean to her and she doesn't know why, but there is no way that I can tell her."

Bev's hands are resting on her knees, but her hands

are shaking. She's tall and she's wild and she doesn't like to be taken care of, but if things were different between us I could still reach out and hold her. Before last night I'm pretty sure she would have let me. And right now, if she asked me again if I got what I wanted, I would tell her that, No, I got the opposite. This is so far away from what I wanted with her.

"It's incredible," she says, "how much damage everyone does to everybody else."

I don't really know where she's going with this, but then she says, "I didn't ever want to break anyone's heart."

I look away from her hands. I focus on keeping my own still.

"I don't ever want to be accountable to anyone for anything again," she says. "I will never make another pact and I will never get married and I will never let anyone think that I am theirs forever."

She stops talking, but I don't know what to say. This is about us but it isn't about us. It's not the conversation I need. I lean my face against the cold window and listen to the occasional murmur of the other passengers, the road beneath us, the almost imperceptible sound of Bev breathing.

An hour later, the bus heaves to a stop and Bev and I go lurching forward, slamming against the seats in front of us, gasping at the impact. I sit back, my hand over my face, and look out the window. The night is so dark that I can't see well, but then my eyes adjust.

Deer.

One after the next, they dart past the window on skinny, graceful legs. For the first time since we left San Francisco, I feel like I might cry. Not because of the deer and how fast they run, and not because my face hurts, although it does, but because of Bev. Because I'm on this bus, because I don't know if my mom still loves my dad and I have no idea what I'm supposed to do with my life. The last deer trots by and then there is stillness, and the bus groans to motion. I lean back against the seat.

"Oh my God," Bev says. "You're bleeding."

I take my hand away from my face, and yeah, I'm bleeding. Around the bus, the other passengers appear unharmed.

But Bev has a red cut on her lip. Her bottom lip, just right of the middle.

I squeeze shut my eyes. Tears come anyway.

More time passes, and it becomes too much—the not knowing.

I get out my phone because I know that *something* will be okay. You don't lose everything at once. When I think hard I can see my mom's face as she watches Dad strumming his guitar. I can see the love in it. Adoration, even. The rightness of it washes over me. My dad will be at the table in the kitchen, and it will be the same time of night for him as it is for me now, and there will be no delay when he answers me, none of the fogginess of sound moving across continents and ocean, nothing foreign or unfamiliar when he laughs and tells me that of course they are fine.

Now the phone is ringing and I feel almost relieved already. His voice sounds hopeful when he answers and I say, "Hey, Dad," and he is glad it's me.

"I know this is going to sound strange but I have a question for you."

Bev looks over at me, brow furrowed, and there may be worry in Dad's tone when he says, "Sure, son, what is it?" But I am probably imagining things.

"Is there anything going on with you and Ma? She's really just away studying French, right?"

I am ready for his laugh, for the worry to lift away.

Instead there is silence.

The clearing of his throat.

The weight of something terrible settling in my stomach.

There are a couple minutes worth of stammered partial explanations and promises to talk about it in depth soon and assurances that they still love one another.

When I don't say anything in response, he says, "Son, the thing is this: I just don't know."

A beep comes and I move the phone away from my ear to see that Jasper's calling.

I manage as many words as I can: "Okay, Dad. I'll call you later. I have to go."

I click over.

"We found them," Jasper says.

At first I don't even register what he's talking about, as if my world has shifted and words that once made sense are now cryptic and strange.

Found who? I almost ask, but he keeps talking.

"They're about to leave for some trip or something so you have to go tonight. They said you could crash there if you want."

He says this so loudly that Bev, sitting next to me, can hear him, even over the rumble of the bus and the loud breathing of all the sleeping passengers. I turn to her.

"You decide," she says.

And yeah, every part of me feels broken and I am exhausted, but it's not the kind of exhaustion that sleep would be able to fix. No matter where we end up tonight it isn't going to be home.

So I tell Jasper that we'll go.

"I have directions," he says. "They aren't simple. So bust out that Sharpie and prepare to take notes."

Bev pulls a torn half sheet of paper from her bag and hands me a pen.

"All right," I say. And Jasper tells us what to do when we get off the Greyhound in Medford. We have to catch another bus to Jacksonville and then walk a mile to get to their house.

"They said they'll leave their porch light on. And they'll wait up for you."

When I hang up Bev doesn't even need to ask what my dad said. I guess it shows on my face.

"Colby," she says.

But I say, "Let's not talk about it," and she doesn't put up a fight.

Bev texts Meg to fill her in as we walk down a gravel and dirt road. We pass a dark house: it isn't theirs. I start to wonder why we're doing this. I know I really wanted to, I know I pushed for it, that it's something that mattered to me as recently as a day ago, but now I can't think of why.

Then there is the shape of a house against the sky in the distance, and as we get closer we see it—the porch light is on.

Before we can knock, the door swings open and a man and woman stand in the doorway. They look around my parents' age, maybe a few years younger.

"I'm Drew," the man says.

"I'm Melanie," says the woman. "Come in."

In their living room, Drew, silver-haired in a Hawaiian shirt, surveys our injuries with an expression that is part concern, part enthusiasm.

"First aid is a hobby of mine," he says. "Come with me."

"I'll make tea." Melanie smiles warmly at us and rounds the corner to the kitchen.

We follow Drew down a narrow hallway lined with photographs that Bev and I don't pause to look at. He flips on the light to the bathroom. It's small and clean and everything in it is covered in shells—shell jars and shell drawer pulls and a shell-lined mirror, all of them pink and white and shining.

"Melanie's hobby," Drew explains, opening a shell-adorned medicine cabinet and pulling out a first-aid kit.

"Have a seat," he says, gesturing to the edge of the bathtub, and Bev and I sit side by side. Our hands touch. Neither of us has the energy to pull away.

He wets washcloths with warm water and soap, unscrews a jar of iodine, lays out medical tape and gauze.

"This might sting," he tells me, dabbing my face, and I feel myself wincing but the burn feels good, like the iodine could heal me.

When Drew is finished disinfecting and bandaging, we walk back down the hallway and into the living room again, where Melanie is waiting for us. She has made us herbal tea in jars.

"Be careful where you hold this," she says, handing me mine. "It's hot."

Steam rises: lemon, ginger, honey.

"Thank you," I say.

"Thank you," Bev says.

When I sip I feel the heat travel from my throat through my chest. I sip again.

"We like your shells," Bev tells Melanie.

"Oh." Melanie laughs. "Well, it's meditative. It helps clear my mind. And somehow Drew puts up with it."

"I love them," he says. "You know that. They're pieces from our other home."

"Where is that?" I ask.

"Kauai," he says. "It's where we met and where we married. We go at least twice a year."

"That's where we're going tomorrow morning."

They turn to one another and smile. So much good passes between them in that single look.

"Are you going to show them what they came for?" Melanie asks. "They traveled a long way to see it."

"Of course," Drew says. "It was a huge surprise to hear from Danielle—it had been years—and an even stranger surprise to hear the reason she called, that you kids wanted to see this old, faded tattoo of mine."

He stands up and turns around. Pulls up his shirt. And there it is, on his back: the bluebird, the telephone wire, the roses, the rain cloud.

"Do you mind if I take a picture?" I ask.

"Not at all," he says, but I'm asking Bev as much as I'm asking him, which feels awful. Normally I would've just reached into her bag and taken out her camera.

Bev nods.

Melanie turns a reading light on and angles the beam toward Drew as Bev hands me the turquoise camera. The photo will turn out a little dark, but hopefully not too dark to see what it is.

"One more?" I pull out my phone and take another picture. It turns out fine.

"So which one is your dad?" Drew asks me, sitting back down. "I remember one of them was a kind of young Jerry Garcia type, scraggly and long haired."

Bev and I both smile.

"That's my uncle Pete."

"So your dad is the more clean-cut one. I didn't know they were brothers."

"Brothers-in-law," I say. "My mom is Pete's sister."

"Colby's mom painted that bird," Bev says.

"Wow." Drew shakes his head in wonder. "Look how it all comes together."

"Tell them the story," Melanie says.

"There isn't much of a story to tell. Danielle said that you were trying to solve a mystery, but I'm afraid it's less of a mystery than a coincidence."

Drew leans back on the sofa.

"So let's see. I was at a café in San Francisco, visiting some friends. That's where they were from, right?"

Bev and I nod. "We still live there," I say.

"Great city," he says. "What a place to grow up. So I was with my friends, and your dad and uncle started setting up. We thought about leaving because we hadn't been planning on seeing any music; we were just looking for a place to talk. One of my friends, he was going through a hard time."

"This was James?" Melanie asks.

Drew nods.

"We decided to stay. I don't know why. One of us must have suggested that we give them a song or two's worth of our attention. See what they were like. We ended up staying through the first set."

Drew pauses, and I can see him figuring out how to say what comes next.

"They weren't the most visionary musicians, but it wasn't about that." He looks at me, making sure that what he's saying doesn't offend me.

"Everything was earnest, you know?" he continues. "Their songs were melodic, sincere. You could tell they felt it. After the set was over, we got up to go, and I thought about buying a cassette but my friends were walking ahead of me and I didn't want to hold them up. But then we got outside and it was raining, so we stopped under the awning to open umbrellas, and I thought: *I want that tape.* So I told them to hold on and I went back in to buy one. I think it was your dad who sold it to me."

He takes a sip of his tea. Melanie rests her head on his shoulder and he puts an arm around her. He does it in this effortless, instinctual way. Bev shifts in her chair, tucks her legs beneath her, and I wonder if anything between us will ever feel natural and easy again.

"So it became a tape that I listened to often. I kept it in my car and it just kind of stayed in the tape deck."

Drew stops and thinks for a moment.

"Meanwhile," he says, "I had met this woman. Here's where you come in, Mel."

Melanie sits up; his arm stays around her.

"I loved her. Trouble is, I didn't know if she loved me."

"I was crazy about you," Melanie says. "You knew that. You just didn't know if I could settle down."

"True," he nods. "I amend that. I was in love with this wild girl, this traveler."

"I was a journalist for a surf magazine," Melanie says. "I was living a few months in California, a few months in Baja, off to Kauai for the winter . . ."

"I wanted her to live a life with me, and she didn't know if she was ready to do that. Long story short, I thought I was going to lose her, and then she changed her mind."

"Best decision of my life," she tells us.

"I took her on a trip to Mendocino. You been there?"

"We drove by it," I say.

"You should have stopped."

"On the way home, maybe," Bev says.

"Everything on the trip was perfect. She told me she would marry me. I felt so goddamn lucky. We got in the car on the morning after she said yes, and I opened the console for something, and I saw the cover of your dad's tape. I felt just like that bird, like the rain clouds were parting just above my head. And I thought, I have to do something to capture this moment, so I can always remember how this feels. I knew that an old friend of mine, Danielle, had a tattoo artist boyfriend who ran a shop right there in Fort Bragg. So we called her up and made an appointment for that day."

"I held his hand all the way through it," Melanie says.

"True," he says. "I didn't want to let you go."

We sit in silence for a little while, sipping our tea.

"That's the story," Drew says. "That's all. Hope it didn't disappoint."

"Not at all," I say, and I try to smile, but there's something so painful about it, that someone's walking around with a tattoo made before my parents were in love. When the future was still wide open.

Melanie sighs pleasantly, stands up.

"It's getting late," she says.

"It's *been* late," Drew adds. "It was past midnight when you got here, and I've been boring you with my first aid and my anecdotes."

"It was so nice of you guys to let us come," Bev says, and I nod, feeling grateful that she's able to speak and say the right things.

"Let me put washcloths out for you," Melanie says.

Drew collects our empty jars.

"Be right back," he tells us.

They both disappear, leaving Bev and me alone in the living room.

I look at the medical tape on her lip, touch the bandage on my cheekbone.

"How's it feeling?" she asks.

"Okay," I say. "A little sore."

"Yeah." She moves to the couch and peers down the hall. Then she says, "That question in the car yesterday, the one about love? That was yours, right?"

I nod.

"I kept thinking about that the whole time we were sitting here."

I picture the way Drew and Melanie looked at one another, the way she rested her head on his shoulder.

"It could be just an act," Bev says.

"Yeah," I say. "But I don't think so."

A long time passes.

Then Bev says, "I don't think so, either."

Bev gets ready first, and by the time I walk back out into the living room, she is already fast asleep on the couch.

"Should we just let her stay there?" Melanie asks.

I nod, and Melanie takes a blanket and drapes it over Bev's feet.

"Come," she whispers. "I've fixed a bed in the study."

The room is cabinlike, unpainted wood walls and hanging plants and a desk cluttered with papers and books. Melanie has made the futon. Soft sheets, a pillow, a green comforter. I climb in.

"Do you need anything?"

I shake my head, no.

She stands above me for a little longer.

"Everything will be okay," she tells me.

She leans over, tucks the blankets around me. I don't mind, because even though it's too intimate an action for a stranger, we both know it suits the moment.

It isn't until later, after she's walked out and shut the door, that I realize I never told her that anything was wrong. Everything about me, it must be obvious to everyone. Like what Sophie said: *You feel it so much*.

I reach for my phone to check the time—2:38—and there's a new voice mail from Dad. I consider letting it wait until tomorrow, but instead I press play:

"Colby, I wasn't finished. I don't want you making something more out of this than it is. This thing between your mom and me isn't something new—it's just that you never asked before. Your mother loves me. She's just a difficult woman to pin down. She always has been. Life . . ." he says. "Life is an extraordinary thing. It has mountains and canyons. I know I'm sounding like a folk song. Actually, I think that might be *my* folk song. *Mountains and canyons . . .*" He does this kind of half-singing, half-humming thing. "Anyway. Here's the thing: if you had asked me last year, around springtime, if anything was going on between us I would have told you the same thing I told you tonight. And if you had asked when you were, say, between the ages of three and five, I would have said, 'It's not looking so hot, kid.' Your mother is a complex creature. She means well, but she's never had any problem with keeping me guessing. So that's it. We're in a state of something—confusion? suspension?—but who isn't. Pete says, 'Tell Melinda hello. Don't forget to check her oil.' I say, Good night, son. Be safe."

Thursday

For the first time in my life, I wake up to the sound of a rooster.

I push the curtains back and look out into the morning. What I find is a grassy field that stretches forever, and on the field are three horses. I've never seen horses like this—so close, just grazing. A white one with brown spots nibbles on grass. An acorn-brown one stands still in one place, then walks slowly to the third, black and white, and rubs his nose against the other's.

I need to draw them. I get out my sketchbook and turn to a blank page and I draw until I hear a knock at the door. It's Bev, telling me that we should get ready; Drew and

Melanie can drive us back to the Greyhound station before they catch their plane.

She crosses the room to me, looks at my drawing. I see surprise flash across her face. She looks out the window, and I can tell she's seeing the horses for the first time.

For a few minutes she stays by me, watching the horses, while I work on my drawing.

"They look so powerful," she says, and I nod yes and assume she's talking about the actual horses but really she isn't looking at them; she's looking at my sketchbook. I keep working. I draw the curves of their backs and their hooves and their manes, the patches of grass beneath them. And then my drawing is finished and I close my sketchbook and for a little while longer we look out of the window together, captivated by a life that is nothing like our own.

"I'll be right back," she says, and disappears. Moments later she's in the room again, holding an acoustic guitar.

"It's Drew's," she tells me.

She sits at the foot of my bed.

"I've been working on a song about my parents. I can't really play it for anyone, so I was hoping I could play it for you."

Her hair is damp and she smells like some good, unfamiliar soap. The cut on her face isn't bandaged anymore; it's already starting to heal. She's watching me, waiting for an answer. I nod, okay.

I know that what she's saying is intentional, a reference to our conversation in the river by the apple farm, and the one later at the Starlight, when I told her that I didn't want to be anyone. And though I don't want to be this person that she has to take care of, that she worries about, at the same time I'm glad that she's playing this for me now, even if it's only to make me know that I mean something to her.

She opens up her gold notebook and thumbs through for the right page. She finds it: messy, lines crossed out, words inserted over those little editing symbols that mean that a new word goes in a too-small space, letters to remind herself of the notes.

She strums one chord and then another one, higher and fuller than the first. Her playing sounds almost folksy coming from an acoustic guitar. She starts to sing, and the melody is more Marvelettes than it is Sleater-Kinney—more slow and solemn than spunky and irreverent. It isn't the angry punk song I would have expected. Instead, it sounds like a song about lost love, which, I guess, it is.

She reaches the chorus and repeats these two lines,

Boots by the door/Not Dad's, not yours, which is simple and great like "Modern Girl," like how the best song lyrics always are. When she switches chords to play the next verse, she messes up.

"Oops, sorry," she says, and I realize that she's nervous. She positions her fingertips on the right fret and continues.

Her voice sounds softer than usual, with none of her trademark breathiness, no yelps or shrieks, just simple notes and a pretty melody. She sings about being a kid, being a part of a family. It could sound corny but it isn't corny—it's just right. She sings the chorus once more.

Then she tells me, "This is the last verse," and sings this:

Our photo album smiles/Faded to a blur

She does this great fingerpicking thing that I've never heard her do before.

Maybe we were never/Who I thought we were

The last chord lingers, then stops, and Bev sets the guitar down. She waits.

"It's really good," I say.

"Thanks."

"It's so sad."

We sit together for a little bit longer. It feels like it could be the moment. It could be now that Bev tells me what happened to us, and why.

But soon Melanie is calling to us from the kitchen, and on the table she's set out orange juice and coffee and scrambled eggs and toast, and Bev and I are both embarrassed, saying that she shouldn't have cooked for us, but she says she needed to use the food before they left and is glad to have people to make it for. We eat. We thank her. We help them carry their bags outside and I try to push away the sadness that comes when they lock their door and I realize that I will never see them again or step foot in their house, and then, as the sadness is threatening to overtake me, I see the most beautiful thing.

It's Melinda, coming toward us. Turquoise and shining and driven by Meg. If we'd left a few minutes earlier they would have missed us.

Meg pulls over across the street, and I tell Melanie and Drew, "Those are our friends," and before I can say anything else, Meg has stepped out of the van onto the dirt road. Her dress of the day is yellow, short enough to show off her tanned legs and brown cowboy boots.

"Hey," she says to Drew. "Are you a weatherman?"

"No," he says. "I'm a geologist," and Meg makes an exaggerated snap—another theory, proven false.

"You smell like breakfast," Meg tells us as we drive away.

"Um, thanks?" I say.

"It's not a good thing or a bad thing. It just makes me hungry. We drove past a restaurant on our way here. We should stop and eat."

"How did you find us?" Bev asks.

"I called the tattoo place last night and talked to Jasper. He went on and on about how bad Saran Wrap is for tattoos, and I told him that I wasn't using Saran Wrap so he had nothing to worry about, and he was like, 'You *promise* you aren't using Saran Wrap?' and I was like, 'Jasper, listen to me: I am not using Saran Wrap,' and then he told me where to find you."

"We thought about calling you," Alexa says. "But we decided it would be a good surprise. You know, to just show up."

"It was," I tell her.

"The best surprise," Bev says.

Meg pulls into the parking lot of a restaurant named Rooster's and we file inside. The waitresses are all middle-aged women who seem like they've been working there forever. The place is dark for the time of day, with brown booths and unpainted wood walls. It feels worn-in and comfortable, and we stand out for several reasons. Among them, we're the only people under forty, and we're the only people with pink hair.

We slide into a booth. Meg and Alexa on one side, Bev and me on the other.

"I'm going to decide what to order," Meg says. "And then you are going to tell us the story."

While Meg and Alexa study the menu I check out the reading material at the table, of which there happens to be plenty. I read Bev a few practically nonsensical riddles off of a pamphlet titled "Kids Jokes," until she rolls her eyes and says, "What's the point? These are impossible to solve."

The waitress comes. Meg and Alexa order breakfast, Bev and I order coffee.

Meg says, "Okay. So he's not a weatherman. What's the deal, then?"

Bev and I tell her Drew's story, about seeing Dad and Pete's show, and falling in love, and being first denied and then accepted.

"That's it?" Meg says, not attempting to hide her disappointment.

"No," Bev says. "I mean, kind of, but it's not everything."

So we elaborate. We tell them about arriving at their house so late at night, and Melanie's seashells and Drew's love of first aid. About Hawaii and the tea and the horses. The way they looked at one another.

When we're finished, Meg says, "These are like magical people. They're your fairy godparents or something. This is not how real people are."

"No." Alexa shakes her head. "Meg, you're wrong. They're each other's soul mates. Someone's going to love me like that one day." Then, more to herself, she says, "Maybe my play should be about *them*."

"Still," Meg says, "that's the mystery? Some dude asked some woman to marry her and she said yes so he got an impulse tattoo? I mean, they sound like nice people, but man. You can't blame me for expecting a better payoff than that."

As if on cue, my phone buzzes in my pocket. I pull it out and check the screen: Jasper.

"Bro, you'll never believe this," he tells me.

"Yeah?"

"So my brother's been out of town at a convention this whole week. Left on, what, Thursday? I don't know for sure. But anyway. He got back last night and I told him the story—you guys, the tattoo, your mom, Spider and that lady he dated, Drew and Melanie. But my brother was like, 'No man, I know that tattoo,' and flipped through *another* book and found a variation that he did on this guy he knew who ended up living in Seattle for a while."

"Whoa," I say. "Another one?"

"Yeah. He's a graffiti artist," Jasper says. "I forgot his name, but my brother says he's kind of a big deal. He's gonna get a hold of him and see if he's still in Seattle."

"Seattle?" I say, and all the girls stop talking and look at me. Alexa's nervous, I can tell. Seattle is not in the plan.

"The tattoo is different but I'm telling you—it's *dope*. I'm not even kidding, if he's in Washington, it's worth the drive."

I doubt that we could make it to Seattle, but I have to admit I'm interested. Just when I thought we'd figured everything out, here it is: something else.

I say, "Let me know what you find out."

"Yeah," Jasper says. "I'm on it."

Crossing the parking lot, Alexa says, "I know we don't have a show tonight, but I just don't think we have time for Seattle."

"Jasper doesn't even know if the guy is in Seattle anymore," I say. "And even if he is, if he's really this big artist why would he want to meet me anyway? Because my mother painted a bird like the one on his tattoo?"

Meg runs ahead of me and jumps into the driver's seat.

"I don't think we have to worry about it," I say. I open my calendar. In today's square I've written, *Portland: dorm.* In tomorrow's, *8pm show.* It's all happened so fast.

"Meg," I say. "This is it."

Only a couple days ago I was standing in a river, wanting to turn back, and now we're almost to our destination, and I still don't know what I'm going to do when I get home.

"This is what?" she asks.

"This is the day we get to Portland. We're moving you into your dorm room in, like, five hours."

Meg doesn't say anything, and then Bev, carving next to me, says, "And tomorrow night is our last show."

"So what happens after tomorrow?" I ask. "The band breaks up?"

"I guess so," Alexa says. "Meg's in Portland, Bev will be in Rhode Island. I'm the only one who will still be in San Francisco. Except maybe you, Colby," she adds. "But you aren't technically in the band."

"We could start a new one," I joke. "Just you and me."

Alexa smiles. "I like boy-girl bands," she says. "What will you play?"

"I don't know. Maybe your sandy harmonica, if you'll let me use it."

"Harmonica and drums," Bev says. "I'm not sure about that."

"Whatever," I say. "It'll be rad."

"We'll be back over the summers, right?" Meg says. "So maybe we can book a couple shows for next year."

"Yeah, maybe," Bev says.

"Did you see that there were cabins at that apple farm?" Meg asks. "I loved it there. We should all go in on a cabin and live there one summer. We could practice all the time."

"I hope so," Alexa says. "We've worked so hard."

For a couple of hours Meg drives and Alexa navigates and Bev carves and I lean against the window with my feet near her lap, looking through the pictures on my phone.

Bev is listening to her Walkman. She keeps stopping and rewinding, stopping and rewinding.

"What are you listening to?" Meg asks when Bev has stopped the tape for the seventh or eighth time.

"Nothing you've heard of," she says.

"Try me," Meg snaps.

"It's nothing," Bev says, and turns up the volume. I hear tinny voices, but not clearly enough to make out what it is.

Time passes. No one says anything.

In the photo I took last night, Drew stands with his back to the camera, his shirt pulled up, the bird spotlighted by the table lamp in Melanie's hands. I had meant to get a closer shot, but I actually like it this way. It shows more of them. In the background I can make out a table and some plants and books.

I press send.

A moment later, my dad texts back: YOU FOUND THE TATTOO!?

I type, YEAH. GUY NAMED DREW. GEOLOGIST. LIVES OUTSIDE MEDFORD.

DID YOU GET THE STORY?

I think for a while, for the best way to put it.

Finally, I write: HE WAS IN LOVE.

WITH ME? Dad shoots back.

HA.

PETE, THEN. NO TASTE.

This is my dad's usual humor. I can't tell if he's laughing as he's writing this, or if he's just forcing it. Maybe it doesn't matter, maybe if we all force ourselves to act like we're okay even if we're not, eventually things will get better.

Halfway between Medford and Portland we decide to stop for lunch.

"We should get it to go and eat in the bus," Alexa says. "We're on schedule, but we should give ourselves enough time to move Meg in while it's still light out."

She is back to herself now, the tour-manager, organized and in control. But Meg says that no, we should eat in Eugene.

"I've heard it's a cute city," she says.

"But don't you want to unpack a little when we get there?" Alexa asks. "We can hang things on the walls. We can make it really feel like your space. I think that's important."

Meg shakes her head no. Turning off the highway she says, "We need a break. We should stay in Eugene and have lunch."

We choose an Italian place with tables outside and pool our money for an extra large pizza and sodas. We are surrounded by college students and stores and cafés, and it feels bigger here than the places we've been, but it's still pretty mellow.

Bev says, "We'll be here for an hour, right?"

Alexa looks unsure, but Meg says, "Definitely."

"Then I'll be right back."

We watch her cross the street with her purse and camera to a one-hour photo lab.

When she comes back, she says, "I was going to wait until Portland, but then the opportunity presented itself."

"Fate," I say.

She smiles at Alexa. "It's possible."

After lunch Meg keeps pausing by shop windows and looking inside. Bev pays for her photographs and we ask to see them but she tells us we'll look later. Every block we walk on the way back to the bus stretches forever, because we have to wait for Meg as she falls behind us. In front of a gardening shop, she says, "I'm just going to run in here for a second. They might have something I want."

"Gardening?" I ask.

Alexa shakes her head.

"Meg. We have to go," she says. "Now."

Each time Bev rewinds, the Walkman wheezes and moans, sounds close to death.

Alexa taps Bev on the shoulder.

"I'm worried you're going to break your tape," she says.

"It'll be fine." Bev puts her headphones back on.

We pass a sign telling us that Portland is only forty miles away.

"Meg, do you have a final playlist for us?" I shout back.

"No."

The answer is so unlike her that I glance in the rearview to try to see what she's doing. She's leaning forward a little—I can't see her face.

Half an hour later, Alexa says, "Look, Meg!" She twists around in her seat, grinning. "We're in Portland."

I catch a glimpse of the welcome sign as we fly past,

but the sign is hardly necessary. For the first time since we left San Francisco, we are in a real city. Freeway overpasses stretch above us. Lanes divide; cars pass us on both sides; we are suddenly inundated with choices.

Also for the first time all trip, Alexa has the directions in her hands but isn't telling me which way to go half a mile in advance.

"Lex," I say, "which way?"

But when Alexa speaks next she isn't speaking to me.

"Where are your pills?" she asks. "Have you been taking your pills?"

I look in the rearview mirror. Meg is pale, trembling. She shakes her head, no.

"Fuck," Alexa says. She sounds so worried that it takes me a moment to realize that this is the first time I've ever heard her swear. She unbuckles her seat belt and dives into the back.

I turn off the freeway, because though I don't always buy Alexa's ideas about energy, this is clear: something is wrong.

Off the freeway is the parking lot for a warehouse. I stop the car as Alexa climbs back over the seat with her black case. I don't know what to do, so I just watch as she takes out the flashlight and the emergency radio and finds the first-aid kit. Inside the kit, all of the pills are wrapped and neatly labeled *Tylenol*, *Aspirin*, and *Meg*.

She unwraps the *Meg* pills and then Bev is next to them,

handing Meg her water bottle. Alexa puts a blue pill in Meg's mouth and Bev takes the water bottle from Meg's shaking hand after she's sipped.

"Fuck," Alexa says again, but Bev doesn't say anything. She doesn't panic; she doesn't even look worried; she just takes Meg in her arms and holds her tightly. She holds her for so long that her eyes focus on something far away. She looks solemn and content, like she would stay that way forever if Meg needed her to.

Once Meg stops shaking, she opens her eyes, looks up to face Alexa.

"I'm sorry, Lex. I just felt so good. I didn't think I needed them."

But Alexa is angry. She gets out of the van and slams the door, paces around the van in circles as she talks on her cell phone.

We watch her out the window.

"She's talking to our parents," Meg says. "I can tell."

"Meg," I say. "What happened?"

She shrugs. "I told you I had my moments," she says.

I nod.

"I panic," she says to Bev. "It comes suddenly sometimes. I've been on meds since freshman year. Not major ones, just something to help with the anxiety. But I stopped taking them a couple weeks ago. I thought maybe I didn't need it. Like I was starting over and I would be okay now."

We are the only people in this parking lot, next to a huge

and empty building, under the overpasses. Above us, the sky is blue and vast.

"No matter what issues you do or don't have," Bev says quietly, "it's a lot of pressure."

It's the first time she's spoken since Meg started acting strangely. Her carving tools are cast aside. She runs her finger across a half-finished figure. The person has short hair, so it's either herself or me—I'm not close enough to tell.

"It's hard."

"What's hard?" I ask.

Bev shakes her head, as if the answer is too big to put into words.

Finally she says, "Growing up."

And there is nothing any of us can say to that. It feels too true for a response. So we just sit in the bus as Alexa orbits us, gesturing wildly, mouthing words we can't hear, held safe by the single year that separates her from us.

We drive down a tree-lined road, past a mansion made of brick-colored stones until we reach Meg's dorm. In front of the building, parents are helping their kids move in. Meg opens the back door and peers up at her new home.

"It looks nice," I say.

Meg nods. "It's like a college from a movie."

"I'm taking a walk," Alexa tells Meg.

"I'm sorry," Meg says.

Alexa shakes her head.

"You don't have to apologize," she says. "I just need to be by myself for a while. Your room is on the third floor."

"I know."

"Number three sixteen."

"I know."

"I'll meet you guys up there in an hour."

Bev, Meg, and I grab boxes of Meg's things and climb the flights of stairs. The top of the third flight opens to a common space with a couple of couches and a table. Bulletin boards with brightly colored fliers announcing clubs and movie nights hang in the spaces between doors along the hallway.

And before we even get to Meg's room—as the college kids and their parents step aside as we pass them in the hall, and I see everyone's welcoming faces, and the notes written on whiteboards on room doors, and the free condoms in a wall-mounted box, and signs announcing open-mic nights and movie screenings—I realize that I was wrong. College *is* something new. It isn't like high school at all.

A guy walks out of the bathroom in flip-flops with a towel tied around his waist.

"Hey," he says to us. "I'm Kevin, your R.A."

"Hi, Kevin," Meg says. "I'm Meg."

"Meg in three sixteen," he says. "I'll swing by later, when I'm dressed in more than a towel."

He laughs and we laugh and he continues down the

hallway, and moments later we find Room 316. Two notes from Kevin hang on the door. One says *Welcome, Meg!*; the other, *Welcome, Julia!* We walk in: white walls, two single beds, two bedside tables, two desks, and two closets. All of it clean and empty.

We set everything down. Meg crosses to the window. I wait for her to turn around, not sure what to expect. She could love it here, or she could tell us to take her home. I leave the boxes taped shut just in case. No one says anything.

Then she turns around. She looks tired, but she still looks like Meg.

"What are you kids waiting for?" she asks. "Let's get to it."

So we do. I run down to the bus for another load of her stuff, and Bev and Meg start ripping tape off boxes, weighing the benefits of each side of the room. By the time I get back, they have taken over the right side. Bev is lining up Meg's shoes on the floor of the right-hand closet; Meg is stacking a few books on her desk. I open the box I just carried up: one bowl, one mug, one fork, one knife, one spoon. A box of crackers, a water filter, a box of Earl Grey, a bar of chocolate, cereal bars. In the next box is a toothbrush and a hairbrush, a razor, lotion, tampons, Tylenol, her Xanax prescription.

"Where do you want these things?" I ask.

"I think I get a locker in the bathroom," she says. "Let's go look."

Meg and I leave the room, go out into the hallway, which is still filled with friendly strangers, and find the bathroom on her wing.

"Let me check if anyone's in here."

She disappears through the door. I hear her calling hello, and then the door opens again and I follow her inside.

There is a row of lockers, a row of shower stalls, a row of toilet stalls, a row of sinks and mirrors. We hunt for an unclaimed locker and find one.

"I'm not looking forward to showering in flip-flops," Meg says. "But I'm all about hot boys roaming the halls in towels."

I place her shampoo in her locker, her hairbrush beside it.

"So you're doing okay?" I ask.

"I'm getting there."

"It seems pretty great here."

She shuts the locker, studies my face.

"What?" I ask.

"Are you regretting it?"

"Not starting college?"

She nods.

"Maybe," I say. Then, "Yes."

"The year will go by so fast. And there are other things to do."

"Yeah, I know. I looked through Alexa's book. I'm trying to decide between delivering mail and arranging flowers."

"Flowers are pretty, and you can listen to music all day if you deliver mail."

She leans against the wall of lockers.

"I guess I can't blame her for wanting this," I say.

"Yeah," she says. "But wanting this was never the problem. The problem was her not telling you."

She's right, I know. And our trip is coming to an end now. There's tonight and tomorrow and then Alexa and Bev and I will drive home in one long day, and Bev still hasn't explained why she kept college a secret.

We don't go straight back to Meg's room. Instead, we explore her floor: the spacious, communal kitchen with two ovens and stoves, the lounge with more couches and a TV, the laundry room with several washers and dryers and tables for folding and lower tables at which to sit and study. Meg swears to me that she is going to bake cookies every night and become addicted to reality shows and always have clean underwear.

When we get back to Meg's room, Alexa is waiting outside the shut door.

"Your campus is incredible! I found this little hidden place on a hill with a couple of benches. And I went into that huge building, the really old one. It's beautiful in there."

As Alexa talks, I just sort of watch her in wonder. When she left us she was all wound up and angry, she took the

236

walk she said she needed in order to be in a good mood, and now she's back, smiling, gushing about how great everything is.

And then the door opens.

Bev.

"What have you been doing in there?" Meg asks.

Bev's eyes are nervous and excited.

She says, "It's okay if you don't like it. You can change it all."

"I'm sure I'll love it. Let me see!"

She steps to the side, lets us in.

One half of the white room is no longer bare. Meg's bed is made with her yellow comforter and green pillows. A silkscreened poster from The Disenchantments' first show is pinned above her desk. A thin wire hangs horizontally over the longer wall, and from the wire dangle several photographs.

We cross the room to look at them. The first is a picture of me.

"Where did this dog come from?" Meg asks.

"She was on the street in front of Bev's house on the morning we left," I say. "Her name's Daisy."

I look from the first photograph to the others. They look at once familiar and unfamiliar. Each photograph is of us, taken in the places we visited, but they look different. The colors are more saturated; in every one of them we look happy; every setting is clean and peaceful. Meg at the apple farm, biting into a green apple with rows of trees behind her. Meg's photo of Alexa at Glass Beach, with the ocean in the background and no sign of junk. Bev leaning against me, asleep in the back row of the bus. The back of me in the driver's seat, with my eyes reflected in the rearview mirror and trees and flowers out the window.

A phrase from school comes to me: "True to life and yet more beautiful," which is what Aristotle said that theater should be.

For the first time it makes sense to me why Bev would have wanted the dog in the photograph to capture the moment: in an ideal world, on an ideal trip, we would have a dog. We would sneak her into our motel rooms and feed her our leftovers and in return, Daisy would curl at our feet in the bus and save us from the cruelties of real life. She would bring us together when we were consumed by personal disappointments with her performance of some simple and irresistible trick, and we would pat her head and she would gaze up at us with an expression of complete devotion and loyalty.

It makes sense, now, why Bev decided against photographing the girl in the Bianchi Market, or Melvin, or the man at the River Bar and Grill. Why Meg would ask to borrow the camera when she saw how pretty Alexa looked standing by the ocean. Why one of the sisters would find a rare moment of Bev and me, together in the way we're supposed to be, and take our picture.

We have photographed the trip we were supposed to have. The one where all any of us felt was happy, and the world was only beautiful, and all of the colors were the brightest versions of themselves.

"They're kind of like your sculptures," I say.

"Yes," Alexa says. "All these perfect little worlds."

"Bev," Meg says. "Thank you." She doesn't go on and on about how amazing her room looks, but there's enough gratitude in the way she says it to put Bev at ease.

"You're welcome."

"Now all I need is my duffel," Meg says, "and we can head to the hotel."

"Your aren't staying here tonight?" I ask her.

"Fuck no." She play-punches my shoulder. "I'm gonna stay with you guys until you pry me from the fender as you drive away."

We park in the lot of the Kennedy School, where they'll be playing their last show tomorrow night, and make our way out to the sidewalk to round the building. I hadn't realized that this place used to be an actual school, but here it is, taking up an entire city block, yellow and white with columns and a lot of windows.

Meg walks ahead of the rest of us, her bass case over her shoulder, plucking flowers from the vines that line the street. Pink flowers with shiny green leaves.

"The flowers match your hair," I say. But she's talking to Bev and doesn't hear me. She leaves a trail of decapitated blossoms behind her. I watch the sidewalk as I walk, careful not to crush them.

We enter through the heavy front doors to an open room with polished wood floors and all of these choices of where to go next: straight through to a restaurant in back, down the hall on the right or the hall on the left, or through the door that says PRINCIPAL'S OFFICE. It's like we're little kids and starting school all over again, but this time around we're not afraid to ask for directions when we need them, so Alexa walks into the office, comes back out with a map to our room and to the theater, where we can drop off the instruments for the show.

She leads us down the hallway to the right. We pass a room labeled DETENTION. Its door is ajar, revealing the tiniest bar I've ever seen, with dark green walls and red velvet bar stools. Soon we reach the theater. I drop my part of Alexa's drum kit off on the stage, and go back out to wander the halls while they talk to a man about logistics for tomorrow night. I find a colorful bathing pool, a couple of restaurants, a cavernous bar that used to be the school's boiler room.

But what really interests me are the halls themselves, because they are covered with paintings and photographs, and all of the images are of little kids. A lot of them are painted in a folk art style, with school-themed borders and smiling children in the center. Others are pure Americana: perfect houses and farm buildings and girls in skirts and boys with book bags. Scattered among the paintings are black-and-white photographs of the real teachers and kids who went to school here. In one, girls stand in the front of the school, dressed in long skirts and black tights, each one of them holding a wooden birdhouse. Another is a class photo. Kids sit at their desks in a crowded classroom, looking up at the camera. Some of them hold books open in their hands; others just smile. A boy in the front row wears round glasses and a striped shirt, suspenders, and a stiff, serious smile.

A plaque under the photo explains that the photograph was taken in 1915, two years after the school opened. I look at the kids' faces. They've all died by now; I can understand that. They were born decades before my grandparents. But even though I can comprehend the fact that they've all died, it's hard for me to imagine that they lived their lives. They must have gotten through school and done some good things and other things they might have regretted. This tiny, pale girl with barrettes and pursed lips, this round-faced boy who forgot to look at the camera, this curly-haired blond girl, peeking out from the back row and grinning—somehow, they all figured out how to grow up.

My phone buzzes.

"All right," Jasper says. "I know you're gonna say that Seattle isn't exactly next door, but it's only three hours away, and I got it all worked out for you."

"He's there?"

"Yeah, and he wants to meet you. My brother said he cracked up when he told him the story. He can see you anytime tomorrow."

"Tomorrow," I say.

Alexa and Meg planned for us to explore the city during the day, not worry about getting anywhere on time. We're going to have to say good-bye to Meg and leave the next morning.

I guess he hears hesitation in my voice because Jasper reminds me, "The tattoo is dope. My brother is straight talented, but this is a level all on its own. You'll be missing out if you don't go, man."

"I'm gonna figure it out," I tell him. "I just have to talk it over."

"Don't let them talk you out of it. I'm texting you his number as soon as we hang up. Peace."

We slip our keycard into the door and enter an old classroom. Chalkboards line the length of the wall, scrawled over by the previous guests. The first thing Meg does is erase everyone's messages and write The Disenchantments in huge block letters.

This time there's one bed, a cot, and a sofa. I just set my stuff on the floor and decide not to worry about where I'll end up.

"I'm gonna get the rest of my stuff," I say.

Bev left some things in the bus, too, so we walk outside together.

"Jasper called," I tell her. "I think I'm going to drive to Seattle in the morning."

"It's our last day, though."

"Yeah," I say. "But it's just a three-hour drive. I'll make it back before the show."

I unlock the bus and we collect what we came for.

"But we found the tattoo," Bev says. "We found Drew and Melanie and they were great."

She's right, but I know that Drew and Melanie aren't enough. If there's something else out there for me, I want to discover it.

"It's important to me to see this through," I say.

"But what's so great about it? Driving all the way to Seattle to meet some random guy? So his tattoo's cool. So what?"

I shut the bus and walk out to the street. And then I realize something.

"We always talk about everything but we never *do* anything," I say.

"What do you mean?"

"I mean everything," I say. I shouldn't have to say more than that. Bev should know.

"We're just talking," Bev says, her voice higher pitched than usual, almost shrill. "It's not a bad thing. Not everything we plan has to be about real life. You don't actually believe that we were going to graffiti that building with The Disenchantments picture, or go live on that apple farm next summer, or take pictures of every single person we meet. All of that stuff, it's just something to talk about. None of it is anything that people actually do."

We're on the sidewalk now, next to the street. The cars pass us, one by one, and years' worth of conversations come back to me like flashes of light, all of these plans we made, all of the things we swore we would do but never did.

"It doesn't have to be a bad thing," she says. "It doesn't mean that we've failed at anything, it's just that we're people like everyone else. There isn't some exception for us just because we feel different."

Another car comes. The wind rushing by is enough to make me lose my breath.

"I just want a normal life," she says. She's looking at me with these wide, plaintive eyes, and when I look away she grabs my elbow so I'll face her again. *A normal life.*

"What does that even mean?" I ask.

She's looking at me like I'm supposed to understand something.

"It means that I want to go to college."

She says this and everything around us fades. The trees in the distance become just black shapes on the horizon. The music from the school becomes the faintest murmur. The cars on the road vanish and all that is left is Bev and me in the dark, and after so many days of wondering why, all I can think or say is, "Oh."

"It sounds like you figured it out already, back at the motel. It was right after I found out about my mom, and all I wanted was to get away. And we kept watching those movies and Paris looked so incredibly far away and I knew that if I said it, you would say yes. At first it was just something we were talking about, like almost everything else. It was a fantasy. Whenever I couldn't handle real life, I could call you up and you would be ready to plan with me. And yeah, it was more elaborate than anything else we had ever talked about doing, but even when we were sitting at the computer for hours looking at trains and cities and drawing maps and researching hostels, there was always a part of me that knew I was just doing it to escape. And I know how that must sound to you and all this time I've been trying to come up with a way to explain it that doesn't make it seem like I thought it was stupid or trivial because it never felt that way. It just felt . . ." She looks up the sky, and I follow her gaze to more stars than I knew could exist, stars you can't see back home because of all the other lights.

She says, "It felt like preparations for an imaginary life."

We're quiet for a minute, and then someone walks past us and the trance is broken.

She takes a breath. "After a while I started to realize that you were completely serious. Everyone was thinking about college and weighing options and every afternoon when we got to your house I watched you throw your college brochures into the recycling. And then we told a few people and everyone at school started talking about it, and soon it was real. It was happening. And I know that it's horrible of me, but I never actually wanted it to happen."

She reaches out, touches my elbow again. I guess the darkness doesn't matter: she doesn't need to see my face to know how much this hurts.

"I love making plans with you because it feels like we can do anything. Like our lives are these amazing adventures where anything can happen and we'll never be limited by stupid shit like jobs and student loans and, like, *jury duty.* Like we can just be spontaneous forever. And free."

"But I think that *can* be true," I say. "At least parts of it."

We stand a couple steps from one another with our arms wrapped around our own bodies, trying to get warm, and I remember looking at ourselves in the mirror on the last morning of school and seeing how alike we looked. And now, it's become clear, we couldn't be more different.

"It might be true," she says. "For some people. For *you.* But I need to know that I'm making the right decision."

She's crying now, shivering, headlights and starlight cast over her bare shoulders and arms.

"I almost told you a million times. Every morning, I woke up and told myself that *that* day would be the day. That I wouldn't let another hour pass without telling you.

But over and over I would start to tell you, and then not say it. I don't know what's wrong with me. I don't know how I could have done this. I knew that going to college was what was right for me, but this is so fucking scary, Colby, because up until now the rightest I've ever felt is when I'm with you."

So here is her reason, what I've been waiting to know for the last five days and eight hundred miles. It isn't complicated, it isn't surprising. It is simple and sad. She told me thousands of lies, so many that it could take forever to forgive her, and there are so many things I could say back to her right now. About being cowardly. About being deceitful. About being reckless with someone else.

But I don't want to say any of that. Instead, I step toward her and she drops her arms from over her chest. I hold her close and she holds me.

And it doesn't take forever, all it takes is this.

Friday

Early in the morning, I climb into the bus alone.

I drive for what feels like a long time, listening to music and watching out the window as the road takes me out of the city, past cranes and water towers, a huge silver sign with a yellow outline of Oregon, letters spelling MADE IN PORTLAND with a deer silhouette leaping below it. Outside of Seattle, I hit morning traffic for a while. A family in another VW bus waves as I inch past them.

Halfway across a green metal bridge is the sign that tells me I'm entering Washington. I drive farther. Out the window, I discover a field of small planes parked in dry grass. A huge granary. Casinos, a body of water to the left, ships, lumberyards. An RV dealership in a patch of wildflowers. Everywhere I look is blue sky, evergreens, metal.

And then, Seattle.

I follow my directions into a neighborhood overlooking freeway underpasses. I find the café where René told me to meet him when we texted last night. It's narrow and long, set between a store with electric guitars hanging in the window and a trendy barbershop.

I take a parking spot on a side street. I'm an hour early, so I decide to walk around, but I don't go far because an art store appears on the corner, and as soon as I duck inside I feel a little bit home. Here is my favorite brand of paintbrushes and the best colored pencils, a blank sketchbook that's exactly like my almost-full one, the paint smell that reminds me of starting something new, of how it feels to mix colors until they are right, of the moment before I touch the canvas with the tip of the brush, when there is still a chance that what I create will match whatever image I've dreamed up.

I grab a basket and wander the narrow aisles until I have found what I want: a tube of silver acrylic paint, two paintbrushes, a new black pen, a sketchbook to replace my current one, and a roll of black butcher paper. I pay with what's left of my road trip money and try not to worry about how little is left. I have a whole account full of money that was supposed to last a year in Europe. So when I hand the guy behind the counter most of what's left in my wallet, I remind myself that cash is not the problem; the problem is the not knowing.

Back outside, under the sunshine, amid the bicycles, I head into the café and order a coffee. The barista grinds up beans, pours hot water through a paper filter straight into my white cup. I still have half an hour before René will get here, so I take my time drinking the coffee, sketching the people around me. A woman sitting in the corner of the room reads a book—John Berger's *Ways of Seeing*, which we studied in our senior thesis class—and takes the occasional sip of her coffee. She has long hair; I try to capture the way it falls over her shoulders. When I've finished with her I turn the page sideways and draw the barista in the white space above where I've drawn the woman. In life, and in my sketchbook, he waits behind the long, sleek espresso machine for the next customer.

I finish my drawing and go up to the counter to ask him if I can have one of the paper espresso cups. He says sure, hands it to me. Back at my chair, I fill the cup with silver paint and unroll the butcher paper, letting the ends hang over both sides of the table.

I want to re-create the design I made for The Disenchantments' first show: the silver, crying eyes with the band name spelled above it. There is no reason that tonight's show will be any different from the others, but it's the last time they'll play together—if not forever, at least for now—and after everything that's happened on this trip, endings feel important.

I don't have Bev here to model for me, but it hardly matters. I close my eyes and a moment later see her face.

I open my eyes to the sunny room and start painting.

At first, the eyes look almost exactly as they did on the shirts. The shape is the same; the shade of silver is the same. The makeup looks a little smeared; I try to make the lashes appear wet and stuck together, which is easier this time around because Bev's eyes have been so sad. When I've finished it, I stand up to see, and though it still looks similar to the first version, it looks more real. I dip my brush back into the paper cup, and paint the words: *The Disenchantments.*

Every letter is perfect.

A man walks in, and I know, immediately, that it's René. I also know that I recognize him from somewhere. He scans the room and I stand up and do this kind of half wave, and he heads over to my table.

"You must be Colby."

I nod and say, "René," and he says, "Yeah," and sits.

And then it hits me.

"Oh my God," I say. "You're René Alvarez."

"Yeah?" he says. He laughs. "You were expecting me, right? Isn't that why you're here?"

"No, I mean," I shake my head, embarrassed. "I knew I

was here to meet you, but I didn't know that you were *you*."

"You mean you know my work?"

"Yeah," I say, "You're *Novio*." And for a second I'm star-struck but then I'm just excited, because when I was doing my senior project René was one of the artists I focused on. It was almost impossible to find anything out about him—he doesn't have a website and he isn't even close to famous like Banksy or Barry McGee.

"I saw your piece on Florida Street."

"In San Francisco?"

"That's where I live. Those trains that you did? Those were amazing."

He looks genuinely happy to hear this, and we talk a little more about that piece before I ask him to tell me about the tattoo.

"All right," he says. "It's like this. Lawrence and I go way back. I was drifting for a while and he let me stay with him in Fort Bragg, and I was just hanging out in his shop one day, looking through the binders and found that little bird. It just made me laugh. I was like, 'That's one lucky little dude.' And it was interesting because it wasn't my style, but the content was the same. I had been doing all these birds, you know, and telephone wires."

"I know!" I say. "There was that one you did in Mexico City with the birds and the wires and that creature—"

"The camazotz. Man, you did your research. So yeah, I was working a lot with those images. And there's such a history, you know, of taking something that is originally someone else's and making it your own. Like how sampling works in music."

"Appropriation art," I say.

"Yeah, well. I'm not the art school type but, yeah, I'm familiar with that term. So I thought, what if I take this little guy and put him into one of *my* scenes, you know?"

He pulls off his white T-shirt. Underneath is a white tank top and, covering the entire upper half of his arm, is the tattoo.

The bird looks identical to my mother's original painting and to the bird on Drew's back, but everything else is different. The rain clouds are more elaborate and foreboding, the raindrops luminous, the telephone wires tangled and thick. If the bird in my mom's painting is lucky not to get a little wet, this bird is escaping some modern-day, Biblical-style flood. Before Meg and Jasper, I never cared that much about tattoos, but there's no denying that this is a work of art.

I'm speechless, and then all I can do is laugh.

"Wait," I say. "I can't believe this. You're fucking *Novio* and you have my *mom's* bird on your arm."

He joins in, bellows so loud it fills the café.

"Yeah, well, you must have quite a mother," he says. "But look at this." He checks out my Disenchantments painting. "This is not too shabby."

"Nah," I say. "It's just something I drew one day."

"That's all you do, though," René says. "You get an image going and you just do it. Lay it down everywhere you go. Get some stickers made and slap them on parking signs in New York and L.A. and suddenly you're someone."

He makes it sound so easy that I think that maybe I should do that, but I already know that that isn't my dream.

"So what's the story? You live in S.F. but you're up here?"

"I drove up to Portland with a few people to drop our friend off at college, and then Jasper told me about the tattoo so I made the drive up here."

"*Hold on,*" René says. "Are you headed back down to Portland today?"

"Yeah."

"I have a friend, needs to get down there by tonight. You have an extra seat?"

"Sure."

He pulls out his phone and keys something slowly.

Soon his phone buzzes and he checks the text.

"What time you leaving?"

"Pretty soon," I say. "I need to be back by, like, seven."

He sends another slow-motion message.

"You sure you're good with this? I mean, the dude's cool. Part of my crew here."

"Yeah," I say. "Definitely."

"All right." He leans back, surveys me. "The camazotz? Shit. You really knew about that?"

I shrug. "It was great," I say. "I've never seen spray

paint used that way. In some places the style was almost, like, Fauvist."

"Almost what?"

"Fauvist. You know, Les Fauves?"

He shakes his head. "Sorry, no."

"They were cool. Matisse started it, but there were a bunch of other painters involved. Camoin and Rouault, and Braque, you know, before he became a Cubist."

He cracks up. "Okay, Art School," he says.

"Whoa," I say. "Did René Alvarez just give me a graffiti name?"

"Looks like it."

"That's cool," I say. "But I'm not going to art school. I mean, it's possible that sometime in the future I might go, like, after I've worked for a while or something, but I'm not going now."

"I'm not talking about what your plans are," he says. "You've been sitting here schooling me about Les Fauves and Matisse and shit, right? I don't pass out names everyday, son, the least you can do is accept it."

"Okay," I say. "Accepted."

René and I drive about a mile through the city, to a strip mall with a Laundromat, a pawnshop, and a check-cashing place. He tells me to park and I follow him into the pawnshop and up to the cash register where it becomes clear that the dude in René's crew is the five-foot-two girl flipping the pages of a gardening magazine behind the counter.

"Abbie, this is Art School, also known as Colby."

She closes the magazine.

"This is my ride? Kid, how old are you?"

"Old enough," I try. But she's narrowing her eyes at me, and even though she's cute and tiny and dressed like a boy in a loose T-shirt and skewed baseball cap, I can tell that she's older, probably in her late twenties, or maybe even thirties, like René.

"Eighteen," I say.

Then René laughs his tremendously loud and happy laugh, and Abbie and I both join in. She has these adorable freckles all over the bridge of her nose, and she steps around the counter, holding her hand out for me to shake.

"If you're surprised by his age, wait till you check out his ride," René says.

"You could drive a pogo stick and I would hop on. My car broke down this morning and I have to get to Portland tonight. No joke, Colby. You're saving me."

"No problem," I tell her. "I have to drive back anyway."

Then she and René launch into a conversation about a mutual friend who it seems has made it into a museum show somewhere in the middle of the country. Abbie thinks it's Michigan but René swears it's Colorado, and the more they talk about it the less I follow. So I take a look at the stuff for sale.

I've never been in a pawnshop before, and the variety is pretty awesome. You could buy an engagement ring and a television, a guitar and a knife, a stereo system and a fur coat. I wander over to the electronics to check out the speakers, and something catches my attention: a record player. It looks like an old model—a blue base with a matching top that snaps onto it so it can be moved from place to place—but, at least from what I can see, it's in perfect condition.

Abbie calls me over to her to plan.

"So I hear you have to be back for something tonight," she says.

I nod. "I need to get back by seven at the latest," I say. I check the clock hanging above the counter. It's only noon, and it's a three-hour drive, so we have plenty of time.

But Abbie doesn't look as relaxed.

"Thing is," she says, "I need to swing by the place I've been staying, because I won't be back in Seattle for some time."

"Sure," I say. "I'll take you."

"It's a trek. We have to drive onto a ferry."

"Really?"

"Yeah."

I've never had to drive onto a ferry before in my life, but then I think of where we are right now, and what a ferry probably means.

"*Waitasecond*," I say. "Do you live on an island?"

"Vashon."

"What?"

"Yeah," she says. "Vashon Island. It takes twenty minutes each way, not considering the ferry line, and then we'll need to get to the farm to get all my stuff."

"You live on a farm?"

René's laugh fills the shop.

"Abbie's full of surprises," he tells me.

Abbie makes a phone call to tell someone she's closing the shop early, and she turns off the lights and locks the cash register so quickly that I don't even get a chance to ask about the record player. But then, as we're heading out the door, I catch sight of it again and can't help myself.

"That record player over there?"

"Uh-huh?"

"How much is it?"

Abbie walks over and checks it out. She stands for a moment, thinking.

Then she picks it up and says, "It's a ride to Portland," hands it to me, and locks up the shop.

Here I am, with a girl who isn't Bev, traveling to an island I hadn't planned to visit. I know it isn't Stockholm but I can almost pretend it is as I inch Melinda forward onto the ferryboat.

We park and turn off the engine and the ferry leaves the dock, and then we are on the water, slowly passing the islands of the Puget Sound.

"Want to get out and look?" Abbie asks.

"Yeah," I say. We lock up the car and head to the top of the boat where the view is better. The sun is shining but with the breeze off the water it's almost cold.

"How did you end up on a farm?" I ask.

She reaches into her bag and pulls out a scarf. "I'm learning how to do it." She ties the scarf around her neck. "Farm," she adds.

I'm impressed. But I mean I guess it's logical that most people who live on farms work on them, too.

"How long have you been there?"

"This one, only a month. I've been moving from place to place for the last six months, though. I'm from Seattle, so I was glad to get back here, but now I'm leaving again."

"René said you were in his crew, so I thought you did street art."

"I mostly gave it up. Sometimes, though, if the feeling strikes me, I'll go lay something down."

"So are you going to Portland for a piece?"

"No, not this time. My best friend is getting married and I'm throwing her bridal shower tomorrow morning. From there I'm heading to a farm outside Bend. I have a farm stay set up for August. But first I have some flower arranging and champagne pouring to do. And a toast."

"Wait," I say. "So you're like, moving? Right now?"

I see why she was checking her watch earlier. I pull out my phone and look at it now. It's past one already.

"Yeah, but I don't have much. Don't worry," she adds. "We'll get back in time for your thing tonight."

Once we pull into the dock at Vashon Island, the drive to the farm is short. We turn into a narrow driveway and up to a house.

"Is this where you live?" I ask as we walk toward it.

She shakes her head. "The owners used to live in it but they had to rent it out to make ends meet." We curve up a path. "Now they live there," she says, pointing to a tiny structure. "The husband and wife and their two kids. It's a studio."

"Whoa."

"Yeah. It's a hard life."

"And you're choosing it?"

She shrugs. "Can't help it," she says. "It feels right."

Now we're really in the farm. To the right, in a fenced-off area, are chickens. To the left are rows of tomatoes and squash and lettuce, and lots of other plants that I can't identify. There's a greenhouse. A couple of goats, chewing on grass. I don't see any other buildings, though, and I don't know where Abbie is taking me until we reach a tent.

"A tent?"

She laughs. "Yeah. Luxury, right? My stuff's all packed."

She unzips the side of the tent and I lean over to peek in:

an enormous backpack, a rolled-up sleeping bag, and a pair of heavy boots.

I grab the backpack and hoist it onto my shoulders. Thing's so heavy it could drag me down this hill.

"What's in this?"

"Everything I own."

"Jesus," I say, trying to get the weight balanced.

"Imagine walking a couple miles with it," she says. "That's what I would have been doing if you weren't here to save me."

She picks up her boots and her sleeping bag and nods.

"That's it," she says.

We make our way back toward the driveway, and on our way we pass a tan woman on a blanket in the grass, her two children on either side of her.

"This is it," Abbie says to them. "I'm going."

I continue down the dusty drive, past a farm stand with fresh vegetables and eggs, until I reach Melinda. I ease Abbie's backpack off of my shoulders and onto the middle seat. I wait, give them a few minutes to say good-bye.

"So, wait," I say to Abbie as we leave Seattle. "Where does the pawnshop fit into all of this?"

Abbie is leaning back on the seat and looking out the windshield with me, taking in what lies ahead. She's part exhausted, part alert. This is a limbo I recognize.

"I really love farming," she says. "But it isn't easy. Not even for the farmers. It pays nothing. You have to believe in it or else it's not worth it. Some gigs are cushier than others, and my first few were nice. I had roofs, and even a bathroom at one of them. The place I was before this one had plenty of food, but when I got to Vashon Island there was a huge sack of rice and some pasta and that was supposed to feed me for a week. We're surrounded by all of this food but we aren't supposed to take it. After the first week there, I started fantasizing about sneaking into the chicken coop in the middle of the night and stealing a chicken. That's when I called my uncle to see if I could work a day at his shop once in a while, just so I could make enough to buy myself some stuff to keep in the refrigerator. Cheese and beans, you know, just enough to keep me feeling good."

It's 3:15 now, so unless we hit a lot of traffic, we're doing fine on time. But tomorrow we'll wake up early and our trip will be over. We'll be heading back to San Francisco, and I still don't know what I'm going to do then. So listening to Abbie talk about her life, the choices she's made, feels important. Becoming a farmer, no matter how pure and good and close to the earth it is, isn't something that I ever see myself doing. But still. I feel like there's something buried in all of this that I need to find out.

"What made you decide to learn to farm?"

"A few things," Abbie says. "My family doesn't understand it at all. You know, they live in Seattle. Uncle owns a pawnshop. Farming isn't exactly the family business. But I've always found myself in unexpected places. For a while I worked at a fire lookout on top of this hill in the middle of a forest. It was great up there. I drew a lot, taught myself the guitar, built planter boxes on the deck and grew lettuce, and then I realized that I was watching my lettuce grow way more than looking out for fires. Plus I saw a ghost one night and it freaked me out."

"Oh, yeah?" I say, curious.

"People don't believe me but I have fifteen pictures to prove it. Here's what happened. I was just up late one night, cooking pasta, and the place that I lived, it had windows on all sides, because, you know, it was a fire lookout, and all the windows were fogged up because of the water I was boiling. I was just messing around, waiting for my dinner to be done, reading this book about country life which is actually really funny because before then I had only lived in cities, when I looked up and there was this face in the glass.

"It was in the condensation, but not like a smiley face, like a real face. It was this old man, looking off to the side of me. Because of the angle only one of his eyes showed all the way but the eye was real. I draw well, but not that well. I wish I had the photos here so you could see them. Anyway, I held it together okay that night. I'm kind of okay with that stuff—ghosts, the afterlife. I'm not afraid of it. But all week I dreamed of ghosts and when the season ended I had to say good-bye to the lettuce I planted. By the time I got out of the forest I decided that I wanted to be a farmer. I do better with the kind of nature I can cultivate. And people. I like having people around."

"So you're an ex–street artist, ex–fire lookout farmer who works part-time in a pawnshop."

"That's about right."

"I know someone who would love you," I say, and tell her all about Alexa's notebook.

"Oh, interesting," Abbie says. "To have that be a goal, jumping around from one thing to another. I don't really see myself like that. I want to find the right fit. I'm getting closer, but I also know that I might never really have everything figured out. I might be searching forever."

After a while, Abbie pulls out her speech, and I let myself fall into the rhythm of driving and thoughts of all these people I've encountered. The farmers, who rent out their house so they can stay afloat, and sleep all together in a studio, but spend their days off outside on a picnic blanket, living the lives they want to live. Drew and Melanie, with their two homes and their horses and their love story. And René, traveling across the world, painting temporary masterpieces. Even my uncle Pete has something good worked out with Melinda and his day trips and his best friend, my dad, who has a nice small house in San Francisco and a dozen neighborhood vendors who know him by name. And me. A son he's proud of no matter what.

All of these different ways of living. Even Sophie, with

her baby in that apartment, with her record store job and her record collection. I imagine her twirling with her baby across her red carpet with Diana Ross crooning, the baby laughing, the two of them getting older in that apartment, eating meals on the red vinyl chairs. Walt, too, as pathetic as his situation is, seems happy in his basement, providing entertainment to Fort Bragg's inner circle. All of them, in their own ways, manage to make their lives work.

We enter Oregon, and I glance over at Abbie.

"Hey," I say. "I have this idea for something. I could use your help if you're up for it."

"What is it?"

I reach back with one arm and feel around the middle seat for The Disenchantments banner I painted this morning. I hand it to her.

"I want to graffiti this," I say. "Somewhere in Portland. I don't really know the city."

"How big?"

"Big."

"You leave tomorrow?"

"Yeah. Early."

"Have you ever done anything like this before?"

I shake my head and grin, because even though she hasn't said it, I can tell she's thinking about how we're going to do this, not whether it's possible.

Abbie asks me a few more questions, and then calls her best friend from the van.

"Hey," she says. "So I'm getting a ride down from this kid and he has an idea for a pretty big piece. He needs help. What do you think?"

She listens for a moment. I change lanes to go faster, past the field with the old planes that I saw this morning, now on my left instead of my right.

"Oh, yeah. I'm in for sure," Abbie says. "We just need one more artist."

Past the same evergreens and cranes and water towers.

"He's staying in Northeast, so I'm thinking somewhere off of Ainsworth." Then, "Yes," she says. "Tonight. I'll see you in an hour. We can scout it out."

She snaps her phone shut.

"It's a plan," she says.

When I get back to the hotel, I get the guy working in the office to unlock the theater for me so I can pin up the banner. I step back, admire it. Then I head to the main wing to look for the girls. I find Alexa, sitting alone on one of the benches in the hallway.

"You aren't getting ready for the show?" I ask.

She shakes her head. "I think I'm fine like this."

I sit down next to her.

"I met this awesome girl today," I say. "She reminded me a lot of you."

She looks interested, but she's so quiet, seems unlike her

usual self, so instead of going on about it I ask her if anything's wrong.

"I've just been thinking. I know what I'm going to write about. I've finally decided."

"Yeah?"

"I'm going to write about Heart."

"The band?"

"Sort of. I'm still figuring it out. Partially about the band. Alisha and Sara are going to be great leads, and they both can sing. So it'll be loosely based on the band. But also just *heart*. You know? Like how it feels and what it means to make music, and to be on the road, putting yourself out there. What it means to be sisters, to be friends."

She turns to me: black hair, blue feather earrings, dark eyes, and a soft, unsmiling mouth.

"I'm just feeling a lot right now," she says. "It's too much to not make something out of it."

I think of that day on the apple farm when Alexa told me that these would be the last days with her sister, of Walt's basement when she fell in love with Heart, of the time she spent on her own when we got to Meg's dorm and how she returned to us so self-possessed, so ready for whatever would come next. I wonder about all of the experiences she had when I wasn't looking, what she was thinking about during all those hours she sat quietly while Meg played the entertainer and Bev and I fought our way through so many things.

"I want to read it," I say. "As you write. I want scenes or fragments or anything. Will you let me see it?"

She says yes, and I start thinking about all of these moments in life that could inspire moments in the play, and I'm still sifting through it all when Alexa stands up and says, "Maybe I will change after all," and she gives me a quick hug and disappears down the hallway.

When the three of them emerge from Meg's room, they are the most glorious creatures I've ever laid eyes upon. Bev is in shiny, skintight black pants, high heels, and a thin white shirt with its sleeves cut off. Her eyes are ringed with dark, shadowy eyeliner and her lips are pink and glossy. Meg wears bright red lipstick and a blue dress she hasn't worn yet on the trip, tighter than her others, showing off her hips and her breasts. Alexa has pulled her hair back, away from her perfect face, and wrapped it in the chiming headband. Her feather earrings move when she walks—she looks like she's flying—and she's wearing a silky green dress.

"Oh my God," I say to them.

"We look hot," Meg says. "We know."

"I made you something," I say. "You'll see it in a minute."

Bev asks, "How was the tattoo?"

"Worth the drive," I say.

And then, without thinking, I say, "Worth all of it."

Bev looks at me curiously and then they head down the hallway, and I'm left to myself, to try to figure out what I mean.

I sit down in an oversize soft chair in the clean, dim theater. When the girls see me they gesture to the banner stretching across the stage, the letters and silver eyes sparkling. Alexa blows me a kiss. Meg gives me an exaggerated thumbs-up. Bev smiles and lifts her hand in a wave.

Slowly, people trickle in, and soon a group of men and women sit on the couch next to me.

"Do you know anything about them?" one of the men asks me, nodding toward the stage where Meg and Alexa and Bev are setting up.

"Yeah."

"Are they good?" the guy asks.

Onstage Meg tunes her bass, and Alexa sets her crash cymbal in place, and Bev connects cords that lead from the microphones to a power strip. And even though I know that soon the sound they create will make people cringe, I feel proud that these girls are my friends.

So I say, "Not really. But whatever, you know? They want to make music, so who cares if they don't know how."

These girls are amazing, whether they can play or not. Even if the feedback is so brutal I want to cover my ears. Because they have beautiful muscles in their arms and de-termined looks on their faces. Because Bev's voice is the best medicine. Better than Xanax or whiskey or all the rest, all anyone would need to keep her calm or help him sleep.

So when they start to play, I try to only listen to Bev's

voice, and I watch them all as they move to create sound—
Alexa's arms crashing down to the drums and rising again;
Meg swaying back and forth as she plucks her bass, confi-
dence restored, in the care of her familiar drug.

And as I watch them I realize that for the first time they
sound okay. What Alexa pounds is actually a beat. Bev's
fingers move quickly across the frets from one clear chord
to the next. Meg's low notes resonate; they pound through
my feet and up to my chest. When Bev starts to sing it all
crashes down on me—the reasons that they want to play
music, the reasons that I wanted to come along.

We all want to feel something, we want to be someone
to one another.

After the show Bev spends a few minutes talking to a guy
who is clearly interested in her. He looks young and nice,
almost like someone we could all be friends with, and I try
to talk myself into feeling okay about this.

I tell Meg that I have an errand to run, and to tell the
others not to wait up, and then I head to the bus and call
Abbie. She shows up in front of the Kennedy School and I
climb into the backseat of her friend's car. I shut the door
and we're off, some great, old hip-hop song playing, the
small space of the car alive with what we're about to do.

"Sienna, this is Colby," Abbie says. And then, to me,
"Sienna found us a great spot. You're going to freak out."

We only drive a few blocks, and then we turn down a small street and then to an alley with a huge brick wall, not unlike the one I found in Arcata when I first had the idea.

"It's so cool that you're doing this," I say as we stand admiring it.

"My pleasure," Sienna says.

"It's her life," Abbie says. "She's always threatening to go into retirement but she never will. In a few years you'll be this like soccer mom, pulling over in your station wagon in the middle of the night to lay down some tags."

Sienna shrugs. "You are who you are, you know? I don't feel right if I go too long without a can of spray paint in my hand. Listen to this sound," she says.

She hops onto the trunk of her car, climbs to the top.

"Abbie showed me the sketch. Should we start with the right eye?" she asks.

"Yeah," I say, and I can't help it—I'm smiling like it's my birthday or something. Standing in the dark on the top of a car, she looks like a superhero, about to get started saving the world. Even when I was imagining doing this, first in Arcata and then today in the bus, the imagining wasn't nearly as great as this moment.

She shakes the can and pops off the top, and soon there is the most fantastic steady hiss, a perfect black arc that will soon be the face's right eye.

She gives me a look that says, So, what do you think?

"That's one beautiful sound," I say.

She nods. "That's right. Now, tell us how to proceed."

We decide that Sienna will rough out the image—I've never done anything on this scale, and every line she sprays seems impossibly long—and then I'll come in after her and add the detail. Abbie keeps watch at the end of the block.

With Sienna moving so quickly, it doesn't take us too long. I spray white paint for the light reflected in the irises and the tear. Black eyelashes as long as my arm. I make the eyeliner like Diana Ross's on the album cover in Sophie's record store, so now the whole thing looks kind of stylized and retro. I keep thinking of René's tattoo—those luminous raindrops, the way Jasper's brother played with light—so we keep going back over our work, darkening sections, adding more highlights.

And then, starting on the far left and ending at the right, I spray "The Disenchantments."

I step back.

It's fucking beautiful.

"We aren't finished," Sienna says. "We're missing the most important part."

"Oh, right," I say.

I'm not gonna lie: when I was doing that report I thought about what it would be like to be one of the guys I was researching. When I got sick of writing and doing Internet searches I practiced tags on pieces of graded homework and college brochures that hadn't hit the recycling yet. But I never actually got good at it. I never thought I'd be in this situation, with the entire side of a building covered with my painting and two experienced graffiti artists waiting to see me tag it.

"You can do it," Abbie says, joining us. "Everyone has a first time."

So I take a can of silver paint and crouch in the bottom right corner. I decide not to try for fast and elaborate, and instead go for slow and even. I spray the Art first and then the School right below it and skewed a little to the left, so that the last letters in both words, the *t* and the *l*, are one long vertical line with the shorter horizontal cross close to the top. Then I decide to extend the vertical line, so that it bends to the left and underlines the word *School*. As I spray I think about the name and what it means, and what it might convey out here, as a part of street art, far away from any actual school with walls and windows and units and semesters. René would probably laugh at me thinking about it like this.

But actually maybe not.

Maybe that was the point. Because as I step back and look at this piece that I designed two years ago that's changed in all of these ways because of what's happened and how we've been living, the name takes on a different meaning. Right now, out in the world, away from my tiny room and my family, for the moment even away from my friends and with these new people I only met hours ago, on a street that was unfamiliar as of this morning, with a new name written in paint drying right in front of me, having just made the best work of art of my life, I realize that this—living—means so much more than art school. That feeling that Bev described by the side of the road last night sweeps over me, and I understand how it can matter to her as much as it does.

Here it is, all at once: rightness.

Not the graffiti itself, even though it's undeniably spectacular, but this feeling of making plans and carrying them through, of meeting people and getting to know them, of being asked to do something and saying *Yes*, of wanting something, asking for it, making it happen.

When we've finished, Sienna and Abbie climb into their car.

"I wish we could wait to see your friends," Abbie says. "But Sienna needs her beauty rest."

"It's true," Sienna says.

They have all of the spray paint in the trunk.

"Wouldn't want to leave you with a stockpile of evidence," Abbie says. "Take care now, Colby. Thanks again for the ride."

I watch them drive away, and then I pull out my phone and call Bev.

"What happened to you?" she asks.

"Come see," I tell her, and give her directions.

Minutes later, they're here. Climbing out of Melinda, tired, still in their makeup from the show but now in more comfortable clothes, walking toward me.

"Where are we?" Meg asks, but I don't say anything. I just lead them around the corner. I step back, lean against the wall across from the painting. They join me. Gasp. Stare. I don't even want to look at the wall anymore; I just want to look at their faces.

"You did it," Alexa says. "How did you do this?"

"I had some help."

"It's incredible," Bev says.

Meg says, "I'm going to come here every day and guard it so that it doesn't get painted over."

"It'll get covered up," I tell her. "But that's okay. It's here for now, right?"

They nod. Yes.

Bev and I are hungry, but Meg and Alexa want to sleep, so we drop them off at the hotel and drive a few blocks through the dark. We park on the street by a diner with a pink fluorescent sign, stand in the dark, and look through its windows.

"Look good?" I ask Bev.

"Yeah," she says.

We walk toward it, past a couple of bikes leaning against a street lamp.

"Someone needs to lock their bikes," I say.

Bev sees them and nods.

Inside, a few tables are taken but overall it's pretty

empty, and the hostess leads us to a vinyl booth and hands us our menus. A radio station plays rock ballads from the eighties.

Soon our waitress appears with two plastic cups of water and her notepad out and ready.

"What can I get you kids this evening," she says.

She's wearing the diner's uniform: short black dress with a white apron, and she doesn't look too much older than we are, and I wonder if calling us "kids" takes effort, if she's trying to prove something.

I order a grilled cheese; Bev orders pie.

"Coffee?" the waitress asks.

We both say yes.

"I've been thinking," I say, when the waitress leaves our table, "about your mom."

Bev stays quiet, but she looks at me, so I take that as an indication that I can continue.

"It's just, I don't know. Maybe your dad already knows about it. Or maybe it's the biggest regret of her life."

The waitress brings us cups of coffee and a bowl of tiny half-and-half containers. I rip the top off one of them and pour it into my coffee.

"Anyway, I know what she did was wrong, but she might be able to explain it, or at least talk to you about what happened. That science fair was *four* years ago."

"So what are you saying?"

"I'm saying I think you should tell her that you know."

"When?"

"I don't know," I say.

And then it hits me, again, that we're leaving in the morning.

So I say, "Now, maybe."

"Here?"

I shrug. "You could play her your song."

She looks around the restaurant, at all the other people.

"Out in the bus?" I suggest.

"Or the bathroom," she says. "It might be hard for her to hear me, and the bathroom probably has good acoustics."

"Sure," I say. "In the bathroom, then."

Bev looks a little pale, but she reaches across the table for my keys and slides out of the booth. I watch her walk fast across the diner floor and outside, and I wonder if this is really going to happen. And then Bev is back with her guitar case and amp, explaining something to the waitress who looks skeptical but nods and says okay.

Bev doesn't even come back to the table. She just motions for me to come with her so I do. We flip on the light of the little room that smells like bleach and urine, and Bev crouches on the blue-tiled floor to snap open the locks of her guitar case. She uncoils the cord and we find a socket on the wall by the door.

"I'm gonna need you to hold the phone," she says. She's trying to act calm but the fear in her voice is impossible to miss and her hands turn the pages of her notebook so fiercely that I'm afraid she's going to rip them.

"Okay," she says.

I scroll through her numbers for the one that says HOME. "Ready?"

She nods, her face pale but determined, and I press Call.

I hear Mary's worried "hello" and say, "Hi-Mary-it's-Colby-everything's-fine," and as I move the phone away from my ear I think I can hear Mary's voice, but Bev has already started strumming. Chords bounce off the bathroom walls.

I hold the phone close to her mouth and, at the same time, reach toward the amp to turn the volume down so the music doesn't drown out the words. Bev sings her first lines, *Sunny afternoon/Empty living room*, and her voice, clear and strong, fills the space.

I don't know if any of this would have happened if we had been at home. Would she have told me about her parents? Would we have crammed ourselves into the bathroom of a San Francisco restaurant to play her song? I doubt it. There's something about distance, being removed from what's familiar, that lets things happen.

So here I am. Gray-white walls, a bare lightbulb in the middle of the ceiling, a toilet with bright blue water. It's one o'clock in the morning and I'm leaning against the yellowed sink of a diner bathroom, guitar chords echoing around me, this girl, my best friend, crouched on the floor, singing her heart out to her mother.

And even though I know how important this is, and that I should be thinking only of what Bev has gone through and what will result from this moment, I can't help watching her and thinking about us, too. I have so many questions about what happened at the Starlight, what it meant to her, what will happen to us now.

She sings, *Maybe we were never/Who I thought we were*, and I think, maybe we always *were* the people we imagined ourselves to be. Able and brave. Maybe we still are. As a chord reverberates through the tiny room, I decide that it can't be that hard to be the person you want to be. What's difficult is finding a place in a world with other people, who want different things for themselves. And then the bathroom is quiet.

Bev's eyes are wide and she hisses, *"Hanguphanguphangup,"* and I fumble with the phone and finally press the button and we look at one another, take a breath in unison, exhale. The phone rings.

I hand it to Bev. She looks at the screen.

"It's her," she says.

"Well, yeah," I say. "Of course."

"Do I have to pick up?"

"I think so, yeah."

She watches the screen.

"Definitely," I say.

So she does.

"Hi."

It takes all my willpower not to ask her what Mary is saying, so I try to distract myself by unplugging the amp from the wall, pulling the cord out of Bev's guitar.

Bev doesn't move, doesn't speak, but when I stand up again, I see her face. She looks suddenly young again. Fragile.

Her mom is doing most of the talking. Bev nods and gives one-word answers. At one point she closes her eyes, and when she opens them again tears run down her face. She's breathing calmly; her voice sounds steady when she speaks. But the tears keep coming.

"Yes," she says.

"I guess so," she says.

A knock comes at the door as I'm placing Bev's guitar into the velvet inside of her guitar case. I click the locks shut. Open the door to a middle-aged woman with dyed black hair.

"I'm sorry," I say to her, "but we're gonna need a couple more minutes."

I smile my nicest smile, and the woman looks confused but not angry, and I shut the door again. I sit down on the ocean-blue tiles and lean against the door. Bev is still silent and listening. I look at her, and then away.

The last time I saw Bev cry was when we were eleven, and my parents and I got home from my soccer game to find her family waiting for us. Her parents were dropping her off on their way to the vet because they had to put Fitzgerald, their cat, to sleep. Fitzgerald was big-pawed and orange and affectionate, and he was older than we were and would follow us from room to room. And though by this point he was feeble and no longer able to eat by himself, to Bev this was murder. She sat between my mom and me on the couch and trembled for an hour, until the call came that it was over and Bev leaned into me and cried until my soccer jersey was soaked through.

I was sad—I loved him, too—but I was also proud to be needed. I'm sure I could have used a shower, I must have had that little kid sweaty smell, but she still chose me. She could have been sobbing on my mom's shoulder but she was sobbing on mine. I remember that I sat very still, overcome by the responsibility of her.

If I had to choose the one moment that I fell in love with Bev, that would probably be it.

Or maybe it would be when she held auditions for *Melancholy Play*, watching the actors intently with her clipboard, making notes. I fell in love with her then, too.

Or every time I drew her, whether she knew I was drawing her or not.

Or when we sat on my living room floor with maps of Europe laid out all around us, and she said, "We have to go everywhere. I don't want to miss anything."

Now, from her side of the bathroom, Bev hangs up, wipes her eyes with her hand.

I wait.

"What did she say?" I ask after a little time has passed.

"She said a lot of things. She asked if that's why she lost me."

"Does your dad know?"

Bev nods yes, and her face clouds over.

"Oh my God," she says. "All these years, I thought I was keeping this horrible secret, but it wasn't even a secret. We could have been a normal family. We could have . . ."

Her voice breaks. I stand up; she steps toward me. I hold still, and she cries until my shirt is wet.

Then we go back to our table.

"I want to show you something," Bev says.

I chew my grilled cheese, sip my lukewarm coffee. Bev leans down and resurfaces with her messenger bag. She takes out the box that holds her carvings, and as I eat, she sets them up on the table. I've been catching glimpses of them throughout the trip, but here they all are, more of them than I realized.

She's lining up the people we met: Walt, Jasper, the lemonade kids, the girl from the Bianchi Motel, Sophie, the redhead from Arcata, Melvin, and other people, too, who I don't recognize but who must have stood out to her for one reason or another. And then I look more closely at one of them. The drunk guy from the River Bar and Grill.

Next comes Melinda, and I notice a dent, right in the front of the fender, from when Pete once hit a pole in a parking garage. She arranges the instruments to the side of the bus, set up as though waiting for the show to begin, and on the other side of the bus come the versions of us. Just glancing at the figures I would think they were more of her usual depictions of people identified by their props: their favorite shoes, their paintbrush, their script. But I look closer, knowing that they'll be different this time.

And they are. Alexa holds the deceptive Magic 8 Ball. Meg's chest is bandaged. In her hand is a tiny bottle of pills. Bev has her headphones on, a barrier against the outside world. I don't have a prop. Instead, I stand, palms empty, facing the sky. There are close to two dozen miniature people here, all flawed and small and gathered together.

"It's just the beginning," she says. "I want to do some of the rooms we stayed in. And I want to make the apple farm, and the beach, too. I've never tried to sculpt water."

I just nod because I don't know how to tell her how amazing these are. However beautiful her sculptures were when the things she depicted were perfect, these, in their imperfection, are so much better.

Finally, I say, "RISD is going to fall in love with you."

"Come with me," she says.

"What?"

"They would accept you in a second. You draw better than anyone I know. Maybe you could even start in the spring semester."

I don't know what to say.

"Come," she says. "You could get an apartment. I have to live in the dorms for the first year, but after that I don't know. Maybe I could move in with you."

She's looking across the table at me, her eyes wide and hopeful and so painfully pretty, saying what I've been wanting to hear her say for forever. But I can't imagine calling my dad and telling him that instead of going to Europe I'm going across the country to rent an apartment because that's what Bev has chosen. I need something new. All I have is a life's worth of school days. What came before school I can't remember. You can only sketch so many desks and teachers and chalkboards. You can only come home to so many dinners and homework assignments and nights of taking the garbage out. You can only go to so many museum field trips before you start to wonder, *Is this it?*

Whatever I decide, I might be making a mistake. But if I'm going to make a mistake I want it to be passionate.

I shake my head, no, and I try to explain.

"So my mom makes this painting for her brother's band, and it's a nice concept and it turns out well. And then it turns out that she falls in love with her brother's bandmate, and a few years later they have me. And maybe that love doesn't turn out to be what they'd hoped, but still, here I am like twenty years later at a tattoo shop in some tiny city and I see my mom's painting and learn that it has to do with other people getting married. And they're still in it, and it helps somehow, for me, that they have this painting my mom did as a symbol of their love. Even if they aren't exactly a normal example. Even if they are, like, magical or whatever. And then it turns out that that tattoo isn't the only one, that a guy saw a photo of the first tattoo, didn't even know it had anything to do with a painting or a band, and he changed the image, made it better, made it a symbol of something else, and that leads to me going to Seattle and meeting these people who are so fucking cool, and coming back here and doing something I wanted to do but didn't really know that I could."

It's all coming together, and as I tell the story I start to realize what I meant when I said that seeing René's tattoo was worth all of it. Because, after everything that's happened, I finally know what I'm going to do now, after tonight, and the more I talk the more the realization grows until I'm shaking a little and my body feels like it's humming and it could be the coffee or the fact that I haven't slept well in over a week, but I think what it actually is, is the overwhelming knowledge that I was right all along.

I always knew what I wanted to do, I just didn't know I could do it.

"I'm going to Europe," I say.

I don't say *without you* aloud because this decision is not meant to hurt her. It's not really about Bev at all. It's about me.

"I really want to go to Amsterdam," I say. "And I want to see those islands."

As soon as I make the decision to go, I want to go *now*.

"Are you still going to visit your mom?"

"Yeah."

The waitress comes and asks if we want anything, and I tell her I want pie. Pecan pie. Because my grilled cheese is too cold to eat and I am suddenly hungry. She walks away and I pull out my phone. All of this planning I did, it's paying off. Because I have the airline's number programmed into my phone and I've learned how to ask the right questions and the best people to ask them of. In two minutes, when I hang up, I have a reservation to fly standby out of Portland the day after tomorrow.

"But what about all of your stuff?" Bev asks.

"I have stuff with me," I say. "I want to travel light anyway."

"But we're going home tomorrow morning. It would be so much easier to fly out of the city."

The waitress sets a slice of pie in front of me, reaches over the table to refill our coffee cups. I put my hands around the mug until it becomes too hot to touch.

"I can't go home yet," I say.

I dial my dad and ask him to send my passport overnight.

"I've had a change of plan," I say. "I'm leaving out of Portland."

There is a moment of quiet, but he recovers quickly.

"What about Melinda?" he asks.

"Bev will drive her."

"Bev?"

"Yeah," I say. "She isn't coming with me."

"Why not?"

I glance at her across the table. She's picking apart her pie, not eating any of it.

"Her plans changed, too."

"Wow," he says. And then: "My son, graduating from high school, solving mysteries, traveling on his own to Europe."

I laugh.

"Tomorrow's Saturday," he says. "So maybe FedEx? I'll see what I can do. But hey," he says in a hushed voice. "Can you hear me?"

"Yeah?"

"Let's not say anything to Pete about these plans until Melinda is safely home. He's in the next room now. We'll wait until Bev pulls up to the house tomorrow night."

"Good idea," I say.

Then, in his normal voice, he says, "I know this must be hard, son. It's hard for me, too."

"I know it is."

It's too quiet for too long on the phone between us.

"We'll be all right," I say.

"Yes," he says.

And then I call my mother. I get her voice mail.

"Ma," I say. "I'm coming early."

On our way out of the diner, the hostess stops us.

"Let me show you something," she says. "Did you know there are no locks on the doors?"

"What?"

"We never close. Ever. Look, no locks."

She points to the doorknob; it's true.

She smoothes her hair, adjusts her name tag, beams.

Above her station, a cuckoo clock announces that it is 3:00 A.M.

"Come back anytime," she says.

We walk toward the van but then Bev stops.

"I want to do something with you," she says. "I don't want to go back yet."

We've already spent hours in an all-night diner and I'm not sure where else we could go. In spite of these obstacles, these are the most glorious words she could speak right now. But we're in an unfamiliar city in the middle of the night. I'm about to suggest that we just drive around, and then I see them. Still leaning up against the streetlight. Waiting for us.

I walk over and Bev follows. They're nice bikes, hipster bikes: fixed gears, one light brown with a turquoise seat, the other yellow and with a wire basket on the handlebars.

"Let's leave them a note," Bev says.

I rip a page out of my sketchbook and get out a pen, hand them to her to write.

"How should we start it?" she asks.

I look at the bikes and think about it. What would I want to read on a note that was left in the place where my bike should be?

"Dear Friends?" I suggest.

Dear Friends, she writes. And then she sits, leaning against the wall. I sit next to her.

> *A long time ago I discovered something I wasn't*
> *meant to know. It didn't have to do with me,*
> *but still, somehow, it became me. I didn't mean*
> *for it to be that way. I fought against it. I tried*
> *to make a perfect life. Everything I saw, I did*
> *my best to correct. Everything I was afraid I*
> *couldn't control, I found some way around. But*
> *people have a way of knowing things, and they*
> *want to know more.*

*So you're going to ask me a question no
one's ever asked me. Here it goes.*

*You: Bev, what was the happiest moment
of your life?*

*Me: Riding bikes with Colby early in the
morning, through Golden Gate Park, when we
were eleven years old.*

*Now that you know the answer, you'll
understand. Colby and I aren't eleven anymore,
and it isn't really the morning yet, and we're a
far distance from home. But it's going to be a
very long time before we're together again, so
we'll have to improvise. Thank you for letting
us use your bikes. We promise to return them
later tonight, right here, to this spot.*

Love,
Bev

Neither of us has tape so I jog back into the diner and get
a piece from the hostess. Then I come back out and we stick
the note to the pole.

"Ready?" Bev asks.

"Yeah," I say.

I straddle the brown bike and she swings her leg over
the yellow one, and in hardly any time at all we're off, sail-
ing through the night air down the empty streets, together
in a way we haven't been in longer than I'd realized.

We ride and ride. Down wide streets and narrow ones, past houses and trees and shops and the river, until, breathless, we reach the edges of an empty park and we tumble off the bikes and onto the grass, and stare into the Oregon night sky.

"Do you feel better?" I ask. "Now that she knows?"

Bev says, "I don't even know. I feel like I'm in a different reality. Like, when I get home, my parents and I aren't going to recognize each other. Or like it was all some weird *Twilight Zone* thing. I'll wake up tomorrow morning and I'll be fourteen, and I'll see those boots and I'll knock on my parents' bedroom door and my mom will know that I know, and she'll confess to my dad and they'll talk to me, and we'll, like, go to therapy and play lots of trust-building games. I'll stand there with a blindfold on and fall backward and they'll catch me. And then we'll be fine or something."

"Do you think you'll get there? Eventually? Even without the blindfold?"

"And the time travel?"

"Yeah, without that, too?"

She's quiet, and I look up at the stars like I did last night. Close my eyes. Try to re-create them from memory.

"For the longest time I thought everything was about the affair, but it isn't so much anymore," she says. "I mean, I know what it's like to make out with a lot of people and still only love one." She's quiet and I let the silence be, let her words hover above me. "I didn't understand it when I was fourteen," she says. "Because things seem so clear when you're fourteen. Now, nothing seems clear. Which makes me less angry, I guess. But I don't know how I feel about everything. I feel stunned."

She turns away from the sky and stares into my face. "Actually," she says. "I *do* know how I feel. I feel like Lorenzo."

"From the play?"

She nods.

"You know how I kept trying to get you to take his lines more seriously? It's because even though a lot of what he said was ridiculous, so much of it felt true. And perfect. There were all of these things that I wanted to tell you, about why I wasn't able to trust myself."

I shake my head. I don't know what she means.

Her forehead creases. "Trust myself with you," she says.

"So all of those times?" I ask. "When you were making out with all of those people in front of me and lying to me about Stewart?"

"I didn't want to do something with you I might regret," she says.

"Do you regret what we did?"

"No," she says.

Time passes. We look up at the sky.

"Those lines, after Lorenzo tells Tilly he loves her?" Bev says. "Those are my favorites."

I try to remember them. I picture opening night, my place on the stage. Bev in the middle seat of the first row. The lights bearing down on us. Meg in a blue dress.

They come back to me: *"I want to tell you all the sad things, and then you will know me better than other people know me and that means we are reserved for one another."*

Bev picks up where I've left off: *"Because we made a reservation like at a restaurant like at a grand hotel and we made this reservation with a certain foreign currency made of secret sad information we told each other in private rooms—"*

"Oh, *I feel a weight on my chest,"* I say.

And then, together: *"What have you done to me, Tilly? Why?"*

Bev and I smile.

"So good," I say.

"Yeah," she says. And then she rolls over on the grass, props herself up, and kisses me.

I can't stop loving Bev just because our lives aren't taking us in similar directions, and to be absolutely honest, I don't want to. I know that if Bev did come with me to Europe, she wouldn't have been doing the right thing. She would have been like my mom, running away from a life she isn't sure of. Searching, always. And yes, we all are, or soon will be, disenchanted, but I still want to know it all: the heartbreak, the fear, the friendship, the anger, the love. All of it.

When I kiss her back, it feels important. It feels like life.

Bev turns over again, reaches for my hand.

And lying here right now, after everything, I fall in love with her again.

We find our way back to the diner and Melinda. Our note is untouched. We lean the bikes against the pole, and decide to leave the note where it is, make one more mark on the world.

When we get back to the motel I offer to stand outside with Bev while she has her cigarette, but she tells me that it's something she wants to do by herself.

"Tour ended tonight," she says. "So this is the last one." She flips the lid, pulls one out. It looks skinny and long resting between her fingers. "Feel lucky you won't be with me on the ride home tomorrow."

She presses the box, a third full of cigarettes, into my palm. At the end of the block, a trash can waits under a streetlamp. I jog over and throw away the pack. When I get back to Bev, she is lighting up. The flame from her lighter illuminates her face and then goes dark. She takes a long drag.

"Good night," I say.

"Good night."

Once again, it's late at night and I've given up on sleep.

Instead, I'm lying on the scratchy motel sheets with Alexa's emergency flashlight propped up on a pillow beside me, drawing the scenes from tonight from memory. The diner with its vinyl booths and our cups of coffee. The bicycles propped against the pole. Bev and me, in the grass, under stars.

I turn over onto my back, so exhausted that I feel like I'm floating. I close my eyes and see Bev's face. Open them and see the dark, shadowed ceiling. Close them and see an airplane in its moment of ascent.

All of the girls are asleep. I can hear them breathing. I listen close, try to determine which breaths belong to whom. After a little while, I give up.

My phone is next to me in bed. I reach for it and move as quietly as I can, off the sheets, across the carpet, out the door into the night. I find the name that I want and press call even though it's 4:49 A.M.

"Hey, bro," Jasper says.

"What's up," I say. "Were you sleeping?"

"No, no," he says, but his words sound heavy. "So how was René?"

"He was cool," I say, but René isn't why I called. I lean against the balcony, above the row of parked cars. The streetlights are lit; the sidewalks are empty.

"So listen," I say. "I was thinking. Do you have a passport?"

Saturday

I want to write Bev a letter on tiny scraps of paper and slip them in her purse for her to find later, mixed in with her own notes to herself. One sentence at a time with no order. Not a puzzle, just fragments. Or yes a puzzle, but a puzzle she could piece together in any way she wanted.

i remember when we were kids.

i wanted to say thank you.

it is what i wanted and it is not what i wanted.

i am afraid of losing you forever.

But I don't do anything like that. Instead, I hug Alexa tightly before she climbs into the passenger seat. And then I stand, empty-handed by the driver's-side door, as Bev gets ready to climb in.

"This is really happening," she says. "You aren't coming back with me."

I take the keys out of my pocket and put them in her hand.

"It's up to you to get Melinda home safe."

She closes her hand around the keys.

Too much time passes while we stand here, not saying anything, while Alexa waits inside.

Finally, I say, "Hey, you know what?"

"What?"

"I forgot to tell you. You guys sounded good last night."

"Yeah?"

"Yeah. Like *good* good."

"Just in time for the last show," she says. "Too little too late, maybe."

She smiles: her nose crinkles, her crooked tooth shows. The cut in her lip is already almost healed, but her eyes are sad.

And then she is hugging me, and then she is pressing her mouth to my mouth, and then she is in the bus with the door shut and the engine running.

Jasper shows up late at night with a duffel bag and backpack, wearing a backward cap and a tank top that shows off the wings and arrows and leaves on his chest and shoulders.

He grabs my hand and we bro hug and he smiles wide and says, "Shit, man, we're really doing this."

"I still can't believe you have a passport."

"Yeah, well, I told you guys I had everything I needed to get out of town. For years I've kept my passport pinned up on the wall of my room, just as a reminder that I'd get out someday. I didn't think I'd actually use it, though. I figured I'd start smaller than this."

He drops all his stuff on Meg's floor and collapses onto her roommate's mattress.

"God, I hope Julia doesn't arrive till tomorrow," Meg laughs.

"What did your boss say?" I ask him.

"He got all sentimental, said he was losing a damn good tattoo artist."

"That's great."

"Yeah. And then he told me to get the fuck out of his shop. Let's see that tattoo, Meg."

She walks toward him.

He looks, says, "Goddamn, that's beautiful."

I can't sleep. Again. I think about getting up and wandering the halls for a while but Jasper and I are not supposed to be here and I don't want to get Meg in trouble.

I try to turn over without rustling the blankets too

much, and then I hear a whisper: "Colby, you awake?"

"Yeah," I whisper back.

"Me too, bro. Can't get to sleep. I keep thinking about that girl I used to date. The sort-of vegetarian?"

"Yeah, I remember."

"She let me give her this tattoo when we were sixteen. I told her she could pick whatever she wanted and she found this picture of a unicorn and she wanted it on the side of her hip so her mom wouldn't ever see it. . . . I ran into her on my way out of town. I told her I was leaving. You should have seen her eyes get all wide when I told her where we were going."

"Oh, yeah?" I say, and he says yeah, and continues his story.

Someone else who feels like talking in the middle of the night—it's pitch black so I'm not afraid to smile at this news.

"Hey, Jasper," I say, "when we get to Amsterdam I want you to do something for me."

"Sure."

"I want you to give me a tattoo. Of tulips."

"Tulips?" he asks. Then he says, "Okay, bro. I guess tulips are cool."

I smile up at the ceiling. "You're not into it."

"No," he says, "it's fine. People want all kinds of random shit. Tulips are fine."

We're quiet for a minute. Then he says, "Hey, you

should sketch me some tulips, you know? Then I can ink your sketch. That could look good."

I picture a sketch of tulips, drawn kind of loose in pencil, like I draw pretty much everything.

"Yeah," I say. "I like that. Maybe we could do some kind of really faint color. Like most of it is just the black ink but there's a little color there. Like inside some of the petals and the leaves."

"What colors? I mean obviously green, but maybe red? Like a pinkish red?"

"Yeah, that sounds good." I know the exact shade from the colored pencils I used all through school. I'll show Jasper at an art store; we can mix the color to match it.

"Maybe yellow, too," I say.

"Yellow's tricky. Doesn't show up that well. We could throw a little orange in there to kick up the tone, though."

"Yeah," I say. "I can picture it. It looks so fucking good."

"You're right. I'm getting into it. These are gonna be some badass tulips."

"I want it on the inside of my arm, like growing up from my wrist."

"It'll show up good there." Jasper yawns. "But it'll hurt."

And I know that Jasper is talking about something specific, about needle puncturing skin, over and over, all the way up the inside of my arm. Yes, it will hurt. But it won't hurt the way leaving will hurt.

Everything that's about to happen, everything that has happened in the last few days—it fills me with an ache so vast it takes me forever to compose myself. After some time, I manage to say, "It's all right if it hurts."

I wait for Jasper to respond, but instead I'm met with the quiet of two sleeping bodies breathing, the familiar feeling of being the only one awake.

Sunday

I wake up on the dorm room carpet, roll over. Meg smiles a sleepy smile off the edge of her mattress.

"Good morning, sunshine," she says.

At two o'clock the delivery guy comes and with it, my passport. We stand in the downstairs dorm lobby and I rip open the envelope. I show the passport to Jasper and Meg.

"I guess this means we're ready," I say.

"Shit," Jasper says. "This is big. We're really doing this."

We go upstairs and pack up until the left side of the room is bare again and everything Jasper and I are going to carry with us on trains and boats and international flights is on our backs and over our shoulders.

Meg sits cross-legged on her unmade, yellow bed, the photographs from our trip hanging above her. In her closet is the record player from Abbie's shop, but she hasn't discovered it yet.

"Don't forget I was the first girl you saw almost-naked," she says. "I don't want to be overshadowed by the following evening's events."

"Colby," Jasper says, "sounds like you have a story to tell me."

I laugh, but as I'm laughing sadness rises in me. I look at Meg. It feels almost impossible to leave her.

But just then a girl in a low-cut shirt and jean shorts, a nose ring, and all these bracelets around both wrists, pushes into the room with her bags.

"Hey, guys," she says, breathless, dropping her bags to the floor.

She looks from me, to Jasper, to Meg, pushes a strand of brown hair off her face and smiles.

"I'm Julia," she says.

Meg and Julia exchange the customary greetings, and I remember leaving Walt's house, wondering if this trip would be characterized by a series of endings. In a way, it has been. But that's not exactly it. More than that, it's been a crash-course in living. You get close to people. You get farther from them. You learn how much you love them, and then you say good-bye, believing that you will be together again, someday, when your lives curve back into one another's.

Meg wraps her arms around me.

"What color will your hair be next year?" I ask.

"You'll have to come see me in order to find out."

"Fair enough," I tell her, and then Jasper and I are walking down the dorm stairs, and into the sun, and to the bus stop, waiting for the shuttle that will take us to the airport.

Even though Jasper hasn't flown since he was five years old, he knows exactly what to do when going through security. He has everything sealed and separated and ready to go.

"I've done my research," he says, pulling off his Vans, tossing them along with his cap and his belt into the plastic tray to be X-rayed. "I even printed out a Eurostar map. We can check it out on the plane."

Portland International Airport is high ceilinged and bright, every surface reflective. As we find our terminal I see us everywhere—in the shop windows, on the silver sides of escalators. We reach our gate and soon after, we've walked the long jetway and down the aisle to our seats in the economy section, where we take our seats next to a dark-haired woman in a fuzzy purple sweater, our neighbor for the next nine hours.

Jasper looks pale.

"You okay?" I ask him.

He nods, but then he's muttering that he'll be right back, and I watch him as he moves against the current of boarding passengers, on his way to the bathroom.

"He isn't used to flying," I explain to the woman, who smiles kindly, reminds me a little of my mother.

I open my backpack and find my calendar. Pull it out, flip to June. I crossed off days as we went, and now the *X*'s look strange. Everything we've done, struck through like it's been accomplished or conquered, when really all we did was drive and talk and eat and kiss and take off our clothes and sing together. I turn to July, and something is written there in Bev's handwriting.

I have no idea when she would have looked through my calendar, or why she would have tried to find it. I feel sick for a moment, embarrassed that I filled every day with a sentence about her.

But the feeling passes.

There are grooves in the paper from where she pressed so hard with her black pen: *Please draw pictures of everything so I can see all I missed.*

I read it over, and then I see something else. Right under where my calendar was, near the top of my backpack, is Bev's Walkman. It feels bulky in my hand when I lift it, and I have to untangle the headphone cord from the drawstring of my hoodie. This will only be a song—I know that—but it matters to me somehow. I want to know what she chose

306

to listen to over and over after everything that happened between us. So, with only minutes until takeoff, with people crowding the aisles on either side of me, trying to cram their possessions into the overhead compartments, I put Bev's headphones over my ears. I press play.

Through the headphones comes a shuffle of fabric or footsteps.

A giggle.

A hushed voice that asks, *Ready?*

Something catches in my chest.

It's us.

Our nine-year-old voices. Singing loudly, in perfect time with one another, with so much confidence it hurts. I lean forward. Close my eyes. Listen.

Near the end of our song, Jasper appears above me. His face is white and he is grinning. I take the headphones off.

"Shit, bro," he says for the twelfth time since last night, "we're really doing this."

And before he's even made it past the woman and me to his seat, the announcement comes to turn off our electronics. I click stop on the Walkman, tuck it within easy reach, and a flight attendant's voice informs us that the doors are secured and we are cleared for takeoff.

Acknowledgments

First and foremost, thank you to my family. My mother reads every single draft and catches the smallest changes and my dad subscribes to my Google Alerts. These are two tiny details that make them officially the best parents in history. Jules, thank you for the French phrases and your musical knowledge and for being such a great brother. You are my definition of fun. Kristyn, every paragraph in this book contains a reason to thank you. I mean that literally, but it also works as a metaphor for everyday life. So thank you x forever.

Thank you to my friends who volunteered to be early readers: Jessica Jacobs, Eric Levy, and Nate Davis, and my supportive, insightful writing group: Carly Anne West, Laura Davis, Lizzie Brock, and Teresa Miller. You all gave me much-needed clarity and guidance when I was fumbling through the early drafts. Mia Nolting, thank you for making the title and the days of the week so pretty

Amanda Krampf: thank you for loving everything I have ever written. Mandy and Eli Harris: thank you for the unwavering support and the many, many celebratory toasts. Vanessa Micale: thank you for choosing to be a farmer so I could put it in my book. Grandmother and

Grandfather: thank you for your wisdom and warmth. The LaCours, Gordons, Proctors, Hoveys, Strobles, Ogulnicks, and Blanton-Hubbards: thank you for giving me such a wonderful family. QPs: thank you for being you. I love you all.

Sara Crowe is the best advocate a writer could ask for. Thank you for your lightning-quick answers to every single question, for egg creams, and for working so hard for my books. Julie Strauss-Gabel possesses the unparalleled gift of asking the right questions. Thank you for asking them of me, and for pushing me beyond what I thought I could do. I am so grateful and honored to work with both of you.

Thank you to Scottie Bowdich, Liza Kaplan, Anna Jarzab, Emilie Bandy, Lisa Kelly, Bernadette Cruz, Shanta Newlin, Emily Romero, Ashley Fedor, Eileen Kreit, Rosanne Lauer, Theresa Evangelista, Marie Kent, and everyone else at Penguin Young Readers Group for giving me such a good home. I can't describe how it feels to have such an amazing team of people working to make sure my books reach readers.

Thank you to Sarah Ruhl for generously allowing me to use lines from her *Melancholy Play*. Thanks also to Sleater-Kinney, The Runaways, The Supremes, Heart, Miles Benjamin Anthony Robinson, Bon Iver, The National, and Camera Obscura for providing the sound track to the writing of this book.

Thank you to Maybeck High School for your energy and quirkiness and warmth. To all the readers who have written to me: your letters and emails are the greatest gifts.

So many friends contributed pieces of themselves to this novel. Thank you for being the beautiful people you are. I'm lucky to have you to inspire me.

Turn the page for a look at

Nina LaCour's

next novel—

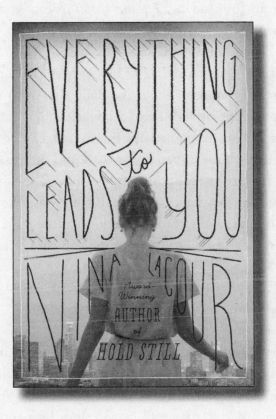

Chapter One

Five texts are waiting for me when I get out of my English final. One is from Charlotte saying she finished early and decided to meet up with our boss, so she'll see me at Toby's house later. One is from Toby, saying, *7 p.m.: Don't forget!* And three are from Morgan.

I don't read those yet.

I head off campus and a few blocks over to where I parked my car in an attempt to avoid the daily after-school gridlock. But of course the driver's side lock won't unlock when I turn the key, so I have to go around the passenger side and open the door and climb across the seat to pull up the other lock and shut the passenger door and go around to the driver's side again—and by the time I'm through with that twenty-second process, the cars are already backed up at the light. So I inch into the road and pull out my phone and read what Morgan wrote.

You okay?
R u coming to set later?
I miss you.

I don't write back. I am going straight to set, but not to see her. I need to measure the space between a piano and a bookshelf to see if the music stand I found on Abbot Kinney Boulevard yesterday will make things look too crowded. The music stand is beautiful. So beautiful, in fact, that if it doesn't fit I will find a new bookshelf, or rearrange the furniture entirely, because this is exactly what I would have in my practice room if I knew how to play an instrument. And if I could afford a nine-hundred-dollar music stand.

As the light turns and I roll my car through the intersection, I'm trying to ignore Morgan's texts and think only of the music stand. This music stand is a miracle. It's exactly what I didn't even know I was looking for. The part that holds the sheet music is this perfect oxidized green. When I texted my boss a picture of the stand she wrote back, *Fucking amazing!!!!* An expletive and four exclamation marks. And when I texted Morgan to tell her that this was the last time I would allow myself to get dumped by her, that breaking up and getting back together six times was already insane, and there was absolutely no way I would take her back a seventh, she replied with, *I don't know what to do!* Indecisive and only mildly emphatic. So typical.

But the music stand, the music stand.

Turning right onto La Cienega, my phone rings and it's Charlotte.

"You need to come here," she says.

"Where?"

"Ginger took me to an estate sale."

"A good one?"

"You just have to come."

"Someone famous?"

"Yes," she says.

"Sounds fun but I need to measure for that music stand."

"Emi," she says. "Trust me. You need to come here now."

So I scribble down the address, make a U-turn, and head toward the Hollywood Hills. I drive up Sunset and roll down all the windows, partly because the air-conditioning doesn't work and it's ninety degrees, but mostly because I'm driving past palm trees and hundreds of beauty parlors and taco trucks and doughnut shops and clothing stores and nightclubs, and I like to take it all in and think about how Los Angeles is the best place in the world.

I turn when my phone tells me to turn and start ascending the hills, where the roads become narrower and the houses more expensive. I keep going, higher than I've ever gone, until the houses are not only way bigger and nicer than the already big, nice houses below them, but also farther apart. And, finally, I turn into a driveway that I'm pretty sure has never before encountered a beat-up hatchback with locks that don't work.

I park under the branches of old, gorgeous trees that are full and green in spite of the arrival of summer, step out of my car, lean against the bumper, and take a look at this house. My job has taken me to a lot of ridiculously nice houses, but this one stands out. It's older and grander, but there's more to it than that. It just feels different. More significant. I'm not thinking about Morgan and thinking instead about who might have owned this house. It was probably someone old, which is good, because an estate sale means someone has died, and it's sad to dig through thirty-year-old people's stuff and think about the futures they could have had.

The double front doors swing open and Charlotte steps into the sun. Her jeans are rolled up at the ankles and her blond hair is in pigtails, and her face is part serious, part elated.

"Guess," she says.

I try to think of who has died in the last couple of weeks. My first thought is our physics teacher's grandmother, but I seriously doubt she would have lived in a house like this one. Then I think of someone else, but I don't say anything because the thought is crazy. This death is huge. Front-page huge. Every-time-I-turn-on-the-radio huge.

But then—there's this house, which is clearly an important house, and old, beautiful trees, and Charlotte's mouth, which is twitching under the tremendous effort of not smiling.

Plus it isn't swarming with people, which means this is some kind of preview that Ginger got invited to because she's a famous production designer and she always gets called to these things first.

"Holy shit," I say.

And Charlotte starts nodding.

"You're not serious."

Her hands fly to her face because she's giddy with the delirious laughter of someone who has spent the last hour in the house of a man who was arguably the most emblematic actor in American cinema.

Clyde Jones. Icon of the American Western.

She leans against the house, doubles over, slides onto the marble landing. I let her have one of her rare hysterical fits of laughter as I take it all in. I can't think of enough expletives to perfectly capture this moment. I would need a year's worth of exclamation points. So I just stare, openmouthed, thinking of the man who used to live here.

Charlotte's hysterics die down, and soon she is standing, composed again, back to her super-brilliant, future museum-studies-major self.

"Come in," she says.

I pause in the colossal doorway. Outside is bright and hot, a beautiful Los Angeles day. Inside it's darker. I can feel the air-conditioning escaping. Even though this is an amazing opportunity that will never come again, I don't know if I should go any farther. The thing is this: My brother, Toby, and I talk all the time about what movies do. They speak to our desires, which are never small. They allow us to escape and to dream and to gaze into eyes that are impossibly beautiful and huge. When you live in LA and work in the movies, you experience the collapse of some of that fantasy. You know that the eyes glow like that because of lights placed at a specific angle, and you see the actresses up close and, yes, they are beautiful, but they are human size and imperfect like the rest of us.

This, though, is different.

Because even if you know a little bit too much about how movies are made, there are always things you don't know. You can hold on to the myth surrounding the actors; you can get swept up in the story.

Clyde Jones belongs in the Old West. He belongs under the stars, smoking hand-rolled cigarettes and listening to the wind. In *A Long Time Till Tomorrow* he lived in a log cabin. In *Lowlands* he lived out of a green pickup truck, sleeping by the side of the road a couple hours at a time, searching for a woman from his past.

Clyde Jones is the savior. The good, uncomplicated man. The perfect cowboy. But as soon as I walk through this doorway he will be an actor who spent his life in a Los Angeles mansion. The ultimate collapse of the fantasy.

"Em?" Charlotte says. She steps to the left, gesturing that I should follow, and I can't help myself. A moment later I'm in Clyde Jones's foyer, the doors shut behind me, gazing at one of the most beautiful objects I've ever beheld: a low-hanging chandelier, geometric and silver and shining.

Clyde Jones was no cowboy, but his aesthetic sensibilities were amazing.

I'm still dying over Clyde's house when Ginger strides past me.

"Oh, good, Emi, you made it." Charlotte and I follow her into the living room.

"Yeah," I say, standing under the high white-beamed ceiling, next to what I can only assume is a pair of original Swan chairs positioned under a huge pastoral landscape with a clear sky as endless as the skies in his films. "It's probably better that I don't go to the studio today."

"These glasses," Ginger says, pointing, and Charlotte walks over to a shiny minibar and takes a tray of highball glasses. "Why should you avoid the studio? Oh, let me guess: Morgan."

"She broke up with me."

"Again?"

"Something about not being tied down. Life's vast possibilities."

"'Life's vast possibilities.' Such bullshit," Charlotte says, setting the glasses next to a group of other beautiful objects that Ginger must have already chosen.

I say, "Yeah," but only because that's what Charlotte needs me to say. Charlotte is the kind of friend who automatically hates everyone who has ever done me wrong. The first time

Morgan broke up with me and we got back together, Charlotte tried her best to get over it and be nice to Morgan. But somewhere around the third time, Charlotte got rude. Stopped saying hi. Stopped smiling around her. By now, Charlotte can't even hear Morgan's name without clenching her jaw.

Ginger shoots me a sympathetic look.

"It's okay," I tell her. "I'm done with movie people."

And then we all laugh, because really. What a ridiculous thing to say.

~

When Ginger is finished choosing what she wants, she lets Charlotte and me explore for a while and see if there's anything we want to buy. We find ourselves in Clyde's study, which has to be the size of my brother's entire apartment. It has high ceilings supported by thick wooden beams and an entire wall of windows with doors that slide open to the land in back. Of all the rooms, this one feels the most Western. There's an enormous rustic table that he must have used as a desk and a collection of leather chairs arranged in a semicircle facing a cavernous fireplace. Shelves line the entirety of one of the side walls, and covering the shelves are hundreds of awards including four Oscars, along with objects from his films: cowboy hats and guns and silver belt buckles.

Most people our age don't know or care very much about Clyde. His career is long over. His roles were rarely sophisticated or smart; there isn't much to recommend him to my generation. But my brother has eclectic tastes, and when he loves something, it becomes nearly impossible not to love it along with him. So over the years I became infatuated with the moment that Clyde appears on the horizon or in the saloon or riding through tall grass toward the woman he loves.

Standing in his study now feels both unexpected and inevitable. And, more than those things, it feels *meaningful*. Like all of Clyde's arrivals. Like, without knowing it, everything I've done has been building toward this moment.

"Are you all right?" Charlotte asks me.

I just nod, because how could I describe this feeling in a way that would make sense? There is no logic behind it.

I pick up one of the belt buckles. It's heavier than I thought it would be, and more beautiful up close: the smooth silhouette of a bucking horse with a rough mountain and waning moon in the background.

"I'm going to see how much they're asking for this," I say.

Charlotte cocks her head. "You're choosing a belt buckle?"

"It's for Toby," I say, and Charlotte blushes because she's been in love with my brother forever. Reminded, I check my phone and see that we're supposed to meet up with him in just under two hours.

Charlotte's flipping through records. She pulls out a Patsy Cline album.

"I can't get over this," she says. "Clyde Jones used to sit on these chairs and listen to *this* record."

We find Ginger signing a credit card slip for over twenty thousand dollars, which might explain why, when we show the estate sale man the belt buckle and Patsy Cline record, he beams at us and says, "My gift to you."

"Charlotte, will you get Harrison on the phone?"

Charlotte does, and hands the phone to the man to arrange a pickup, and then we are back in Clyde's hot driveway, out of his house forever.

—

Toby lives in a classic LA courtyard apartment, like the one in David Lynch's film *Mulholland Drive*, which chooses to focus on the darker side of the movie business, and also the one in *Melrose Place*, which was a nineties TV show set in West Hollywood that my dad lectures about in his Pop Culture of Los Angeles course at UCLA. Toby's courtyard has a tidy green lawn and a pretty fountain, and from the side of his cottage you can see a tiny strip of the ocean. We walk in, and there is his stuff, packed, waiting by the door. A set of matching suitcases that look so grown up.

He hugs us both. Me first and long, Charlotte next and quicker. Then he stands and faces us, my tan brother with his crooked smile and black hair that's always in his eyes. I feel sad, and then I push the sadness away because of what we have to tell him.

"Toby," I say. "We spent the afternoon in Clyde Jones's house."

"You're shitting me," he says, his eyes wide.

"No," Charlotte says. "Not at all."

"His house was full of the most amazing—" I start, but Toby puts his hands over his ears.

"*Dont'tellmedon'ttellmedon'ttellme,*" he says.

"Okay," I say.

"The collapse of the fantasy," he says.

I know, I mouth, all exaggerated so he can read my lips.

"I love Clyde Jones," he says, dropping his hands.

I nod. "Not another word on the subject," I say. "But I do have something for you. Close your eyes."

My brother does as told and holds out his hands. I pretend I don't notice Charlotte staring at him, and place the belt buckle in his cupped palms. He opens his eyes. Doesn't say anything. I wonder whether I chose the wrong object, and then I realize that tears are starting.

"Oh, please," I say.

"Holy. Shit." He blinks rapidly to compose himself. Then he rushes to his bookshelf of DVDs and pulls one out. He's mumbling to himself as he turns on his TV and waits for the chapter selection to appear on the screen. "Saloon door . . . I'm a man of the law but that don't make me honest . . . Round these parts . . . Yes!"

He's found the scene, and we all squeeze onto my parents' old sofa, me in the middle acting as a buffer for the sexual tension between my brother and my best friend.

Toby presses play and turns up the volume. I recognize it as *The Strangers*, but I've only seen it a couple times so I've forgotten a lot of what's happening. The scene begins with a shot of a saloon door. We hear the voices of the people inside but the camera doesn't turn to them. When one person matters so much, all you can do is wait for his arrival. And then boots appear at the bottom of the door, a hat above it. The doors burst open and there stands Clyde Jones.

The screen fills with a close-up of his young, knowing

face, shaded by a cowboy hat. He scans the saloon until he sees the sheriff, drinking at a table with one of the bad guys. The camera shifts to his cowboy boots as they stomp across the worn wooden floor toward the sheriff and his buddy, who both spring up from the table and draw their guns as soon as they see Clyde.

Unfazed, Clyde deadpans, "I thought you were a man of the law."

Sheriff: "I'm a man of the law but that don't make me honest."

The bad cowboy doesn't say anything, but looks borderline maniacal as he points the gun at Clyde.

Then Clyde says, "Round these parts, lawlessness is a disease. I have a funny suspicion I know how to cure it."

The camera moves down to his holster, and Toby shouts, "Look!" and presses pause. There's the belt buckle: the horse, that hill, the moon.

Charlotte says, "That's amazing!"

I say, "Toby. I am seriously worried about you. Of all the Clyde Jones movies and all the belt buckles, *how* did you know that this buckle was in this scene of this movie?"

But Toby is doing a dance around his living room, ignoring me, reveling in the glory of his new possession.

"Thank you, thank you, thank you," he chants.

After a while Toby calms down enough that we can watch the rest of the movie, which goes by quickly. Clyde kills all the bad guys. Gets the girl. The end.

"Okay," Toby says. "I asked you both here for a reason. Come to the table."

I'm trying to hold on to the good feeling of the last hour, but the truth is I'm getting sad again. Toby is about to leave for two months to scout around Europe for this film that starts shooting soon. It's stupid of me—it's only two months, and it's a huge promotion for him—but Toby and I spend a lot of time together so it feels like a big deal. Plus he's going to miss my graduation, which I shouldn't care about because I've been over high school for a long time. But I do care just a little bit.

Toby opens the door to the patio off the kitchen and the night air floods in. He pours us some iced tea he gets from an Ethiopian place around the corner. The people there know him and sell it to him in a plastic pitcher that he takes back and gets refilled every couple days. They don't do it for anyone else, only Toby.

When we're seated at the round kitchen table, he says, "So, you know how I put up that ad to sublet my place? Well, I got all these responses. People were willing to spend *mad* cash to live here for two months."

"Sure," I say. Because it's obvious. His place is small but super adorable. It's this happy mix of Mom and Dad's old worn-in furniture and castoffs from sets I've worked on and things we picked up from Beverly Hills yard sales, where rich people sell their expensive stuff for cheap. It's just a few blocks from Abbot Kinney, and a few blocks more from the beach.

"Yeah," he says. "So it was seeming like it was gonna work. But then I had a better idea."

He takes a sip of his tea. Ice clinks. Charlotte leans forward in her chair. But me, I sit back. I know my brother, the master of good ideas, is waiting for the right moment to reveal his latest plan.

Finally, he says, "I'm letting you guys have it."

"Whaaaat?" I say. Charlotte and I turn to each other, as if to confirm that we both just heard the same thing. We shake our heads in wonder. And then I can't help it, I think of the third time Morgan broke up with me, when her reason was that I was younger (only three years!) and lived with my parents. Would it make a difference to her whether I lived here instead? Or is this time really about the vastness or whatever?

Charlotte says, "Are you serious?"

And Toby grins and says, "Completely. It's my graduation present to both of you. But there's a condition."

"Of course," I say, but he ignores me.

"I want you to do something with the place. Something epic. And I don't mean throw a party. I mean, something great has to take place here while I'm gone."

"Like what?" I ask. I'm a little worried, but excited, too. Toby's the kind of person whose greatness makes other people want to rise to any occasion. Everything he does is somehow larger than life, which is how he worked his way from a summer job as one of the parking staff to a full-time job as the location manager's assistant. And then, last month, at the age of twenty-two, he became the youngest location scout in the studio's recent history.

"That's all I'm gonna say on the subject," he says. "The rest is up to you."

We try asking more questions but when we do he just sits back and smiles. So the conversation shifts to *The Agency*, the film he's scouting for. I get to design a room for it, too, which will be my biggest job yet. It's a huge-budget movie with a young ensemble cast—Charlie Hayden and Emma Perez and

Justin Stark—all the really big young actors. It's a spy adventure, but the room I'm designing is for one of the girls when she's still supposed to be in high school, before they all become spies and start traveling around the world. It's probably going to be a stupid movie, but I'm thrilled about it anyway. A few weeks ago, Toby and I got to go to a party with the director and the whole cast and crew. I hung out with these stars whose faces are on posters all across the world. That's just one example of the kinds of things I get to do because of Toby.

Too soon, a knock comes on Toby's door—what is now for two months my door—and the film studio driver sweeps his suitcases into the trunk and then sweeps up my brother, too. Toby dangles the keys out the window, then looks out at me and says, "Epic."

The car pulls away and we wave and then it turns a corner and is gone. And Charlotte and I are left on the curb outside the apartment.

I sit down on the still-warm concrete.

"Epic," I say.

"We'll think of something," Charlotte says, sitting next to me.

We sit in silence for a while, listening to the neighbors. They talk and laugh, and soon some music starts. I'm trying to push away the heavy feeling that's descending now, that has been so often lately, but I'm having trouble. A few months ago it seemed like high school was going to last forever, like our college planning was for a distant and indistinct future. I could hang out with Charlotte without feeling a good-bye looming, take for granted every spur-of-the-moment plan with my brother, sneak out at night to drive up to Laurel Canyon with Morgan and lie under blankets in the back of her truck without worrying that it would be the last time. But now the University of Michigan is taking my best friend from me in just over two months, and my brother is off to Europe tonight and who knows where else after that. Morgan is free to kiss any girl she wants. I expected graduation to feel like freedom, but instead I'm finding myself a little bit lost.

My phone buzzes. *Why didn't you come to work?* I hide Morgan's name on the screen and ignore Charlotte's questioning look.

"Hey, we should listen to that record you got," I say, and Charlotte says, "Nice way to avoid the question," and I say, "Patsy Cline sounds like a perfect way to end the evening," which is a total lie. I don't know why Charlotte likes that kind of music.

But I fake enthusiasm as she takes the record out of its sleeve and places it on Toby's record player and lowers the needle. We lie on Toby's fluffy white rug (I got it from a pristine Beverly Hills yard sale for Toby's twenty-first birthday, along with some etched cocktail glasses) and listen to Patsy sing her heart out. Each song lasts approximately one minute so we just listen as song after song plays. Truthfully? I actually like it. I mean, the heartbreak! Patsy knew what she was singing about, that's for sure. It's like she *knows* I have a phone in my pocket with texts from a girl who I wish more than anything really loved me. Patsy is telling me that she understands how hard it is not to text Morgan back. She might even be saying *Dignity is overrated. You know what trumps dignity? Kissing.*

And I might be sending silent promises to Patsy that go something like *Next time Charlotte gets up to go to the bathroom I'll just send a quick text. Just a short one.*

"That was such a good song," Charlotte says.

"Oh," I say. "Yeah."

But I kind of missed it because Patsy and I were otherwise engaged and I swear that song only lasted *six seconds.*

"I wonder who wrote it," she says, standing and stretching and making her way to the album cover resting against a speaker.

This is probably my moment. She'll look at the song list and get her answer and then she'll head to the bathroom and I will write something really short like *Let's talk tomorrow* or *I still love you.*

"Hank Cochran and Jimmy Key," she says. "I love those lines 'If still loving you means I'm weak, then I'm weak.'"

"Wow," I say. It's like Patsy is giving me permission to give in to how I feel. "Are the lyrics printed?" I ask, sitting up.

"Yeah, here." Charlotte steps over and hands me the record sleeve, and as I take it something flutters out. I pick it up off the rug.

"An envelope." I check to see if it's sealed. It is. I turn it over and read the front. "'*In the event of my death, hand-deliver to Caroline Maddox of 726 Ruby Avenue, Apartment F. Long Beach, California.*'"

"*What?*" Charlotte says.

"Oh my God," I say. "Do you think Clyde wrote that?"

Read *Nina LaCour*'s
award-winning debut novel!

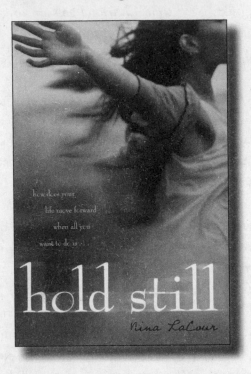

★ "What is most impressive about LaCour's tale is her ability to make the presence of an absent character so deeply felt."
—*Publishers Weekly*, starred review

★ "Poignant and beautifully crafted."   —*VOYA*, starred review

"A smart voice, an engrossing story, and genuine emotion."
—*Kirkus Reviews*

A William C. Morris YA Debut Award finalist

An ALA Best Books for Young Adults selection

A *Publishers Weekly* Flying Start selection